Kiss Me If You Dare

Also by Nicole Young

Patricia Amble Mystery series

Love Me If You Must

Kill Me If You Can

Kiss Me If You Dare

A PATRICIA AMBLE MYSTERY

Nicole Young

a division of Baker Publishing Group
Grand Rapids, Michigan

Published by Revell
a division of Baker Publishing Group
P.O. Box 6287, Grand Rapids, MI 49516-6287
www.revellbooks.com

Second printing, March 2009

Printed in the United States of America

Library of Congress Cataloging-in-Publication Data
Young, Nicole, 1967–
Kiss me if you dare / Nicole Young.
p. cm. — (A Patricia Amble mystery ; 3)
ISBN 978-0-8007-3159-5 (pbk.)
1. Amble, Patricia (Fictitious character)—Fiction. 2. Dwellings—Remodeling—Fiction. I. Title.
PS3625.0968K57 2009
813'.6—dc22 2008044857

This book is a work of fiction. Names, characters, places, and incidents are the product of the author's imagination or are used fictitiously. Any resemblance to actual events, locales, or persons, living or dead, is coincidental.

To Katey with love
on your eighteenth birthday

1

In the sweep of the headlights, the house on the hill looked like a gaudy mansion dating from California's gold rush era. I felt a surge of exhilaration. I could imagine the view of the mighty Pacific I'd have in the morning from windows overlooking the cliffs. And the thought of crumbling plaster around the panes got my blood pumping. Digging my teeth into this place would make the perfect distraction.

Chunks of heaving cement led to an old-fashioned carport at one side of the home. The vehicle pulled behind an older model Honda and stopped.

The driver cut the engine and touched my arm. "Despite her appearance, Ms. Rigg helps where she can. Please don't undermine her desire." He held my gaze for an extra beat, an Einstein look-alike with his shaggy white hair and Coke-bottle glasses. The lab-coat look with mix-n-match clothes beneath screamed "permanently out to lunch." He got out of the vehicle and disappeared inside.

Relief swept over me with his departure. We'd been cooped up in the car together on and off for the past seventy-two hours. And while Professor Denton Braddock obviously meant well with his endless stream of words to the wise, I felt like a four-year-old trapped in Mr. Rogers' neighborhood.

A blast of pain shot up my arm. The moist ocean air with its tinge of salt seemed to add to the agony. I rubbed at the bandage that extended from elbow to shoulder, ready for another painkiller. I grabbed at the handle with my good arm and opened the car door.

A single bulb dangled above me in the weathered porch area. Shadows shrank and grew as the stiff breeze sent the light scuttling. I shivered, though the early summer evening was balmy.

I stared at the entry to my newest renovation project and sighed. Fixing up houses and selling them for a profit had been my living for much of the past decade. But I'd intended to make the log cabin back in the deep woods of Michigan my final project. I'd been ready to settle down. Thanks to the redneck mafia, I had to live with Plan B—at least until I could return home and make my dream a reality.

Ahead, warped steps led up to a screen door and into the house. I put a foot on the bottom tread. This was the first time I'd arrived at a renovation empty-handed. No cot. No sleeping bag. No coffeemaker. No tools. No Goodwill bargains. No identification.

Just the clothes on my back. I even had to live under another name while I hid out in Del Gloria. No more Patricia Louise Amble, the name on my birth certificate. I was now Alisha Marie Braddock, the professor's supposed niece visiting from Galveston.

"Why Galveston?" I'd asked him somewhere between Minnesota and Wyoming.

"I like how it sounds."

"I've never been to Galveston," I said.

"Then you can't give any details about your previous life, can you?"

I hated his answer. I'd walked away from great romantic possibilities with Brad back in Rawlings in order to dig into my past. I hadn't felt right starting a relationship when I couldn't give an intelligent account of my ancestry. According to Denton, I was now supposed to brush off any questions that would give clues to my identity.

I scuffed across the porch and through the screen door. It slammed behind me.

Beyond an entryway, I found the kitchen, tall and narrow with cupboards stretching beyond human reach along two walls. A library ladder would have been at home in the galley layout.

Far overhead, two bulbs cast a dim light on the room. The cream-colored walls seemed in perfect condition. The finish on the dark cabinetry shone to a high gloss, without a fingerprint in sight. I ran my hand along a cool stone countertop. Though clearly a replacement, the flawless surface looked original to the home. All in all, a remarkable restoration job.

I crossed my arms and leaned against the counter. When Brad set me up with this hideout, he'd assured me that Denton was offering food and shelter in exchange for my restoration skills. I could only assume the rest of the house, minus the kitchen, needed my expert touch.

The thought of Brad delivered a new dose of pain, starting at my heart and radiating to every limb.

A door swung open at one end of the room.

"Welcome, Miss Braddock," said a woman's voice.

Remembering my name change, I stood to attention at the brisk Irish accent.

"I'm Ms. Rigg." She spoke the title as if Mizz was her given name as she shuffled into the light. "Do you need help with your bags or can you get them yourself?"

Ms. Rigg was a tiny woman wearing a black cotton dress over black socks and black sneakers. White legs poked out beneath her hem with each step. As she drew closer, I realized her small stature could be attributed to a curved spine. The hump on her back rose almost as high as the top of her head.

I tried not to stare. "No. I'm fine. I have no bags."

"Then what about food? You must be hungry."

I focused my mind on my stomach. It growled on cue. "Food would be great. Thanks."

The words seemed to trip a switch. The woman moved with purpose to the stove and lifted the lid on an oversized pot. "Beef stew. The professor's favorite."

Steam billowed as she stirred. The succulent scent of juicy tomatoes and spice filled the air.

"Mmmm. Smells delicious." I liked the thought of a built-in cook during my stay in Del Gloria.

She plopped the lid back and retrieved a stepping stool from a corner of the kitchen. She set it down near the sink, climbed up, and pulled open a cabinet. Even with the added height, she struggled to reach the bowls. At her grunt, I intervened.

“Here. Let me help with those.” Just a smidge under six feet, my height came in handy in the restoration business. Those hard-to-reach corners were easy for me. Long arms, long neck, long legs . . . I either resembled a supermodel or an ostrich.

The fingers of my good arm barely touched the smooth ceramic bowls before Ms. Rigg swatted me away.

“Don’t you be interfering in my kitchen.” Her voice rose to shrill peaks. “It’s bad enough the professor agreed to take you in. Barely through the door and you think you own the place.” Gray hair in a bun shook loose with her anger. “Well, you don’t own it yet. Relation or not, you’ll not be taking my place in this house.”

I recoiled at her words. “I’m sorry. I just meant to help. And please, don’t worry about me. I’m not really—”

The far door swung open.

“Alisha.”

Professor Braddock strode in. For a moment he seemed strong and decisive, not the awkward nerd-type I’d ridden here with.

He took me by the arm. I winced at the pressure on my bandage.

“I’m showing Alisha to her room. She can help herself to stew later.” Denton led me out of the kitchen. We stopped just outside the door.

He turned me toward him, showing no mercy to my wound. “Heed my words. You will not survive if anyone suspects you are not who I say you are.”

I shook off his grip. “Sorry.” I cradled my arm. “She got so defensive. I didn’t want her thinking I was here permanently.”

"Perhaps you are here permanently. We won't know for some time." His lips pursed under a bushy moustache as he started to walk. "I warned you about Ms. Rigg. I specifically asked you not to help her."

I hurried to keep up, thinking back to his parting words in the car. "I had no idea she'd be so offended."

He halted at the foot of a grand staircase. "Now you know. Don't help unless she asks."

I stared at a mole on his cheek. Denton certainly offered asylum—as in loony bin, not sanctuary. What had Brad been thinking? When I found the body in my basement two projects ago, the killer had been behind bars within six months. Could I last around here for six months?

I sighed and followed Denton up the stairs. It wasn't as if I had a choice.

2

Denton jogged up the steps, speaking to me over his shoulder. "Ms. Rigg has been with my family since I was a boy. When my parents died, I continued to employ her—not only out of obligation, but also from gratitude. She served us well over the years, always treating my home and family as her own. It's rare to find that kind of loyalty in today's world."

He led me down a hallway, gloomy in the fading light.

"Why was she so offended when I tried to help?" I asked. "She practically snapped my head off when I reached for that bowl." It had been a brown bowl, deep chocolate brown, not unlike the color of Brad's eyes.

Denton paused in front of a closed door. "She may only be the housekeeper, but Alexa Rigg fancies herself mistress of Cliffhouse. She takes her work seriously. Perhaps too seriously. Her duties have become a heavy weight on her shoulders."

"Can't you tell her to ease up?" I said. "I'd love to help where I could. It's silly to have her wait on me hand and foot when I'm perfectly capable of helping myself. And I really don't think she enjoys it."

His hand rested on the doorknob. "Her world is one of conflict. I can't make her choose peace when she prefers drama."

The door swung open to reveal an airy bedroom with a row of windows along the far wall. I strode to one and peered through the blackness at a thin rose-colored glow where the water met the sky, like a view of Earth from outer space, a fringe of sunbeams defining the horizon. I drew in an awed breath. Who could embrace conflict within sight of paradise? Ms. Rigg must be living with her eyes closed.

I turned to Denton. "What about you? Don't you prefer peace in your own home?"

Taking a step back, he smiled. "Yes. That's why I stay out of the kitchen." He gripped the doorknob. "Sleep well, Patricia. You'll need it." The door shut behind him.

I waited awhile after his footsteps died away before tiptoeing to the kitchen for a serving of Ms. Rigg's beef stew. I erased all evidence of my meal, then took a stealth tour of the house, roaming from one amazing room to the next—avoiding those with closed doors. By the time I found my way back to my bedroom, I was convinced Cliffhouse presented the finest renovation I'd ever seen.

The next morning, lying in a big four-poster with the morning light filtering through silk curtains, I absorbed more of my new home. The room was fit for a princess. The whole house fit for a queen. Not one area seemed in need of repair. I could almost feel my muscles going limp from lack of hard labor.

The ceiling soared well past the acorn-shaped tips of the bedposts. A single imperfection in the drywall, a tiny lump of paint almost directly above me, gave my eyes a focal point as my mind drifted Brad-ward. I strained to remember the expression on his face as I drove off in his SUV, headed to Del Gloria. He must have waved. Said "I love you." Maybe even had tears in his eyes. But all my mind could produce was white static, like snow on an off-the-air station.

What could I remember? The way his eyes sparkled like stars in a sky of midnight blue just before he kissed me on the porch and promised to pick me up a few hours later to shop for an engagement ring.

I shifted under the covers and held my left hand above my head, examining the third finger over, wondering which set I would have chosen if my world hadn't crumbled that day. White or yellow gold? A solitary diamond or a dazzling cluster? Simple or flashy? I smiled at the thought. Simple, of course. Brad loved a woman with dishpan hands, not some ivory-skinned debutante.

I lay there a few minutes more, wishing I could pick up the phone and give him a call. Then I swung my legs over the side of the mattress. A groan accompanied my efforts. The three-day trip to Del Gloria had been excruciating with my bum arm. I rubbed at the ache near my shoulder. The bullet had torn through the flesh, but missed the bone.

A drug deal gone sour and I'd been caught in the middle. Brad had been there too . . . but the details were hazy. The blast of a weapon, pain knifing through my body, the steady glare of the sun as I drove west in a race for my life.

The next thing I knew I'd rammed into the back end

of a mom-and-three-kids minivan somewhere this side of Minneapolis. My arm was bleeding, but other than that, no one had been hurt. I was brought in for medical attention, lucid enough to evade questions by claiming I couldn't remember anything—including my name. Weirdly, it was mostly true at the time. I'd handed them the slip of paper in my pocket, the one that said DENTON BRADDOCK in Brad Walters' handwriting. They dialed the phone number. Denton must have known all the right things to say because they left me alone after that.

"It appears you're suffering from trauma-induced memory loss," the physician told me later as he treated my injury. "Dr. Braddock is flying in from California. We'll release you into his custody." He made it sound like he knew Dr. Braddock personally, as if he was confidently turning me over to the care of some renowned practitioner. How could I have known he meant Dr. Frankenstein?

Now here I was. An inmate of the coastal sanatorium.

I walked to a window. At least this time my prison had a view. The lawn in front of the house sloped down to meet a two-lane road flanked by guardrail. Beyond, the land dropped away into a wispy blue ocean that disappeared into the morning fog. I lifted the sash a few inches. Through the screen came the crash of water against rocks. I'd expected the sound to be soothing. But the ebb and swell along the cliffs seemed vicious. Ferocious. Unsettling. I pushed the pane back into place. The roar died, swapped for a muffled *whoosh*.

A morning routine was out of the question. I had no soap, shampoo, or makeup. Not even a change of clothes since my own had been too bloodstained to salvage. The professor said all I had to do was ask and he'd get me everything I needed. But how foolish was that? I was thirty-three years old. I'd provided for my own needs practically my whole life. I had no intention of begging him for money or anything else.

In the adjoining bathroom, I splashed water on my face one-handed, thinking that at the very least, soap should have been provided for guests. Denton hadn't remembered all the basics when he'd speed-shopped for my wardrobe, though his thoughtfulness let me check out of the hospital fully clothed instead of with my skivvies peeking through the gap in the back of my gown. And at least he'd remembered a toothbrush and toothpaste. Still, I wished I'd grabbed a bar of soap and a mini-shampoo before checking out of the Lumpy Mattress Motel yesterday.

I toweled off, pausing as I got a glimpse of myself. The woman in the mirror looked strained, with dark smudges beneath her eyes. I touched a finger to the skin. Time was catching up to me. Subtle crow's feet splayed my temple area, a testimony to periodic heartbreak. A deeper gash across my forehead labeled me a worry-wart. A crop of gray highlights tufted from the center part of my below-the-shoulder auburn hair, the effects of chronic anxiety.

I forced a smile. My bottom lids arched up. Brad told me it made me look exotic. But squinty-eyed was a more apt description.

Letting my smile fade, I ran a finger across the frown lines framing my mouth. I looked haunted, like the ghost of Tish Amble. Something more than disappointment had changed the appearance of my face.

Sure, I got frustrated with life when a visit from the Yooper Godfather put my marriage proposal on hold—*Yooper* being the name you call somebody from the U.P., as in Michigan's Upper Peninsula. But there was something else, something beyond dejection in my eyes. Something I couldn't finger . . .

A heavy knock sounded at the door.

"Alisha. We're leaving in ten minutes."

It was Denton, barking orders in a voice so unlike the soft-spoken one he'd used at the hospital to schmooze the staff.

I looked in the mirror one last time, helpless to do anything about my appearance.

I shrugged at myself in apology. "Coming," I called.

With one arm working and the other too tender to be of much use, I slithered into my Levis, and topped them with a five-dollar tee in blaze orange. The jeans fell a tad on the short side. I managed to roll up the bottoms a few turns, making them into pedal pushers, my cure for everything that landed at or above my ankles. I checked my trim silhouette in the mirror and raked fingers through my hair, having no choice but to leave it down. There was no getting around the fact that ponytail holders required two operating arms. I gave the overall look a thumbs-up, grateful I didn't know a soul west of the Mississippi.

The hall was empty. I made my way past closed doors painted white and trimmed with gold leaf, then down the sweeping staircase to the kitchen, where Ms. Fussybritches busily buffed the stovetop with a white cloth.

"Good morning," she said with her lilting Irish accent.

"Morning," I returned in my strictly Midwestern one. "I'm just going to grab a quick bowl of cereal." I paused, nervous my words may have offended her. "If that's okay," I added.

"Cereal is next to the icebox. And you already know where the bowls are." Her cloth never missed a motion.

I got busy with my breakfast, unable to shake the feeling that evil hate-beams radiated from the direction of the oven. Through the crunching of all-natural granola, I could hear Ms. Rigg's cloth making meaningful swoops across the surface, first quiet, then faster and louder as the cotton caught the ring around a burner and banged at it over and over, as if determined to make the metal pay for my sins.

I forced down the last swallow. Without a word, I rinsed my bowl and squirted it with dish soap.

"Leave that for me," the drill sergeant commanded. Her cloth screeched to a halt.

My hands froze in place.

"I'm the only one who'll be doing the dishes around this house." Alexa Rigg's face torqued into an angry scowl. "Can't say what you hope to gain at Cliffhouse. But whatever it is, you'll not be gaining it at my expense."

At the threat in her voice, I backed away from the sink, scrounged up a paper towel to dry my hands, and hightailed it out of enemy territory, abandoning the thought of a cup of coffee.

I found Denton in the dining room, swigging down his last drop of caffeine. He stood as I entered. His white hair was combed neatly to one side. He must have popped in contacts. And his shirt, tie, and slacks actually matched.

"What's going on?" I asked, unnerved by his transformation from Mr. Dweeb to Mr. Ooh La La.

He looked at his wristwatch. "Time to go."

I ran to keep up with him as he swooped to the portico and started the rental car.

I slid into the passenger seat, nursing a tender bicep under day-old bandages. He turned the car around and headed down the driveway. At the bottom of the hill, he stopped for traffic.

"Do you smell that?" Denton wrinkled up his nose and took a few whiffs. "Is that you?"

"Pardon me?" I didn't like the new, debonair Denton. At least Dweeby Denton had manners.

"I'm sorry, but it smells like body odor in here."

Blood rushed to my face. I hadn't taken a shower since yesterday before dawn and hadn't had a change of clothes in three days. On top of it, my overworked bandage carried a salty aroma this morning. But come on, I couldn't reek that bad. I subtly aimed my nose toward my armpit. *Oof.*

I cleared my throat. "It's not as if I have a change of clothes or the stuff to take a shower, you know. I don't have two nickels to rub together yet."

"And when do you plan to have those two nickels? A week from now when I couldn't even ride in the same car with you?"

He pulled onto the main road.

My jaw dropped. "How rude. Stop the car. I'm getting out."

He kept driving.

We neared a three-way stop. Straight ahead, the road followed the cliff's edge along the coast. The fork to the right led up a hill toward civilization. One phone call from the McDonald's we'd passed on the way in last night and I could escape this isolated promontory. I grabbed my emergency escape handle.

His voice softened. "That was not meant as an affront. I feel that if a person needs help, she should ask for it. You probably don't even realize you are behaving like Ms. Rigg."

I stiffened, surprised at his observation. Ms. Rigg was the last person I wanted to pattern my life after. I blew out a breath. "Where are we going, anyway?" When the professor had knocked on my door this morning, I'd assumed he'd be taking me to the restoration project Brad had mentioned. Now, I eyed Denton's dress clothes, wondering why I hadn't questioned him earlier.

"I am going to teach. You are going to meet with the Dean of Admissions at Del Gloria College. Summer classes have already started, but I've arranged a late enrollment."

My mouth gaped. "Me enroll in college? Are you crazy?" My last attempt at a bachelor's degree ended when I'd been thrown in the slammer. With the recent drama in my life, I wasn't sure I was ready to take another stab at it.

"Tish—isn't that what Brad called you?" Denton asked.

I bristled to hear him use my nickname. He hadn't earned that right. I nodded my acknowledgment.

"Then, Tish, let me put things in simple terms. You don't have a choice." He punctuated each word.

Waves of rebellion swept through me at his attempted coup. Apparently, with my current situation, Denton figured he owned me.

My teeth clamped in defiance. With no options coming to mind, I'd have to make the best of things until I could get out of Dodge. Anyway, what could it hurt to take a few classes? Hadn't I always wanted to finish college?

I gave a sigh of reluctance. "Fine," I said, crossing my arms. "I'll go."

3

Denton nodded his approval. "Wise choice."

The car accelerated.

I glared his way. "You said I didn't have a choice."

"Then see what a good decision you made? Now you don't have to be angry with me for making you do something you didn't want to do."

My jaw wiggled back and forth. With a course of action set, I thought ahead to my admissions meeting. "I take it I should clean up a little before my interview."

"Another good decision."

I flicked a wrist toward my stale clothing. "I don't have anything to wear. And I'm going to need a shower."

He looked over at me as if waiting for something, then went back to driving.

I studied his profile as we drove past homes converted into law firms and dentist offices. Without his chunky glasses, Denton was actually quite handsome. He'd trimmed his moustache to a slim white line. A few errant curls above his ears added a dash of mystery. His shoulders were pulled back in proud posture, completely

opposite the slouchy sag he'd carried on the drive from Minnesota. If the guy hadn't been in his sixties, I'd have sworn I was attracted to him.

"I suggest you take a shower and change your clothes if that's what you need to do," he finally answered, taking a left past the McDonald's at the WELCOME TO DEL GLORIA sign.

The road widened into a highway, and a minute later we left the town behind and drove along a flat, open stretch. At a road marked DEL GLORIA INTERNATIONAL AI -PORT, the doc turned right.

I twiddled my thumbs. "If there's an airport nearby, how come we drove all the way from Minnesota?"

"Two reasons. First, you had no identification. Only false documents would have allowed us to fly without giving away the whereabouts of Patricia Louise Amble."

That made sense. "And second?" I asked.

"Second, it gave me time to analyze you and design your course of study." He pulled into the rent-a-car lot and stopped the car. "So what have you decided?"

I fidgeted under his stare. "Decided about what?"

"About how you're going to obtain the shower and change of clothing you mentioned."

Oh, the humility of it all. I swallowed my pride. "I guess I was hoping you'd help me out with that for today. I have no money. No checkbook. And you cut up my debit card."

"For your own safety." He gave me an inquiring look. "So exactly what do you need?"

I grunted in frustration. "Money. For clothes and

things." I wasn't about to give him a shopping list that included personal items.

"Do you remember what I told you that first night at the hotel?"

I nodded.

"Just ask and anything you need will be provided. Anything at all," he said.

The rent-a-car attendant stood outside, writing on a clipboard as he waited for us to get out of the vehicle.

I blinked back tears and cleared my throat. A muscle in the side of my face twitched. Then my chin launched into a stubborn quiver. Right under Denton's probing gaze, I felt my whole face collapse into a wrinkled ball. My gasping sobs filled the car. Tears landed in puddles on my jeans.

How had my life come to this? Thirty-three years old and I was begging for my bread. Me, the woman who'd broken free of that pit I'd called home in Walled Lake. It hadn't been easy, but I'd done it through my own hard work. And later, after sinking into the mire those three years behind bars, I'd grabbed myself by the bootstraps, given them a mighty yank, and gotten back on my feet. Then I'd saved and slaved and bought my first home to renovate. And today I had stocks in my name. Bonds about to mature. Certificates of Deposit ready to be cashed.

I sniffled and raised my head. I wasn't desperate and destitute. I was just temporarily barred from accessing my funds. This layman's witness protection program might be humbling, but I could survive it. It wasn't what I'd expected, but Brad meant the best when he'd set me up with Denton.

Brad. The name gave my already-raw heart another twist. He'd rescued me from the clutches of a scam artist in Rawlings and saved me from death at the hands of slime-ball drug dealers in Port Silvan. He'd been eight hours away from making me his official bride-to-be when—

The sound of a gunshot cracked through my mind. A stab of pain gripped my arm. The momentary burst of memory launched a migraine across my forehead.

Candice LeJeune's face swirled red before my eyes. She'd ruined everything. My life had been coming together for the first time. Then she'd lured me into her illegal activities. All the thanks I'd gotten was a bullet in the arm. I rubbed my bandage, trying to wrangle up the details of that crazy morning. In the end, all that mattered was I'd done what Brad had told me to do: get to Del Gloria and Denton Braddock.

Now, sitting under the disapproving glare of Sir Grump-a-lot, I wish I'd argued with Brad a little more.

I wiped my cheeks with the back of my hand.

"Feel better?" Denton asked. He said it without condemnation.

The softened response came as a surprise, and I let my guard down. "Yeah. I guess I needed that."

"It was overdue." He unfolded a tissue from his pocket and passed it to me.

"Thanks." I dried my tears. I'd held myself together pretty good over the past several days, despite the events in Michigan. Today, it felt good to have a moment of relief.

We exited the rental car, Denton signed the clipboard, and we headed toward the parking lot.

"Thank you," the attendant said with a cheery wave, as if the extra ten minutes I'd needed to pull myself together were no big deal.

Denton jangled a set of keys. "I'll have you drop me at the college. Then you can take my car to do your shopping and go back to the house to get ready. Your appointment is at two o'clock at Walters Hall."

Walters. The same as Brad's last name. It seemed I couldn't avoid reminders of him today.

Denton pressed the security button on his key chain. A bleep sounded to the left. He walked to the passenger side door of a sleek, black Jaguar and threw me the keys.

I stared at the vehicle. "Your real car is a Jag?"

"Surprised?" he asked, getting in.

I settled myself in the soft leather behind the steering wheel. It smelled as good as Brad's hunky SUV, which was probably sitting in a Minnesota body shop.

I glanced at the distinguished-looking man beside me. "Today nothing surprises me. Yesterday, I would have been shocked."

"Oh, you mean because of your mistaken first impressions?"

I listened to the purr of the engine before putting the car in reverse. "Exactly. What was that all about anyway?"

"It was necessary in order to ascertain your level of spiritual growth. At Del Gloria College, we want to know if a prospective student takes the world at face value, or if they look deeper, past the exterior, to discover a person's core. Now that I've observed your behavior, I can assign you to the appropriate classes."

I pulled to the end of the row. My arm only hurt a little. "Excuse me? You had to act like a dweeb so you could tell where I'm at spiritually? You could have just asked."

"Words mean nothing. Only actions."

I'd been tolerant of his whole geek show all the way to California. Of course I'd passed his simple test.

He pointed. "Get back on the main road and take it to the other end of town."

I pressed on the gas. A tumbleweed, blown loose from the open field, cut across the road in front of me. "So you're not the Nutty Professor, you're really some richer-than-thou instructor at a Christian college. And I should have been open-minded enough to guess the truth." I gave a disgruntled humph. "If it's all about actions, then I fail to see how I'm supposed to feel good about living under your roof the next few months."

"That's too optimistic," he said. "You'll be here longer than a few months. Much longer."

The flat expanse turned into a residential zone as we crossed town. Then the route became tunnel-like as we passed beneath a canopy of trees. Birds fluttered from branch to branch seeking cover from the hot sun.

"You know," I said to Denton, "Brad is going to tie up the loose ends of that whole drug-deal thing and then contact me to come home. I'll be here six months at the most."

He sighed deep and heavy, as if the entire matter were beyond my understanding and he didn't have time to explain. "It's a complex situation. You'll have to be patient."

I heaved a sigh of my own. Seven days since my world fell apart. It had only been seven days. I tapped my foot on the gas pedal, surging past the foreign landscape. I did some math as I pulled onto College Boulevard. The median burst with the stunning pink blooms of some exotic bush, the perfect color for bridesmaids' dresses. I pictured the delicate shade on Brad's sister Samantha and wrinkled my nose. She'd look like a swirl of cotton candy.

I swung my mind back around to my calculations. About a hundred eighty more days before I could be with Brad again. Then I'd be back in Port Silvan and I'd finish the renovations on my log cabin in the woods. And somehow Brad and I would find a way to be together. Only a hundred eighty more days.

I already suffered being away this long. My lungs couldn't seem to fill with air. My stomach churned more than usual, leaving an acid trail in my throat. And an ache hovered at the front of my neck, as if I might launch into another round of tears at any moment. Somehow being near Brad put my body, mind, and spirit in proper alignment. As long as I was with him, I was feeling no pain.

"Turn right," Denton said.

The Jag responded to my one-armed commands as I angled around a corner toward a low glass building at the end of a circle drive. I pulled up to the curb.

"Here." Denton opened his wallet and counted out a thousand in crisp hundreds. He held the stack toward me.

I gasped and put up a palm to stop him. "Oh my. That's overkill. One of those should be enough."

"Get what you need today so you don't have to think about it anymore. You'll be glad you did."

I studied his face for hidden meaning. He seemed sincere, but something screamed "Warning, warning!" Really, what kind of person carried a thousand dollars' cash in his wallet on a daily basis?

He nudged the bills into my hand.

The kind of guy that owned a Jaguar, I supposed.

"Thank you." My voice was barely a whisper.

"You're welcome. I'll meet you after your interview, there," he pointed across campus to a domed building that could pass for a state capitol, "at Walters Hall." He got out of the car. "Oh," he added, "driving without a license is illegal in all fifty states. So don't get pulled over until we can get your new identity set up."

The door slammed shut with the discreet hush of a luxury vehicle.

I stayed for a moment and watched my guardian ogre enter the building, disappearing behind silver glass that reflected a black Jaguar parked at the curb out front.

My fingers rubbed at the stack of hundred-dollar bills. A thousand bucks, a luxury car for the day—life wasn't so bad. The woman in the reflection smiled at me, waving the money in her hand.

I put the car in gear and drove toward town, caught up in the thrill of the hunt.

4

A sign pointed the way to BUSINESS DISTRICT. I turned up a hillside blooming with early summer splendor. At the top of the rise, the road ran straight. A gap between the farthest buildings showcased the blue Pacific. I drove down the three-block stretch and checked out the shop selection. From the timeworn building fronts, I got the overall impression that Del Gloria was a hardworking town, one without the time, money, or inclination to cater to snooty tourists. I patted the wad of money in my jeans pocket. That attitude would bode well for my hardly earned dollars.

I spotted what I was looking for and slammed on the brakes. I eased the Jag into a slanted parking space in front of the Del Gloria Thrift-Mart. For a moment, I felt at home in this strange land. Even on California's rocky coast, folks had a yen for secondhand clothing.

The door *ding*ed as I entered. To one side, a circular rack of women's tops were marked 75 percent off. I headed toward it like a paint splotch to a new pair of jeans.

After thirty minutes of scrutinizing stains, checking sizes, and tracking down a variety of work-wear, I proceeded to the register.

The cashier rang up my items.

I pulled out a hundred-dollar bill and waited for change. She counted it into my hand with barely a glance at my face. It was nice to be in a college town. The steady influx of strangers gave me the anonymity necessary to pull off this crazy safe-house scheme.

A moment later, I was on the sidewalk headed for the department store. Inside, I picked out my interpretation of interview clothes: a deep blue jacket over a white blouse topping a pinstriped knee-length skirt and navy Mary Janes with a spunky heel. Completely conservative. And *so* not me. But neither was impressing people with my clothing. I brought the ensemble up front, loaded up the counter with socks, undies, and a few modest bras, and pulled out my bills to pay.

The clerk tallied and bagged my items, then I scooted out the door.

One block down was the drugstore, where I splurged on an assortment of cosmetics, personal care items, and fresh bandages. I even bought a hair dryer and curling iron.

The black Jag was waiting for me, crowded between standard issue Toyotas and Hondas. I got behind the wheel and headed for Cliffhouse.

An hour later, I was showered, dressed, and driving to Walters Hall for my interview.

My chest constricted with nervous tension and my knees shook. With only a few hours' notice to prepare,

I couldn't think of a thing I had to offer DGC. What college would even want me? Besides marrying Brad and settling down and possibly continuing to renovate homes on the side, I had no spectacular future plans.

At the thought of Brad, the ache near my shoulder flared up. I rested my arm in my lap. I'd done too much already today. The doctor had told me to take it easy. Shopping wasn't exactly a contact sport, but my body would need a few days to recover from the exertion. I gritted my teeth, determined to make it through the interview before giving in to the pain.

I eased the Jag past a group of students on the sidewalk. They waved as I drove by.

I found a parking space close to the door and got out.

A woman stopped at the front bumper. She held a stack of books in one hand. The other was on her hip. Short, kinked brown hair, a few shades darker than her skin, lifted at random in the breeze.

"I thought you were the doc," she said, annoyance in her voice.

"Oh." I looked at the Jag and a lightbulb came on. "No, he lent me his car for the morning." I smoothed my skirt and auto-locked the doors.

She gave me a probing once-over. "Who are you, a recruiter from the naval base?"

Her attitude got to me. I pulled rank. "No. I'm the professor's niece from Galveston." I thrust my good hand toward her. "Alisha Braddock. Nice to meet you. And your name is?"

I detected a flush creeping up her cheeks. She switched

her stack of books to the opposite hand and shook mine in a quick salute. "Portia Romero. Nice to meet you."

I gave a final thrust. "I'll make sure to let Uncle Denton know you're looking for him. Bye." I flung a smirk over my shoulder and headed to my interview.

The nerve of some people. I steamed about Portia Romero's hoity-toity attitude all the way to the front entrance of Walters Hall. I stopped at the stone steps, took a deep breath, and tried to clear my mind.

My big second chance at college. A re-do. A turning back of the clock. All I had to do was make the best of the next six months. Maybe the credits would transfer to a college back in Michigan and I could finish school there. As soon as Brad called me home.

Inside, I scanned the directory. Dean of Admissions, Suite 401. I swallowed hard at the other words that popped off the marquis: Dean of Bible Studies, Philosophy, Theology . . . not exactly my cup of tea.

I took the elevator. My heart rate increased with the altitude. The doors opened. Stark black marble and a potted plant gave a sober welcome.

Inside, the acrid scent of just-installed industrial carpet matched its blackberry-pie hue. A tawny counter, the color of flaky crust, separated visitors from staff. I folded my hands on the textured surface and forced them to be still. Near a bank of windows overlooking the campus, an attractive redhead sat behind a desk.

"Hi," I said, getting the woman's attention. "I'm Ti—" I caught my blunder and swallowed. "I'm Alisha Braddock. I'm here for an interview with the dean."

A smile lit her face. She toyed with something on the

arm of her chair and the whole thing backed out from the desk and wheeled over to the counter. She reached up a hand in greeting. "I'm so pleased to meet you. Professor Braddock is a favorite around here. He's told us so many wonderful things about his niece from Galveston."

"He has?" I leaned over the counter and shook her hand.

"Of course. And I can see why. You're beautiful. Just beautiful."

I dropped my arm, dazed. "Oh, that Uncle Denton," I played along. "He shouldn't have." For the moment I was glad to be decked out in my dress duds. It felt good to be considered beautiful by a complete stranger, even if she was just trying to butter up the niece of the beloved "Doc."

"Dean Lester will see you in just a moment. Go ahead and have a seat." She nodded to the row of chairs by the door.

An assortment of Del Gloria College literature was scattered in tidy array on a coffee table. I picked up a course catalog to peruse while waiting. The cover showed students in caps and gowns looking off toward some rosy future. I flipped to an inside page and scanned photos surrounding a Bible verse. More smiles. More hype. I read the quote, written in flowery script. "Jesus said, 'It is not the healthy who need a doctor, but the sick . . . For I have not come to call the righteous, but sinners.'"

The words hit at some deep level, wriggling their way into my brain. I tossed the catalog back on the table, not caring for the feelings evoked by a few simple words and images. My fingers instead found the zipper on the patent leather pocketbook I'd bought to match my heels. The doc's remaining five hundred dollars were the only items inside. No driver's license, insurance card, cell phone, or checkbook. *Zzzt . . . zzzt . . . zzzt.* After a minute of the mind-numbing noise, I tucked the thing under my arm and resorted to clicking my heels instead. The leather made a funny squeak.

The secretary was talking to someone.

"Miss Braddock." The words found their way through my mental wanderings.

I whipped my head up and blushed. "Oh, I'm so sorry. You're talking to me." I put a hand to my temple.

I jumped up and followed her to a glassed-in office.

"Dean Lester, this is Alisha Braddock, here for a two o'clock interview." The secretary wheeled out, shutting the door behind her.

"How nice to meet you, Alisha," came a lilting southern accent. "I'm Dr. Jordan Lester. Please. Be seated." The African-American woman indicated the overstuffed armchair opposite her desk. Her persimmon blouse and bold turquoise jewelry made the exact opposite statement of my conservative garb.

I sat, sinking into soft chenille.

Dean Lester came around to the front of the desk and perched on a corner of it. One leg of her black slacks rode up slightly to reveal ballet flats with a touch of sparkle.

I had a feeling this wasn't going to be a typical college entry interview.

"Tell me about yourself."

Her gentle voice and sincere smile nearly put me at ease.

I cleared my throat. "Well, to begin with, I'm Professor Braddock's niece from Galveston." I hated the lie, but it came easier every time I told it.

"Galveston? You sound more like you're from Minnesota."

I blinked fast. "Well, yes, I was in Minnesota before Galveston." That first part wasn't a lie.

I waited for another question. She just kept smiling.

Crossing my legs, I smiled back. The silence dragged on.

"Well?" she prompted. "Tell me more."

I blew out a nervous breath. I grew up an orphan, nearly married a con artist, was best friends with a murderer . . . My arm throbbed at the thought of Candice LeJeune. I rubbed at it as I devised a suitably vague answer for the dean.

"I like houses," I said. "I like to fix them up."

"Why?" The sparkles on her shoes glinted like a disco ball as she swung her foot.

I shrugged. "I like to fix broken stuff. I like to take things that are ugly and make them beautiful again."

She looked at a notepad on her desk. "Then I think it's appropriate Professor Braddock has assigned you to our Revamp Department."

I perked up. "Wow. Sounds like it's right up my alley."

She wagged a finger. "The program has less to do with renovating houses and more to do with building character. I hope you're up for a year of intense introspection."

Introspection. Didn't that mean looking inside myself? I wasn't sure I was ready for that.

Her face retained its pleasant expression. "I'm looking at the course list the professor put together. Pending transfer of your credits and taking the maximum course load, you can receive your degree in as little as one year."

My eyes studied a speck of lint on the blackberry carpeting. In one year I could have my college degree. Too bad I wouldn't be here that long. I thought about Brad doing his police thing and making sure the bad guys got locked up so I could go back to Michigan and be his wife. Out of nowhere, my arm sent off a shot of pain that bent me into my lap.

"Are you all right?" The dean touched my shoulder.

"Yeah." I took a minute to breathe. "Sorry. It's almost time for more aspirin."

"Your uncle informed me of your injury. Would you like to finish this later?"

The pang passed and I straightened. "No. Let's get it over with."

She paused, then looked back at her notes. "Professor Braddock left a few notations about your childhood. Apparently your parents died when you were young?"

I hesitated, not sure what Denton's story line was. I figured it would be best to stick as close to the truth as possible so I wouldn't confuse myself, let alone everyone else.

"My mom died when I was eight. I think my dad is still alive. I just don't know where he is right now."

The dean raised her eyebrows. "You say that like you have plans to locate him."

"I do. Someday." I'd often wondered how my life would

have been different if my father hadn't turned in the local drug lord and gotten himself on the man's hit list. Would he have stuck around with my mom and me? I guess I'd never know.

"How does that fit into your studies?"

I blinked, knowing I didn't have the first clue where to look for my dad. "I'd like to finish my degree, but sometimes things get in the way." I was an expert at letting my college career get derailed.

Dean Lester sighed and walked around her desk. She sat in the oversized executive chair. "Miss Braddock. Your uncle has agreed to support you for the duration of your study at Del Gloria College. Should you choose to leave the program, that support will be withdrawn."

My blood surged. "Uncle D doesn't own me. I agreed to start classes. I never promised to finish them."

The dean stared at me in silence. Then she leaned forward. "I'll leave that between you and your uncle. In the meantime, I feel you are an excellent candidate for the program. Highly qualified, in fact."

The tone in her voice didn't exactly imply that was a good thing.

The dean rose to shake my hand. "You can pick up your schedule from my assistant. Congratulations on your acceptance to Del Gloria College."

I dropped her hand, bewildered as she shooed me out the door.

5

I made my escape, not wanting to question the dean's logic. How she figured I was highly qualified for any college program was a mystery to me. I stepped off the elevator and turned toward the bright sunshine glistening beyond the massive stone porch of Walters Hall. I pushed through the doors, and ground to a halt at the sight of Denton Braddock standing on the steps out front, surrounded by students.

Exhausted from an afternoon of whirlwind shopping and flat-out fibbing, I was impatient for my new room and the creature comforts of Cliffhouse, namely, Ms. Rigg's beef stew. Surely Denton didn't plan on standing around chitchatting much longer.

His voice echoed under the portico. "Always do the right thing. That way you won't suffer self-reproach later," he was saying.

Great. A Mr. Rogers episode on doing the right thing. I gave a private snort. And this from the guy putting together my fake identity. I maneuvered into the fringes of the crowd.

A man in his fifties moved to the front with a question. "Sometimes it's hard to know what to do. How can you be certain of what's right?"

Birdsong filled the silence as the undergrads held their collective breaths for his answer. I crossed my arms and tapped my foot, more worried about how long the performance would drag on than what the prof had to say.

He raised his voice, making sure those of us in the back could hear his answer. "Ask yourself, is it within man's law? Is it within God's law? Always make the choice not to hurt yourself."

My new archenemy Portia Romero wriggled her way toward the professor. "Isn't that selfish, if I'm thinking only of me?"

Yeah, like she was some big saint and actually cared about others.

"Check your motives," Denton answered. "If your intentions are pure, you're on the right track. Otherwise, you may be hurting yourself by setting out to hurt someone else, the principle of reaping what you sow."

Denton caught my eye. His mouth widened into a Cheshire cat smile. Somehow I felt like I'd just been targeted for termination.

He moved a step higher and looked over the crowd. "Alisha, come up here." His voice reached out to me.

I rooted my feet and crossed my arms.

Everyone turned to look. Those nearby nudged me toward the front and before I knew it, I was next to Professor Braddock, two steps above the crowd.

"Students," he turned to the faces, "I'd like to introduce

my niece, Alisha Braddock. She'll be staying with me at Cliffhouse and studying in our Revamp Program."

The mob broke into applause, sending a rush of blood to my cheeks.

As the clapping subsided, Denton raised one arm in a goodbye gesture to the gathering, like a rock star bidding his audience farewell. The other arm firmly about my shoulder, he walked me to the Jaguar and helped me into the passenger seat.

The door slammed. I stared at the silver carpeting. Opposite me, Denton got in and started the engine.

"Why did you put me on the spot like that?" My voice came out a choked cry.

He backed the vehicle into the road, then pulled ahead. "It's better to come right out and tell them who you are rather than making them guess. Curiosity can be dangerous. Now that I've explained your presence, you can safely be Alisha Braddock, the professor's niece from Galveston."

He turned at the intersection.

Shrinking in my seat, I massaged my temples, waiting for the pressure in my head to subside. "Do you really have a niece in Texas?"

He shot a glance my way. "Of course not. I'm an only child."

"Oh. How many people know that?"

He shrugged. "Nobody. I'm a private man."

"What if somebody does know? Who will they think I am then?"

"They won't question it." His tone assumed an end to the conversation.

We passed beneath the arching trees on the way to the main highway.

"Well," I said, massaging my arm, "suppose they do question it? Then what?"

"We'll cross that bridge when we come to it."

Any sense of security I might have felt washed out with the bridge comment. I sat straight. "What if someone figures out who I am? It's not like my face hasn't been on the front page of the national news." One little felony and I'd become a household name. Had it really been ten years since my release?

The ocean glimmered straight ahead as we pulled to the stop sign above the cliffs. When traffic cleared, the Jag angled left.

"If there's trouble, I'll take care of it," Denton said, eyes on the road.

"You sound like a mob boss."

"Boss's son, perhaps. My father was Stanley Braddock."

I filtered the name through the databanks. "Sorry. Doesn't ring any bells."

"He was a U.S. Senator and Ambassador to Ireland."

"Now I see where the Ms. Rigg connection fits in. But how does Great Uncle Stanley take care of trouble when it comes calling?"

"My father is dead. But he had many friends."

"Ooooh. A secret society." My eyebrows arced.

He half smiled and shook his head. "A network of good friends willing to help out when needed."

"I suppose you inherited the network"—I patted the Jaguar's leather seat—"along with everything else?"

He gave me a cock-eyed grin. "Basically."

I stared at the heaving waves. "A man of privilege. Lucky you."

"Humph. Just as I suspected."

I whipped my head to look at him. "What?"

"You feel sorry for yourself."

I crossed my arms. "I do not."

"When Brad first mentioned you, I knew you'd be the self-pity type."

I rubbed my injury. "Brad talked to you about me?"

Denton rested his hand on the shifter between us. "Of course he did. Brad and I talked often."

The Jag slowed for the turn up the driveway.

I blinked hard. "Did he tell you we were planning to get married?"

Silence. I turned to look. A muscle in Denton's jaw popped in and out as if he were forcing his words back down his throat.

"What? Brad didn't tell you?" My arm surged with pain.

Denton stared straight ahead. "He talked to me about it. I advised against it."

"Advised against it?" My nostrils flared. "Brad loves me. He ignored your advice. We were going the next day to pick out the rings." I looked down at my injury. "Then this happened."

The Jaguar pitched to a stop under the portico.

Denton cut the engine. "I can only say I'm grateful for divine intervention."

My fingernails dug into the leather seat. "This has gone far enough." I groped for the door handle and pushed my way outside. My heel sank between patches of concrete. "I'm not staying here a moment longer. I've had enough of you and your superior attitude." I pivoted toward the porch. My body turned, but my foot stayed embedded in the crack, jerking me off balance. Too late to catch myself, I plunged to the cement.

I landed on my bad arm. Stars and spirals filled my eyes. Ringing filled my ears. The glare of the sun blinded me as I sucked in shallow breaths and waited for the pain to pass.

A face blocked the light. It seemed familiar. "Brad? Is that you?"

6

"Stand up, Patricia." Denton's voice.

Not-so-gentle hands helped me to my feet.

Denton, not Brad. The perpetual ball in my throat squeezed tears from my eyes. "I thought you were Brad. I need Brad. I have to talk to him." I looked around for some phone booth or magic portal that would let me communicate with my boyfriend.

Boyfriend. I choked on the word. It should have been fiancé. I looked at my left hand, scuffed from its tussle with the concrete. The ring finger was bare. Just one more day and it would have been sparkling in the rays of a setting sun.

"I need to talk to Brad."

Denton led me up the steps. I leaned into him, limping on my weak ankle, newly raw from the fall.

"I'm sure you know as well as I do how impossible that would be."

In the door, down the hall, through an arch. Denton plunked me on a velvet settee.

I looked around the formal sitting room at the coved

ceilings and window nooks. Furniture and accents came in various shades of ivory, gold, and green. Opulent. Decadent. Very appropriate to the period of architecture, and right in line with the owner's impervious attitude.

"Ms. Rigg," Denton's voice boomed. "Bring an ice pack, please."

A few minutes earlier I'd been convinced the best thing to do was get out of Del Gloria. Now, I didn't have an arm or a leg to stand on.

Denton unfastened the buckle of my Mary Jane and pulled it off, checking my injury.

I gave a sigh of defeat. "Listen. I'm sorry I overreacted out there. I'm kind of stressed right now. This not knowing is starting to get to me."

"Not knowing about what?"

"You know, like is everyone okay at home? Is someone taking care of my house? Is it safe to go back there? How close are they to putting the bad guys behind bars? Stuff like that."

Ms. Rigg arrived with the ice. "Will she be alright, Professor?" The housekeeper leaned in to give her beady eyes a better view of the swollen area.

He wrapped the cold pack around my ankle. "It's too soon to tell, Ms. Rigg."

"Aye."

I flipped a hand toward the injury. "It'll be fine. I landed on it funny last fall. It acts up every so often."

"Your ankle is the least of my concerns." Denton stood. "Keep it elevated the rest of the evening. Ms. Rigg can bring your supper out here."

I didn't relish the thought of reclining all night in

dress clothes. My nylons were already twisted around my thighs and the waistband of my skirt dug in. The tag of my blouse scratched at the back of my neck. But the humble pie I'd already been forced to eat today made the clothes on my back far more comfortable than the bloating in my stomach.

With a final pat on my foot, Denton left the room, the loyal Ms. Rigg just behind him.

Alone in silence, I took a deep breath and leaned my head against the wooden arm of the settee. I stared at the concave ceiling, its perfectly smooth surface the work of an expert craftsman. Brad told me specifically not to contact anyone once I got to Del Gloria. But I couldn't take it. I was going crazy. I had to talk to somebody. I had to know what was going on back there.

The wood dug into my skull. I looked around for something soft. A green chair nearby offered a matching bolster. I hobbled over and swiped it. Comfortable once more, I drifted back to that morning at the lodge.

Just hours before doomsday, Brad had practically popped the question, implying that we'd drive to town for an official engagement ring—and fitting proposal—the next day. But then I'd gotten that call from Candice. She needed the box of photos, the culmination of years of evidence against a prosperous and violent drug ring. And I'd been stupid enough to bring them to her.

I glanced down at my arm. Then she'd shot me. I blinked in concentration, trying to fit the pieces together. That morning Frank Majestic, the local trucking tycoon drug lord, had come to the house wanting to know where my father was—as if I had a clue. Then Candice snuck in, grabbed Frank from behind, and stuck a gun to his head.

My fingers twiddled aimlessly. She was there to save me, right?

But then she pointed her weapon . . .

The sitting room flashed white.

"Ahhh," I cried out as pain shot through my arm at the memory.

Gasping for breath, I determined that this time I would see past the white light that blotted out more than twelve hours of my life. But no matter how hard I concentrated, I couldn't see beyond the blast of Candice's weapon. It was as if a scratch on a music track merged the echo of the gun with the crumpling of steel on the back bumper of a minivan. Nothing existed between the two sounds.

I blew out air slowly. If I kept up the brooding, I'd fall into a panic attack.

That was why I couldn't afford to lounge around and nurse my ankle. I flipped my feet to the floor. More than anything, I needed a project to keep my mind off things. It was bad enough I had only one arm going for me. My foot would just have to take a number and get in line.

The staircase beckoned just outside the doors. I hopped on one leg and gripped the rail. Teeth clenched, I made the climb to my bedroom. A long soak in the tub, then jammies and *The Count of Monte Cristo* from a shelf of classics. Snuggled in a corner chair, I paged through the story of the naïve Edmond Dantès. The setting sun dipped the pages in gold, illuminating the account of the Frenchman's conniving foes, jealous of his good fortune in business and love, as they schemed to be rid of the young Dantès. I grunted as I read, indignant at the power others held over a man trying so hard to live right.

A knock sounded at the door. I looked up.

"Miss Braddock," came the housekeeper's voice, "I have your supper."

"Yes, come in."

The doorknob twisted and Ms. Rigg entered with a tray of meat and potatoes smothered in gravy. Silverware rattled as she set the tray on the table next to me.

"Thank you," I said, mouth salivating.

"Not at all." She gave me a pursed-lip, flared-nostril, squinty-eyed look and turned to go.

When she was halfway to the door, I got up my nerve. "Ms. Rigg?"

She halted, her back still to me.

"Can I speak with you a moment?" I asked.

She turned. "Did you want something more, miss?"

"Have you already eaten?" I plodded ahead, hoping to win the old gal over.

"Aye."

"Well," I tried for a weak spot in her armor. "Won't you sit and enjoy a cup of tea?"

She looked at the upholstered armchair opposite me as if I'd just insulted her. "I'll not be shirking my duties."

"I won't tell." I gave her my friendliest smile. "I'd love to hear about your life in Ireland."

A look of surprise crossed her face. Her fingers fidgeted a moment, as if torn between duty and desire. She shuffled to the chair and sat.

"Ireland," she said as if speaking the name of her lover.

One hand rubbed along her jaw. Her eyes took on a faraway look. "I was beautiful there. The most beautiful woman in all of Dublin."

At the memory, her face seemed to become younger. Wrinkles smoothed from her forehead, her mouth grew from a frown to a smile, and the hump on her spine seemed to straighten.

"I loved to dance. You should have seen me in my red dress." She shook her head and gazed toward the windows, perhaps lost in the memory of an Irish ballroom.

"Did you work at the embassy? Is that how you met the Braddocks?" I pictured the bustling streets of Dublin, the young Ms. Rigg in a fifties coatdress and coiffed hair skipping up the steps of an old-fashioned building ready to type letters for the day.

"I was a waitress at a gentleman's club." She flicked a glance my way as if to watch my reaction.

I kept my face placid. "I forgot to pour you some tea."

"I don't drink it." She settled back in her chair. "The ambassador would request me at his table." Her pride was evident. "A generous man, he was." A shadow fell across her features and her shoulders drooped. "After he returned to America, I contacted him for work. Times were hard and I had a daughter to raise."

"You have a daughter?" For some reason, Ms. Rigg hadn't struck me as the motherly type.

"Jane. She lives in Los Angeles now, but she was raised alongside the young professor. He's always looked on her as a wee sister."

Perhaps the professor had a heart after all.

"Do you miss Ireland?" I asked.

She gave a vehement shake of her head. "Never knew if you'd live through the night. Revenge. Everything was about revenge. No end to it." Her eyes glazed. "I had my fill." The thought seemed to remind her that she wasn't supposed to like me. Her lips returned to their tightly pursed position. "I'll be going now." She stood and smoothed her black cotton.

"Thank you for the meal. I enjoyed talking to you. I hope we'll do it often."

Ms. Rigg's face reddened. "If I thought for a minute you were true kin of the professor, I might agree." She adjusted the blousy front of her dress. "For his sake I'll treat you kindly, whoever you are. Don't ask more than that." She spun to go.

Sharing tea had been a once-weekly event with Candice LeJeune. But judging from Ms. Rigg's sudden attitude change, I doubted she and I would ever find common ground.

I poked at the meat on the plate and read awhile longer, grateful that cooking skills and social graces were independent gifts.

Half an hour later, another knock interrupted my tale.

"Come in." I folded a tissue to mark my page and closed the book.

Denton peeked over the threshold. "Take the weekend to rest up. You're welcome to come to church with me Sunday if you want. You've got class Monday morning, eight a.m. I'll be in meetings, so you'll have to take the Dogpatch."

I nodded. DGPTC, pronounced Dogpatch, stood for Del Gloria Public Transportation Carrier, a fancy name for the local bus. I'd found my ticket to ride, a swipe-n-go pass, in the admissions packet.

"Thank you."

"Good night." He nodded his head once.

I smiled. "Good night."

The weekend dragged by in utter boredom. I skipped out on church, using my sore foot as an excuse. But the truth was, I didn't feel up to meeting new people and lying—at church, no less—about my name, my hometown, and my bogus relationship to the doc. I'd been working hard to simplify my life. Weaving more webs went against my grain.

Monday morning I woke refreshed, ready for my first day of classes. The pain in my foot had dulled to a mere throb. I ignored it as I showered, gave my arm a clean wrap, and dressed in a thrift-mart tee and blue jeans. Breakfast, coffee-to-go, and a short walk to the bottom of the driveway. The Dogpatch squeaked to a halt. I boarded and found a seat. Mud-colored rocks and gray-blue ocean sped past. The view here was bland compared to the soothing sight of Lake Michigan from the windows of my lodge back home.

The bus turned inland and a few minutes later I disembarked on campus. A short walk found me in front of a plain, two-story building. I sighed, preparing to have Denton's ideals stuffed down my throat. I plowed forward through the double doors to Room 117.

Fluorescent lights made a dull buzz in the tiny classroom. Seven or eight students were scattered around. Not one turned as I entered. No smiles, beckoning hands, or pats on the adjoining desk. My choice to sit against the back wall was a no-brainer.

Moments later Professor Braddock entered, fresh from his early morning staff meeting.

He flipped through a stack of papers, barely glancing up. "Students, I hope you'll welcome my niece, Alisha Braddock, as she joins the Revamp Program."

A couple mumbled hellos, the turn of a head. Couldn't feel more welcomed than that.

The prof paced the front as he gave his lecture. "This year's final project for the Revamp Program is on a grander scale than in previous years. The city has donated a block of abandoned houses, in various states of disrepair, in the Old Town District. Your job is to make the homes functional, livable, and comfortable for the disadvantaged families that will be occupying them on completion. You'll use every skill you've studied in your college career—from the details of home renovation to the arts of negotiation and team building."

I couldn't imagine that the prof, in his high-falutin' suit, knew the first thing about renovating homes. He was probably relieved I showed up on the scene. At least someone could get the work done and line up the various inspectors.

I tuned out his discourse on the nitty-gritty details of the renovations, having lived them firsthand for most of my adult life. Every now and then I'd hear him give a Scripture reference, reminding me that I was now in religious territory.

My pen slid along the lines of my paper, as I pretended to take notes. *Alisha Marie Braddock*, I wrote. Big, bold cursive. Tiny, neat print. Medium, sloppy strokes. None felt natural.

I scribbled my true signature just to remember how it felt. *Patricia Louise Amble*. Then I crossed it out.

In front of me, the backs of heads provided new fodder for a bored mind. One hairdo reminded me vaguely of Portia Romero. I could only hope I was wrong.

Partway through, Denton shifted gears, recapturing my attention.

"Many of you have survived tough circumstances in life. Someone cared enough about you to nominate you to the admissions team at Del Gloria College. Once you were selected, you accepted the invitation, choosing to get the most out of this once-in-a-lifetime opportunity. We designed specific coursework to help you overcome your personal challenges. We believed in you and provided encouragement throughout your time here." He paused and met each student's eyes. "But one year from now, you'll be back in the real world. You'll be dealing with people who are not sensitive, understanding, or catering to your needs. The Old Town Renovation Project bridges the two worlds, preparing you to interact with today's culture, without being dragged down by it." Walking to his desk, Professor Braddock gathered papers into a pile. "To make the project more real-world, we'll add a dimension of capitalism by splitting you into two competing teams."

He clapped his hands once, like a coach dismissing the huddle. "Take a break and be back in ten."

Students stood and made their way to the exit. My eyelid gave a twitch of annoyance. The kinky head in front of me had indeed belonged to Portia Romero. She caught my glance.

"So how's The Niece today?" she asked in her snotty voice.

"Doing great." I scooted past a slow-moving classmate and hurried down the hall to the line at the soda machine. Portia joined me. I kept my back to her, tapping my foot, hoping the wheelchair-bound woman in front of me would hurry and make a selection.

"So how come you're at DGC? You look fine to me," Portia commented.

I turned. "Same reason you are. Get my degree and get out."

The line cleared. I stepped up to the machine and put in my change. A bar lifted, dumping my selection into the access hole. I pulled out the citrus-flavored water and turned to go.

"Hold up," Portia said. "I'll walk back with you."

I actually waited.

Portia fed her change piece by piece into the slot. With a squint, I watched, stunned. The hand holding the quarters wasn't really a hand. A few tiny nubs, like baby fingers, seemed to grow from a stunted palm. I swallowed, feeling guilty for my earlier behavior. She obviously had enough challenges without catching flack from me.

Soda in hand, she started down the hall, me scurrying to keep up.

She tilted her head my way. "If you end up on my team, don't think for a minute you can slack off just because your uncle is the instructor."

So much for treating her with kid gloves. This girl could dish it out.

"Just try to keep up with me," I said in my best attempt at a good comeback. At least my arm was back in action. She wouldn't have that luxury.

"No problem there, sister." She sashayed into the classroom and took her seat.

I slid into mine, trying not to let Portia's superiority complex eat away at my confidence.

Denton strode in and started writing on the whiteboard. Two lists of names went up beneath the headings "Team A" and "Team B."

My name landed just under Portia Romero's on Team B.

I held back a groan. Around me, others were grumbling as well, apparently dissatisfied with their assignments.

To one side, a man in his midtwenties raised his hand. A backward ball cap and megajewelry screamed "gangster."

Denton turned toward the class and wagged a finger. "Uh, uh, uh. Much thought has gone into these teams. Absolutely no changes will be made."

Groans.

Professor Braddock wrote on the board again, printing a list of four addresses under each team.

"As this is a seniors-only curriculum, you'll have to complete the project prior to graduation in order to participate in the ceremony. That gives you approximately eleven months to renovate four houses per team. That's approximately one per quarter."

I stared slack-jawed at the board. It took me at least one year to do a home. Even with four people working together, the task of finishing four homes in less than a year was simply impossible. I only hoped I wouldn't be around to see the team's complete failure.

I crossed my arms and poked out my lower lip.

"Gwen Hart is leader for Team A. Alisha Braddock for Team B."

I stammered some kind of objection. I'd never been a leader of anything. I only worked alone.

Denton's palm shot out. "No changes." He stacked papers together on the desk and inserted them into a carrying case. "The winning team will be in the running for the college's Covenant Award." He looked my way. "If you're not familiar with the award, it's the highest honor that can be received at Del Gloria College. The top students from six departments are eligible. Former recipients have gone on to head missions in the U.S. and around the world. They've become leaders of charitable foundations. And they've changed their communities for the better." He paused and smiled. "Not to mention that fifty thousand dollars in seed money comes with it."

The professor dropped a packet on the desk of a mousy blond—Gwen Hart, I presumed—tossed one on mine, and headed toward the door.

"You know my office hours," he shot over his shoulder. Then he was gone.

7

The class sat speechless at the professor's hefty assignment and hasty departure. The thought of fifty grand apparently wasn't enough to generate enthusiasm for the year of grinding labor ahead. I couldn't even fathom what to do with that kind of money. I supposed Brad and I could finish the renovations on my rambling lodge back in Michigan and fill the bedrooms with foster kids or something. But I sure didn't know the first step toward saving the world.

I rubbed the stitches on my arm as the room came to life with a purposeful rustling. Binders slammed closed. Zippers zipped. Students rose from their seats, as if about to leave.

"Hold it." Portia's voice ricocheted off the walls. "Nobody's leaving yet. Class is only half over. Get in your teams. Talk about how to tackle your project. Come on. Don't waste time."

Almost reluctantly, the class split into the assigned teams. I stayed in my seat, waiting for my groupies to gather around me.

On the other side of the room, Gwen, the blond from Team A, stared at the packet in front of her as if it contained the Twelve Labors of Hercules. The gangster guy scooted a desk up to hers and slouched into the seat, wiggling one leg impatiently. They were joined by a man in his thirties with a deep purple birthmark covering half of his face. The last to join them was a fidgety young brunette, playing with her pencil like it was a baton.

When nobody from Team B turned up at my desk, I glanced over and saw my teammates hunched around Portia. I could already tell things were getting off to a bad start. With a resigned sigh, I brought my "leader" packet to the huddle.

Not willing to meet Portia's eyes, I smiled instead at the redheaded assistant from Dean Lester's office.

"I thought I recognized you," I said to the woman in the wheelchair, glad to have a friendly face in such hostile surrounds. She introduced herself as Celia Long. I looked to the fourth member of Team B, a twenty-something youth with a cane.

"Koby Rider," he said with a nod.

"Great." Portia snagged the instruction packet from me and dug into it. "Now that we all know each other, let's get this show on the road." Quiet for a moment, she scanned the pages.

My fingers gave an irate tap on the desk. Denton had assigned me to be team leader. Portia had usurped my authority in the first thirty seconds. I had a feeling this whole project thing was going to be one long, uphill battle.

"Okay," Portia said, straightening the stack, "let's get over to the homesite and see what we've got ahead of us."

The other team was still bickering as we got up, gathered our totes and backpacks, and headed out.

At the curb, we stood in silence, watching for the next bus. At some point I'd have to grab the reins from Portia. She seemed like she knew what she was doing organization-wise, but when it came to bricks and mortar, I'd have to reclaim my authority and get the job done right.

The bus belched a diesel cloud as it drove up to the curb. Celia boarded via a wheelchair lift. Inside, the rest of us sat on adjacent benches. I dropped my black canvas tote on the floor, studying Koby from the corner of my eye. Light brown hair, a pensive aura, and a cane with a snake's head on the handle.

I cleared my throat. "So, what's the meaning of the cane?"

He tapped it once on the floor of the bus as if annoyed. "I don't have any legs." He looked down at his slacks. "These are prosthetics."

"Oh." There really wasn't a good response to a statement like that. "I guess what I meant was how come you have a snake's head on your cane? Is there some significance?"

He shifted his gaze out the window. "From the Bible. Moses put a snake on the pole and when people looked at it, they were saved."

"Oh." At least he wasn't a member of some violent gang called the Fangs or the Serpents or something.

"How about you?" he said after a beat. "What's your problem?"

Blood rushed to my face. "I don't have a problem. I was just striking up conversation."

"Yeah?" Portia said from her place across from me. "Everybody at Del Gloria has a problem. Just 'cause we can't see yours doesn't mean it's not there." She leaned back against her seat. "We'll figure it out. It's just a matter of time."

I looked down. The last thing I wanted was my muddled past to follow me to Del Gloria. At least here, I'd hoped to have a shot at a fresh start. But fibbing about my name, my hometown, and my relationship to the professor wouldn't earn me any brownie points if people caught on. I'd better try to act more natural before Portia connected the dots and blabbed to the world that I wasn't really Alisha Braddock.

The bus rolled to a stop and we got off at an olden-days train depot. A modern-day Amtrak was just pulling from the station.

Portia glanced at the paperwork as we waited for the train to pass. "Just down a few blocks," she said over the din of clanking metal.

As the sound died, our group of misfits crossed over the rails to Del Gloria's historic district. Rows of tiny bungalows lined the streets. Portia guided us down a block to Rios Buena Suerta.

"Good Luck Street," she translated.

We paused at the crossroads, gazing at the line of dilapidated homes we had only eleven months to complete.

I shook my head in dismay. "We're going to need more than good luck. This will take a miracle."

"No way," Portia said. "It'll just take hard work."

I rolled my eyes. "Look at us. No offense, but half of us don't have the use of their legs. The other half barely have arms." I held up my bandaged bicep while nodding toward Portia's fingerless hand. "How much can we actually get done before the deadline?"

"Watch it," Portia spat in my direction. "I've already overcome my handicap. You're the one with all the hang-ups."

"It's okay, Alisha." Celia edged her chair close to me. "We'll get done in time."

Koby lifted his cane in the air. "Announcing the winners of the Covenant Award . . . Team B!" he said in a dramatic voice.

I shot a glance at the guy I had pegged an introvert, then looked at the row of homes. One had a dislocated front porch. Another had a roof caving in. Down the way, a foundation crumbled.

I put a hand on my hip and mumbled under my breath. "I'm holding out for a miracle."

Celia led the way down the sidewalk to the first house. Portia and I team-lifted her in the wheelchair up a step onto the sagging porch.

Celia drove toward the threshold and stopped. "Great. I wondered about this." The width of the wheelchair exceeded the measurement of the doorway by a couple inches. "I'll just wait out here." Her voice sounded glum.

"Not a chance," Portia said. "Koby, collapse that chair and push it through while I pick up Celia."

I rushed to intervene. "Here, I better do it." I grabbed at the back handles the same time Koby did. Portia hefted the tiny Celia into her arms and walked through the door.

"I've got it," Koby said, reaching in to take over my hold.

"I'll get it. You could fall." I nudged him with my hip to back him off.

"Somebody get that chair in here," Portia ordered. "I'm not made of muscles, you know."

Koby practically body-slammed me out of his way. "And I'm not made of glass." He pushed the chair over the threshold and opened it on the other side.

Portia lowered Celia into her seat.

Koby threw me a look of triumph as I rubbed at my hip.

"Truce." I put my arms up in surrender.

He nodded. "Just don't do it again."

With our first disagreement behind us, the hodgepodge members of Team B surveyed the project ahead, giving each house a once-over. Celia kept a list of major issues and ideas as we brainstormed a plan of attack.

The last home was in the best condition. Nineteen thirties or forties with an updated feel. Ahead of me, my teammates moved with determination, performing their routine to get Celia in the door. I hung back, wondering if I'd be up for the work ahead. From the looks of my ragtag team, I'd have to bear the brunt of it. And my motivation seemed to be missing. Financial strain had always been enough to hustle me from the end of one project to the start of the next. But here in Del Gloria, thousands of miles from everything that mattered, my heart felt like a lump of coal pressed against my lungs, robbing me of breath, stifling my inspiration.

Inside came Portia's voice, followed by laughter from Celia and Koby.

"Face it, Tish. You've landed in Oz," I whispered to myself. But like Dorothy, it was only temporary. Soon I'd get the phone call that would whisk me back home. And all would be well.

I gave a sigh and followed the group into the dim interior. Nodding in robotic agreement to all of Portia's suggestions, I kept a mental log of all the ones I'd have to do right when the rookies weren't looking.

The lunch hour had come and gone as we wrapped up our tour. Our gang had just stepped off the porch when a voice called to us from across the street.

"Hey, you guys." The brunette from Team A waved to us from the coarse lawn of a cockeyed bungalow. Behind her, Gangster Guy and the rest of the crew exited the building.

"Hey! You finally getting to work over there?" Portia's toxic tongue went to work.

The girl on the lawn crossed her arms.

Gangster Guy stepped to the curb. "Yo. Eat our dust."

Portia inhaled a deep breath, ready to fire back a response.

I grabbed her arm. "Why do you provoke them? Can't you just be nice?"

She shook off my grip. "Back off, Miss Priss. Maybe you've got Uncle Denton to take care of you. But me," she thumped her chest with a fist, "I'm on my own. I'm getting a piece of that Covenant Award. Whatever it takes."

"Yeah? Well, I'm the team leader. And I'm telling you we're not going to harass our competition." I hoped I came off as having more gumption than I actually felt.

Portia snickered. "Leader? Yeah, whatever." She started walking back toward the bus station. "Come on, team. Follow me."

I brought up the rear, hoping Brad would hurry up with his plan to save me.

8

The bus pulled away, leaving me alone on the driveway. I'd ridden home in silence, putting an impermeable wall between me and my teammates. Celia had made an attempt at conversation, but gave up when all I offered was a cold shoulder. I hated to push her away, but the day's overwhelming events had caught up to me.

Across the road, the Pacific glared white in the sunshine. Gulls circled a rocky promontory down the way, beckoning for company. Cars zipped past on the two-lane in front of me. I waited for a break in traffic, then crossed over, climbing the metal guardrail onto a flat shelf of rock.

I eased close to the edge for a peek at the drop-off. A narrow trail, hewn over time, clung to the face of the cliff. Should I or shouldn't I?

Why not? There was no schedule to keep.

I dropped my tote behind a clump of brush, then stepped down onto the narrow outcropping, slippery with pebbles. I picked my way along the zigzagging route to the patch of sand at its base. Sunrays beamed hot onto my newfound hideaway. I slid off my tennies and scraped my feet through the burning earth as I made my way toward the water's edge. The sand buzzed with each drag of my foot.

I stopped well back from the surf, watching the shoreline shift beneath the surging and subsiding waves. I'd take the pleasant pull of Lake Michigan over the powerful Pacific any day. I stared out over the endless expanse of water, feeling farther than ever from the places—and people—I loved.

The sand cushioned my head as I lay with eyes closed, trying to imagine what Brad was doing that very moment back home. He'd have rounded up the bad guys by now, with help from the local and state authorities that had already been investigating the case. So today, Brad would be focused on tying up the loose ends, making things safe for my return. I pictured him settling in at the lake house after a good day's work, hanging out in the living room with Puppa—my pet name for my grandfather—and Great-grandma Olivia, having a good laugh over the whole escapade. My temporary boarder Melissa Belmont and her two kids would be back in their own home, safe from her abusive husband. And Brad's sister Samantha would soon be heading to her Coney Island diner in downstate Michigan, having outrun the bad choices of her past once and for all. With my last guest gone, the log cabin would be sitting empty, anticipating my return.

I had only to wait for the convictions that meant jail time for Frank Majestic and his cronies. Then I could go back to Michigan. Back to Brad. Back to the time when it was just the two of us and one joyous, long-lasting future ahead.

A swirl of sand choked me. I sat up, eyes watering in the glare. I rubbed at the bandage on my arm, hoping to brush away the feeling that there was no future with

Brad to return to. Sure, this whole safe-house thing had stalled our wedding plans. But it was only temporary. Nothing would change between us. The next time I saw him, I'd run into his arms and we'd kiss, long and tender, just like we had that last morning in the woods.

Still, the feeling persisted that things were different now. Would Brad meet someone new while I twiddled away time in California? Would he decide that Denton was right and I wouldn't be the best choice of brides?

I pitched a shell toward the water. I didn't care for Denton Braddock. Not one bit. And I couldn't shake the notion that Denton knew more about what was going on back home than he was willing to tell. The professor must have been in contact with somebody—Brad, the authorities, or whoever—since the day he'd claimed me at the hospital in Minnesota. His vague answers to my status checks had become annoying.

I lingered in the sand awhile, soaking up more vitamin D and deadly solar rays than I got in a week in Michigan. I dusted the grit off my clothes, tied my sneakers, and began the climb to the top of the cliff. Halfway up, I panicked. The task had been so much easier going down. Now, my shoes couldn't seem to find a hold in the sliding pebbles. The narrow shelf left me clinging to smooth rock, fighting the pull of gravity that threatened to keel me backward onto the sand so far below.

"Crazy flatlander," I muttered to myself, frozen in place with sweat stinging my eyes.

"Okay, God," I whispered to the rocks, "this is where we start bargaining. You get me up this cliff and I promise never to do anything this stupid again."

Behind me came the scream of a gull. Or maybe a vulture. I was too petrified to turn around and look. The crushing din of the water, an occasional passing car on the road above, and the squeaking cries from my throat became the only sounds to register as the minutes passed. A stone bounced down from above, landing in my hair. A cramp crawled up my leg. It gradually occurred to me that God wasn't going to send a host of angels to airlift me to safety. It seemed the most the winged beings would do was cheer me on while I figured my own way out of the conundrum.

Eyes closed, I spread my arms against the rock, feeling for the slightest indentation. There it was. A small bump to my left, providing my fingertips with just enough leverage to let me hoist myself another twelve inches along the path. Then I found another hold, and another, until my knees were on fragments of asphalt torn from the road next to me. I clung to the guardrail and let my strength return.

Cars honked as they passed, their blaring horns a substitute for the crazy-lady insults the drivers must have been hurling behind closed windows. I dropped to the ground and leaned against the hot metal.

Such a close call. My hands were still shaking. I took a deep breath and stood, reaching for my tote.

Gone.

I dropped to all fours, patting the ground in disbelief. It had been here. Right behind that shrub. I glanced over the drop-off. No black bag in sight. Had someone pulled over and stolen the thing?

I pondered the unlikely thought as I headed up the

hill to Cliffhouse. Losing my tote was no big disaster. The project packet, my notebook, and the bus pass had been its only contents. I could always get a copy of the packet from Denton. Celia could probably help me get a new bus pass from Dean Lester. And notebooks weren't hard to come by.

I entered Cliffhouse through the side porch. Voices came from the kitchen as I passed. I paused, lingering to identify the speakers. Two women. The one with the Irish accent was no doubt Ms. Rigg. But the other?

My stomach growled. I used it as an excuse to snoop.

"Hello," I said, passing through the swinging door into the room.

The visitor stood to attention, shoving her hands in her pockets and wiping a smile off her face. She looked in her late forties. Bright orange hair dye failed to hide the tell-tale gray. A pale blue shirt over jeans and sandals highlighted her tanned, freckled skin.

"It's Miss Braddock, Jane dear." Commandant Rigg nearly clicked her heels at the introduction. "Miss Braddock, this is my daughter. She's visiting from Los Angeles."

Jane offered a hand. I shook it. Behind her on the countertop was my missing tote.

"Oh my goodness. I thought I'd lost that." I stepped around the Rigg daughter and sifted through the contents. All accounted for. "Where did you find it?" I turned toward the women.

Jane shrugged, hands in her pockets. "I spotted something behind the guardrail when I pulled in. I investigated," she pointed at the tote, "and that's what I found."

I thought about the pebble that dropped on my head and wondered if it hadn't been Jane who set it loose.

With a sheepish tilt of my head, I explained. "The bottom didn't look so far down when I was standing at the top, so I thought I'd check out the surf." An embarrassed titter. "But coming back up was a different story." I grinned at Jane. "Wasn't sure I'd make it up alive to claim my tote. Thanks for keeping it safe."

"No problem, dear." Jane gave me a condescending city-slicker smile. "Try taking the stairs next time. They're just down a half mile."

"Oh. Thanks." I nodded. "So, what do you do in LA?"

She smiled like a baby boomer magazine cover model. "I'm an actress. I've worked with De Niro, Streep, and Barrymore."

"You worked with Lionel Barrymore?" I loved him from my favorite film classics.

Her face turned red. "Please," she gave a snort, "I'm not that old. I was speaking of Drew Barrymore."

"Oh, she's one of my favorites. Which movie were you in with her?"

"The classic Cinderella tale, *Ever After*."

"I've watched it a million times." I squinted at Jane's face. "I don't remember you offhand. Which character were you?"

"I had a bit part."

Ms. Rigg could barely restrain her excitement. "She served the prince his supper." The Irish accent was in high gear. "'Would you care for more wine?' Jane asked him. It was a beautiful moment. Lovely, she was."

I shook my head in confusion. "I don't remember that scene."

Jane's glowing smile had simmered to one of annoyance. "Ever hear of the cutting room floor?" She turned to Ms. Rigg. "Please. I can blow my own horn, Mother." A renewed smile as Jane looked back at me, somehow still in front of the camera. "It won't be long before I get my starring role. I'm auditioning for a part opposite Crandall this week."

I hated to tell her I'd never heard of Crandall.

"In the meantime, it's good that your uncle Denton is a generous provider." Her voice became sharp. "Though he's not nearly as generous as his father was."

Ms. Rigg turned red and her eyes bugged out. "Be careful, Jane. The professor is under no obligation to support you."

"I see no reason he should support me at all." Jane's lips toyed in false thought. "Why, it's my own inheritance he doles out to me in such very stingy portions."

I tried to follow along. "Oh? He's the executor for your estate?" I had a hard time imagining Jane as Denton's ward.

A twitch of Jane's eyebrow. "We share the same father," she said. "Dennie is legit, so he got the money, while I, the illegitimate daughter, was conveniently left out of the will."

Ms. Rigg's face spasmed. "Jane, dear. I've told you again and again the ambassador was not your father."

A wave of her hand. "Honestly, Mother. I figured it out by five years old. I'm sure Lenore Braddock did too. That explains why she hated me so much."

Ms. Rigg's trembling fingers tapped across her lips. "No, no. She didn't hate you. She let us stay. She had a million reasons to throw us out, but she never did."

"My point, exactly. As long as she kept you in her snooty little sight, she knew you wouldn't go blabbing that the ambassador slept with an Irish barmaid. Nothing but an unspoken form of bribery." Jane gave a roll of her eyes. "The things the bored and wealthy will do to uphold their reputations."

An uncomfortable silence descended.

I swung my arms, hoping to get myself moving. "Uhh," I pointed toward the fridge, "I'm just going to grab a little snack. It was very nice to meet you, Jane."

I dipped into some cottage cheese as Ms. Rigg and her daughter hightailed it out of the kitchen, Jane laughing like a mischievous seven-year-old as her mother dragged her by the elbow. I leaned against the counter as I ate, detoxing from my crazed climb up the cliff and the equally crazed conversation that followed. Jane dear didn't strike me as a sugar-and-spice kind of girl. There seemed to be a little more naughty than nice to that woman. I set down my fork and peered through my tote again. The fact that everything was accounted for didn't ease my suspicions.

Shrugging, I finished my snack. Under the circumstances, I probably couldn't help but be a tiny bit suspicious of everybody. After a quick cleanup, I slung my tote over my shoulder and headed upstairs.

9

I met Team B at the worksite at 8:00 Wednesday morning. Portia had come up with a detailed schedule that would theoretically allow us to attend our other classes and still finish the project on time and in style.

Today was marked "Demolition Day" on the calendar.

"Grab a hammer," Portia said as I walked in. Koby and Celia apparently hadn't arrived yet.

"Hello to you too." I dug through a toolbox, picking out a mini-sledge. Bold orange letters on the handle marked it property of DGC. The Revamp Program supplied the tools and materials for the project. The students provided the labor and know-how. But when it came to imagining a timely completion, I just didn't know how it was going to happen.

Overwhelmed, I sighed. We'd just have to take things one day at a time. A narrow staircase took me to the second story. Cracked and bowed plaster covered the walls. I snapped a dust mask over my face, slid on a pair of safety glasses, and whaled away with my sledge. My neck jarred with every blow. Muscles in my back flexed and stretched. My heart raced and my ears rang as I lost myself in the mindless battering. An hour or more

passed with barely a letup. I'd be sore tomorrow, but nothing beat the feeling of accomplishment that would come when all the walls were bare.

One final swing and I stopped for a break. I sat on the top step and leaned against an exposed stud, listening to the easy chatter going on downstairs between Portia, Koby, and Celia. We'd agreed that I'd cover the second floor work with Portia's help so Koby and Celia could stay on the main floor. But it sounded like Portia was having too great a time to help me out.

I clomped downstairs. "Hey. Anybody working down here?"

Portia flung me a look. "Back off. We're allowed to have fun."

I gave a snort and shake of my head. "Nobody said you weren't. I was just playing around."

"Yeah? Well, your jokes aren't funny." Portia planted her wrists on her hips.

I lowered my voice. "You're supposed to be working upstairs with me. I'm not trying to pick a fight, just trying to keep things on schedule."

She opened her mouth, but nothing came out.

"Go ahead, Portia," Celia said. "Me and Koby can handle things down here."

"Fine." The ice queen tromped up the steps ahead of me. Huffs of indignation melded with the squeaking treads.

Backs to one another, we slung our sledges. After a while, my arms lost feeling.

"Ugh." Portia dropped her sledge to the floor and leaned against a two-by-four. "It's eleven. Let's call it a morning."

I trekked down the steps behind her, my body protesting as much as the old wood.

"Good work, guys," Portia said, looking at the progress on the first floor. "Get to class, get a good night's sleep, and we'll see you back here in the morning."

"I'm getting my stitches out tomorrow, so I'll be running a little late," I said as we put away the tools and grabbed our bags. Koby and Portia helped Celia through the door and down the steps. Portia checked the lock and hid the key under a stone, and we all headed up Rios Buena Suerta.

"There's enough money in the budget for a wider front door and a ramp," Portia said in her all-business voice. "Koby, you want to order the supplies so we can get those in right away? That way if Celia gets here ahead of the rest of us, she can start right in."

I hated to admit it, but Portia was doing a good job as team leader. It made sense for each of us, including Celia, to have access to the project at any hour. With so much work and so little time, we'd all have to be here every spare second to get the project done on deadline. Eight families were already lined up to occupy the renovated structures once they were completed. We couldn't let them down.

"Thank you, Portia. That's so thoughtful of you," Celia said over the whir of her wheels. "I'm so used to being independent, you can't believe how helpless something like too narrow a doorway can make me feel."

We turned the corner, bringing the bus depot in sight.

"Oh, I believe it," Portia said. "Probably about as helpless as I felt when my car got stolen. Thank God for Dogpatch."

"When did that happen?" I asked, glancing over my shoulder at her. In the background, I saw a form coming down the porch of our current undertaking.

"'Bout three years ago," Portia was saying.

"Hey." I stopped in my tracks and pointed. "Hey!" I dropped my bag and took off at high speed, running along the sidewalk toward the bungalow. "Hey!"

The figure stopped and waved his hands at me. "Whoa. Whoa."

It was what's-his-name, the purple-face guy.

"What do you think you're doing?" My lungs felt like they'd fall out with my next exhale.

"Peeking in the window. That's all. Seeing how far you got today."

His voice sounded a little too full of schmooze. I didn't trust him.

"A spy, huh?" I only hoped that was all he was doing. I wiggled the doorknob. Still locked. "Don't start playing dirty." I gave him my most threatening glare. "Neither team has time for it."

"Kind of suspicious, aren't you?" He rubbed at his jaw.

Portia slid to a halt next to me. "What's going on?"

"Just seeing what he was up to on our porch," I said.

Portia stuck her nose inches from his. "What's your name again?"

"Simon Scroll."

"Well, Simon," she said, "you just transferred in, so I'll cut you some slack. But if you cross the line, I'm going to have to teach you a thing or two. *Comprende*?"

"Sí, señorita." He turned his back to us and stepped off the curb, mumbling something unintelligible under his breath.

I watched him cross the street to his own project. "Gee. For some reason I thought this was a Christian college. With guys like him around, guess I don't have to worry about the behavior police coming after me."

"News flash. We're just beggars telling other beggars where to find food."

"Well, I guess that excuses your attitude." I turned and started walking toward the waiting Koby and Celia.

Portia grabbed my arm. "What do you mean by that?"

I pulled away. "You're so defensive all the time. And pretty bossy, I might add. But I guess beggars can act any way they want."

For a second she looked like she might cry. Then her expression hardened. "I don't have time for all that nicey-nicey talk people do when they say one thing to your face and something else behind your back. I just tell you what's on my mind right up front. If you don't like it, that's your problem." She walked past me.

"I don't like it. And I don't think anybody else likes it, either. That makes it your problem." I caught up to her.

She snarled over her shoulder and walked faster. "I'm doing the best I can. I'm not going to worry my little head about anybody's feelings but my own."

"We can all see you're hurt. Do you have to take it out on us?" I raced to keep up.

"You don't know the meaning of hurt until you've read my file. So back off."

Celia and Koby scooted aside as Portia barreled by like a steam engine without brakes.

"Oh," I shouted at her back, stooping to grab my bag as I flew past, "you have a monopoly on pain? Maybe you should read my file."

"Yeah," she flung at me. "It starts with 'Once upon a time' and ends with 'Happily ever after.' Who can feel sorry for the Little Princess?"

The air rushed out of me. She obviously didn't know anything about my background. And I'd gladly keep it that way. "Hey, just because my uncle owns half of California doesn't make me royalty. So back off."

Portia reached the bus stop and leaned against the metal signpost, panting.

"Besides," I gasped for air and took a stand next to her, "if all you're looking for is sympathy, you're doing a terrible job. I'd rather slug you than feel sorry for you."

"Good," she said and flashed a smile, "then it's working."

I leaned over and held my knees, drawing noisy breaths of air. "You are so messed up."

She laughed. "I know. That's what you like about me. We're so much alike."

I shook my head. "I'm not that messed up."

"Hey"—she grinned—"the only difference between us is I admit it. You're still floating your boat down a river in Egypt."

"De Nile. I get it." I let out a chuckle.

Koby and Celia arrived, concern on their faces.

"What's going on with you two?" Koby asked.

"We're bonding."

Portia said the words so seriously, I burst out laughing. "Yeah. We're so close, she's starting to get under my skin."

The bus pulled up, the roaring diesel killing any comeback. While Celia and her chair were loaded, I took a seat next to Portia.

"So that guy back there, Simon Scroll, I thought you knew him."

"He's new to Del Gloria. He showed up in class the same day you did."

"I probably shouldn't have been so suspicious, but I get a little possessive when it comes to my projects."

"I don't blame you. Simon Scroll has to prove himself on his own merits. Being a student at a Christian college doesn't mean squat." She rolled her eyes. "And so far I'm not impressed."

I liked how Portia put it. We all had to prove ourselves on our own merits. What had Denton said? Words meant nothing. Only actions.

The bus jerked to a halt in front of the campus fitness center. I waved goodbye to the gang and grabbed a quick shower in the locker room before heading to my next class.

The relaxing flow of water washed over my aching muscles. It felt so good to be working on a project again. I lathered my hair, picturing what was happening back at my lodge in Michigan. Maybe Puppa was there cutting grass today. The yard wasn't much of a lawn, mostly woods, so it would just take a few minutes of his time. I hoped he'd weed whip the foundation too. I hadn't gotten to it yet this season, and it was already out of control when I left. One quick phone call would ease my mind. Soap bubbles crowded the drain as I rinsed. Better not. Brad made it plain that I wasn't to contact anyone until he gave me the all clear.

A thud came from the locker area. I'd been alone when I arrived. Someone must have come in. I turned off the water and toweled dry.

"Hello?" I came around the tiled wall.

A rustling sound. Footsteps. The door squeaked open, then shut.

I checked the rows of lockers. Nobody.

"Hmmm." My voice bounced against bare surfaces.

Back in my own row, my bag lay open on the bench. Fresh jeans, socks, and a tee were stuffed chaotically in the top. Just the way I'd left them. And my dirty clothes lay in the same crumpled pile on the floor.

I took a deep breath. It would probably be awhile before I could relax, even though I was certain nobody knew I was holed up in Del Gloria.

The tee kept its wrinkles even after I pulled it tight. Dressed, I brushed out my hair under the dryer, then flipped it back, checking my reflection. All I needed was a little ponytail on top and I'd look like one of those mop-haired show dogs.

I grabbed my bag and headed to my twelve o'clock.

The lecture hall was half filled with students, some sitting in chatty groups, others, like me, in a space of their own.

The instructor arrived—dowdy skirt, blouse escaping from the waistband, wrinkled jacket, oversized eyeglasses, and hair that defied any style. Her unkempt appearance said she'd sandwiched class in between a nap and a late report.

I cut the woman a good dose of slack on account of our inner similarities. Like me, she was probably more comfortable in jeans and a cotton shirt. She launched into her lecture, capturing my attention with her comparison between ways of dealing with anger. Was I a Stuffer, an Escalator, or a Director?

I grappled with my bag, feeling around for my notebook and pen. I flipped to a blank page and scribbled my notes.

Stuffer—avoid confrontation at all costs

Escalator—blame someone else for problems

Director—express anger to others in healthy ways

The business class was supposed to help me manage employees and deal with upper-level peers. But forget them. I flipped the page and kept writing, fascinated to realize I'd been stuffing anger my entire life. The perpetual stomachaches I suffered were probably a direct result. But then wasn't I also good at blaming others for my problems? Still, I'd confronted Portia about her slacking on the job this morning. The results had actually turned out pretty good. That had been directing my anger.

Yippee! I scrawled at the bottom of my notes. I was making progress.

I flipped the page. My hands froze in place. My heart skipped a beat.

HELLO PATRICIA AMBLE. The words were scratched across the paper in giant script.

I slammed the cover shut, trapping the words in the book, pretending I hadn't seen them.

10

The instructor's voice swirled like gibberish around me. Had Frank Majestic sent a hit man to take me out? Was someone watching me right now, waiting to line me up in his sights? Or had some conniving student discovered my true identity and was playing a sick joke?

Lots of people had access to my tote, starting with Jane dear, Ms. Rigg's daughter. Then there were the members of Team B. Celia would never have snooped, but Koby or Portia? I wouldn't put it past them.

My foot tapped uncontrollably. And there was whoever had been in the locker room with me today.

But how could anyone know who I was? Unless they put two and two together regarding Denton's only-child status. Or . . .

I flipped through my notebook, looking for the page I'd used to sign my new name. If someone had come across my practice sheet and been vicious enough to read *Patricia Louise Amble* through my scribbles . . . How low could you go?

The page wasn't there. A line of paper scraps where it had been ripped out was all that remained.

That devious, black-hearted, two-faced, backstabbing Portia. It must have been her. She'd had plenty of time to do the deed this morning before Koby and Celia arrived, knowing I wouldn't suspect a thing until I came across her cute little HELLO PATRICIA AMBLE note.

She'd had it out for me from the beginning. The question was, what did I plan to do about it? I could be just as devious, black-hearted, two-faced, and backstabbing as her.

But did I want to be?

Around me, students shuffled to get their notes put away and head to their next class. I gave a disgusted sigh, realizing I'd stewed through the rest of the lecture.

I gathered my items into the tote and walked to Walters Hall. Birds chirped and the sun shone, but the sidewalk in front of me was the only thing on my mind. Feet passed by and I ignored an occasional hello.

A quick scan of the directory in the lobby provided directions to Professor Braddock's office. I took the stairs, sprinting up five flights, letting the flow of adrenaline clear my thoughts.

I knocked on the door and barged in, scaring off a wide-eyed, twenty-something coed.

Denton folded his hands on the desk in front of him. "I'm sure you have a good explanation for your intrusion."

Dropping my tote, I pulled out my notebook and flipped to the fateful page.

"Look at this." I threw the words on his desk and tapped at them with a heavy finger.

He straightened. "I see." He studied the page silently. "Any idea who wrote it?"

"Portia Romero." I spat the name.

He stared at the paper. "Are you certain?"

"Ninety-five percent."

He crossed his arms. "If by chance it was someone in the other 5 percent, whom would you suspect?"

I counted on my fingers. "Ms. Rigg's daughter, Koby Rider, and whoever was in the locker room today."

His eyebrows lifted. "When did you see Jane?"

"She was at Cliffhouse Monday when I got back from town."

"Hmmm." He handed the notebook back to me. "That's all," he said with a little wave of his hand.

I stared at him, indignant, before stomping out the door. Brad couldn't have been more wrong about putting me under Denton's protection. Clearly the man would enjoy having me turn up dead.

My eyes were blurred with rage as I hit the elevator button. The bell dinged and the doors opened. I hesitated. If I stepped inside, then I'd be back to my habit of stuffing my anger. But if I went back in there and confronted him . . .

I swung around and burst through the office door. His back was to me.

"Uh huh," he said.

"Hey. Sorry for the intrusion again," I tried to keep my voice steady, "but I just have to tell you that I don't feel safe right now. And I feel like you don't care."

His chair turned toward me. He held up a finger. "I don't have to remind you that her safety is of the utmost importance," he said into the phone. "Thank you. Goodbye."

He hung up the receiver and stared me down. "I'm not going to dance around my office in a panic, if that's what you expect. I made a phone call that should resolve this situation. You can go about your life without giving that note another thought." He opened his desk drawer, took out a pen and tablet, and started writing.

"O-kay. Thanks." I lingered, confused. "So who was that on the phone?"

"Your bodyguard."

"Ha ha." I wasn't in the mood for jokes.

"Really. I hired a man to keep you under surveillance. He's one of the best. Highly recommended."

"Who is he? Do I get to meet him?"

"No. He's been operating undercover since your arrival. I've just informed him of the note and he will let me know if there is any imminent danger, or simply take care of it should it arise."

Wow. My own bodyguard. Oddly, I didn't feel any safer. Where had the guy been when I was dangling on the side of that cliff? I couldn't recall a pair of arms waiting below to catch me. He was overpaid, whoever he was.

Defused, I took the elevator to the lobby, mulling the whole way. Denton made it seem like I should drop the whole thing, simply because he said so. But it wasn't that easy. It hadn't been so long since I'd been jailed, framed, chased, set up, and shot at. I wasn't about to let down my guard.

I took the bus to Cliffhouse, snuck a sandwich from the fridge, and climbed up to my room.

—✤—

The alarm clock woke me at the crack of six the next morning. I slammed the snooze. My shoulder paid me back with a shot of pain. Too much time on the sledgehammer yesterday. I should have broken in my body gently.

Even my brain hurt. I hadn't really slept, just dozed in and out of a bad dream. I'd been chasing a doe through the woods. The crunch of shoes through the underbrush. The scrape of branches against my face. I had to catch the doe. But she was gone, and I was standing at the edge of a babbling brook wondering what I was doing there. Someone called my name from the bushes behind me. I crept close. A pair of muddy Nikes stuck out from beneath a shrub. Everything in me wanted to run away, but I had to see who was there . . . I pulled back the leaves . . .

A face.

Brad's face. And there was a bullet hole between his wide-open eyes.

The sheets had been damp with sweat when I sat up in the pitch-black, awake. I'd had a hard time falling back to sleep. Each time I dozed off, the doe would be there, and I'd have to chase her again.

I shook off the images and got out of bed. Of course I was dreaming about Brad. I missed him so much.

The shower took a minute to warm up. I brushed my teeth while I waited. It seemed an eternity had passed since Brad and I had last been together. Had it only been two weeks?

I finished my routine and headed downstairs, meeting Denton in the dining room. By now I understood why he sat in the formal area rather than the kitchen. Less drama. Thankfully, Ms. Rigg treated me kindly in his presence, even pouring my coffee.

"Do you recall your doctor appointment at eight, Alisha?" Denton asked.

"Mmmm." I chewed my bagel and swallowed before answering. "Yep. All set."

"How have you been feeling?"

I glanced at the gash on my arm, the skin now neatly knit together. "Great. These stitches are ready to go."

Denton squinted at the wound. "It seems to have healed nicely. You were very fortunate to have such a minor injury."

I tossed a third of a bagel back onto my plate, losing my appetite at the reminder of the worst day of my life.

Denton took a sip of his coffee, looking at me over the rim. "I understand the gunman was at very close range."

"Gun*woman*, actually." I saw Candice's pistol go up, heard the explosion, then lost everything in the flash of white that followed. As always, pain rushed up my arm at the memory.

I must have flinched, because Denton reached over and touched my wrist. "Give it time. The pain will lessen."

I nodded, pushing away from the table. "Well, gotta go. Have a good one."

"Goodbye, Alisha."

I grabbed my tote and dashed outside for the bus.

—w—

The single-story medical building was at the edge of campus. I signed in at the seventies-era sliding-glass reception window. *Alisha Braddock*, I was careful to write on the sheet. I sat in a corner by a low, square coffee table covered in tattered, outdated magazines. The room carried a faint musty odor. Dark wood, patchy wallpaper, plastic tub chairs, and mite-laden carpeting screamed for a remodel.

A few minutes later, a woman called my name. I followed her down a narrow hall.

We entered Room 3. She gestured toward the exam table. I hopped up, hands suddenly clammy. As she ran through the temp, weight, and blood pressure routine, I pondered the significance of the multicolored fish that swam across the blue background of her jumper.

"Everything looks good," she said, writing her findings on my chart. "Dr. Vandenberg will be just a few minutes."

While waiting, I redecorated the tiny space with brighter lighting, new ceiling tiles, modern wallpaper, and fresh flooring. The re-do disappeared as the doctor entered the room, chart in hand.

Sleek and elegant, the woman looked more like a movie star than an MD. Skin the color of mocha, full lips, and sparkling brown eyes. I wondered why she wasn't doing her internship at U of C Hollywood instead of here in Del Gloria.

"Hello, Alisha. I'm Dr. Vandenberg. I see you're new to

campus." She set the chart on the counter and proceeded to feel the glands in my neck.

"I've been here a week or so." I swallowed at her command. "Um, I'm just here to have some stitches removed. Everything else feels fine."

A stethoscope slid down my back.

"Breathe in," the doctor instructed.

I took a breath.

"Your chart says you've been assigned to the Revamp Program. I understand that is a very rigorous curriculum. I want to make sure there are no other health issues as you go into it."

"They sure put a lot of extra information in those medical charts." I couldn't remember my major being printed next to my weight back at Michigan State's clinic.

She tapped a rubber hammer to my knee. "At Del Gloria we don't separate physical, mental, and spiritual health. The mind and soul are parts of the body. We treat them as one."

"And what does that have to do with me getting my stitches out?"

"Say ahhh."

A bright beam panned over my mouth, then into my eyes. The doctor clicked the penlight off and leaned back against the counter, arms crossed. "Let's talk about your stitches. Tell me why you have them."

A bead of sweat broke out on my forehead. I rubbed at it, pretending to have an itch. How much could I tell without giving myself away? Perhaps it was better to just keep pretending I couldn't remember the details. I closed my eyes and concentrated, picturing Candice's weapon, aimed and loaded. The white flash, then the pain in my arm again.

My breath came in gasps. "I was shot." I avoided her eyes.

"By whom?" She hugged my chart to her chest as if to hide the answers from me.

I shrugged. "A woman with a gun."

The doctor stared at me, perhaps waiting to see if that was my final answer.

"Well," I felt compelled to keep talking, "she was a friend of mine. At least I thought she was."

"And this friend shot you?"

I nodded.

"Are you having difficulties with your memory?" she asked. "Do you forget where you put things, forget what you were about to do next, draw a blank when you try to remember your childhood?"

"No. I remember stuff."

Dr. Vandenberg nodded and set my chart on the counter. "It can take time to recover from a traumatic event like the one you experienced. Let's take a look at those stitches." With a few swift moves, she pulled what looked like fat fish line from my arm. "There. That didn't hurt a bit."

I cranked my arm around for a look. The stitches were gone. A patch of red skin remained to prove my tale.

"That will lighten up over time. Nobody has to know about your adventure unless you tell them."

"Thank you." I scooted to the edge of the table, ready to make my run to freedom.

"Alisha," the doctor said, "I want you to start writing

things down. Keep a daily journal of what's going on in your life. Then read back over it once a week to remind yourself what you did."

I sighed and slid to a standing position. "I don't really see what that has to do with anything. I have a great memory."

"I'm sure you do." She clicked her pen and hung it in the hinges of the clipboard. "It's just an exercise to keep your mind sharp. Nobody reads it but you. I think you'll be fascinated by what's revealed."

She made her exit.

I stopped at the front desk then hustled outside. Glaring sunshine washed out green lawns. The chatter of birds rang from tree branches as I headed to the curb to wait for Dogpatch.

I sat on the weathered plastic bench, one leg jerking rhythmically. Dr. Vandenberg might have a degree in medicine, but if she knew anything about me, she'd understand why keeping a journal was a bad idea. Three simple words from my past—Patricia Louise Amble—had already stirred up trouble in this new life. Imagine if I had an entire notebook filled with memories. A shudder coursed through my flesh as I imagined the Grim Reaper plunking down next to me on the bench.

11

I arrived at Rios Buena Suerta in time to start shoveling plaster into black plastic bags for disposal. Portia's way of handling the task alone was to hang the bag from a doorknob, slide the shovel in the top opening, and dump it. I was certain the task would go faster if I held the bag while she scooped.

"Pull the plastic away." Portia's frustration came out in her voice.

"I'm trying." I slid the bag's opening farther under the shovel. "There. Now go ahead and tip it."

A fog of dust rose as the debris landed. I pulled the neck of the bag up . . . and a pile of plaster landed on the floor.

"It was easier before you got here." Portia stamped the shovel on the floorboards. "Do your own pile. My system was working just fine."

"It'll go faster if we help each other," I insisted. "Why don't you hold the bag and I'll shovel?"

Portia held up her stunted hand. "You're brilliant. How's that going to work?"

"Watch this." I forced a corner of a fresh bag over the doorknob and showed her how to hold the rest of the bag wide with both arms.

"Like I said, you're brilliant." She scooped up a load of debris.

"What are you doing? I'm supposed to be shoveling."

Dust rose as she dumped it in. "Looks like you're an expert bag-handler. Stay right there." Another scoop landed in the bag.

I tested out my new anger management techniques.

"You know, Portia. You act like you know it all when it comes to this renovation project. But Professor Braddock put me in charge and I'd like you to stop acting like you're the leader."

"Professor Braddock?" she asked in a mocking tone. "Don't you mean Uncle Denton?"

The bag fell out of my hands and I straightened, hands jammed on my hips. "You make it sound like you don't believe he's my uncle. Is there something you'd like to confess?" I waited for her to tell me she'd snooped through my notebook and written Hello Patricia Amble just to agitate me.

Instead, a look of surprise flashed across her face. "I meant that of course he put you in charge, being your uncle and all." Her eyebrows scrunched together. "Are you saying he's not really your uncle?"

Her sincerity took me off guard. Maybe she hadn't been the one to rip out my signature page. "No, that's not what I'm saying," I stammered. "Of course he's my uncle. I mean, why would he tell everyone I was his niece if I wasn't really his niece?"

She stared at me squinty-eyed. "Good question."

"Oh, come on, Portia, he's my uncle. I just thought you were trying to say he wasn't. You know, trying to imply that I'm not really Alisha Braddock." Backtracking didn't seem to be doing the trick.

She shook her head, a disgusted expression on her face. "Then who are you?"

I waved my hands through the air, like an umpire calling it safe. "Come on. I'm me. I really am Alisha Braddock, the professor's niece. Who else would I be?"

She put a hand on her hip. "I'm dying to find out."

I gave a sigh of exasperation and ruffled my hair. "So, I take it you weren't the one who left that note in my binder."

"What note?"

I shook my head. "Nothing. Just forget about it, okay?"

"It's a pretty tough conversation to forget about."

I tied up the top of the bag, avoiding her eyes.

She touched my hand. "Are you in trouble or something?"

I jerked upright, tears threatening to flow. "Of course not. Why would you even suggest it?"

Portia rolled her eyes. "The girl doth protesteth too much. You want to talk about it?"

I wavered, lured by the temptation of stepping out of the lie and into the light. "There's nothing to talk about. You're being ridiculous."

She turned her back to me and pushed the remaining mess into a central pile. "If you ever change your mind, give a holler. We might have more in common than you think."

As we worked another hour in silence, I couldn't help but wonder. If Portia hadn't written that note, who had? And besides informing my so-called bodyguard, what did Denton plan to do about this threat to my security?

Downstairs, Koby and Celia had their own cleanup system in place. Celia acted as bag lady while Koby did the dirty work. They stopped at our arrival.

Koby leaned on the shovel like a cane. "Time to go already?"

Portia looked at her dust-covered wristwatch. "Yep. We've got an hour to get to class."

Koby wiped a hand across his cheek, leaving a smear of white. "How do you think the other team is doing?"

We helped Celia out the door and down the steps, each of us sending bold glances toward the competition's row of houses.

"I don't see anyone over there," Portia said, locking the door and stashing the key. "I'd sure like to know how far they've gotten. Who wants to come with me?"

I shook my head. "Not on your life. After the way we chased Simon out of here the other day, I don't think they'd appreciate us snooping."

Portia got a mischievous look on her face. "Come with me, Alisha. They owe us a peek."

"No way." I put my foot down on spying. It only brought trouble.

She grabbed my arm and dragged me toward the street. "We'll meet you at the station," she called to the others.

I pulled back in token resistance, still following as she went up the steps of the opposition. She gave a quiet knock at the front door.

"Nice time to be neighborly," I said under my breath.

"Nobody's here, anyway." Portia shielded her face against the glare and looked through the window. "Wow."

At her exclamation, I crowded next to her at the window, looking inside.

Portia gave a low whistle. "It doesn't look like they've done anything."

"How do they expect to finish on time?" I asked. "They're behind us already—and we'll barely make it at the rate we're going." Thank goodness Portia's schedule and determination kept Team B on track.

"I wonder what's up with Gwen. She carries a 4.0 GPA. This isn't like her." Portia moved to the next window for a peek inside. "Sure takes the fun out of winning if there isn't anyone hot on your heels."

I followed. "The professor did a pretty poor job of putting the teams together. All the best workers are on our team."

Portia dropped her hands. "You changed your tune since that first day. What happened to 'half of us don't have legs and the other half don't have arms'?"

I looked to the boards that covered the porch. Mold grew between the splitting seams. "I guess I learned my lesson about judging everybody by operational body parts."

Portia pointed to her temple. "We've got it where it counts . . . up here. We're going to win because we're working smarter."

I peered through the window. "I'd say it's probably more that we're working harder. At least we're working."

A squeak of the porch steps sounded behind us.

"Can I help you ladies with something?"

We whirled. I gave a startled scream. Portia landed in a defensive karate pose.

"Simon," I exclaimed, relaxing and laughing it off. "You scared us."

His birthmark was a faded purple along one side of his face. Dark plum last week, lavender today. Was it my imagination, or had it changed color like a mood ring?

"Now who's spying?" he asked.

Portia stepped toward him. "We're worried about you guys. It looks like you haven't even started. What's going on?"

He put a foot on the porch rail, leaning into it. "Everything's under control."

"Whatever you're doing, keep it up." Portia smiled in my direction. "Looks like Team B has the Covenant Award clinched."

Simon shrugged. "It's all yours. Don't expect anything out of Team A. Bunch of whiners." He flicked his hand. "What's her name, Gwen, she's having a panic attack. Things weren't going perfect so she quit showing up. Some leader, huh? And Maize. There's a doozy. She can't stay on task for more than ten minutes, then she's off starting something else. And that Dagger kid." He shook his head. "Who enrolled him? He's a hard enough worker, but I'm not sure he knows the time of day."

Portia's jaw twitched back and forth. "Well? What about you? I don't see you in there making progress."

"I'm a professional student. I'm just here so I don't have to face life out there." His head jerked toward Del Gloria proper.

"If you were professional, you'd do a better job faking that you wanted to be here," Portia said. "How'd you get into DGC, anyway?"

A happy-go-lucky smile. "I'm doing the professor a favor." Simon looked me straight in the eye, his crooked grin full of hidden meaning.

I drew in a sharp breath.

Simon's gaze traveled to Portia. "The prof needed another person to round out the class and make even teams."

I sighed in relief.

A quick goodbye, and we cut across the grass at a brisk pace, hoping to catch the bus.

"I don't trust that guy," Portia commented as we turned the corner. "Gwen's apartment is only one building down from mine. I'll go over tonight and see what's going on."

I huffed to keep up. "I'll see Denton tonight and make sure he's got the scoop."

The bus pulled around the far corner, heading toward the bus stop.

"Hurry!" I ran ahead of Portia.

Celia was already loaded when we sprinted up the steps and swiped our transit passes through the scanner.

Still laughing from our race, Portia and I piled into seats next to Koby.

"I didn't think we'd make it." I gasped for air.

"No problem," Portia said. "I love running to catch a bus. It beats the old days, when I was running to dodge a bullet."

I looked at her, shocked. "You're kidding, right?"

She shook her head. "Dead serious."

"Who was shooting at you?"

"Which time?" she asked.

I gulped. "Oh, my. Where were you before you came here?"

"Can't tell you where I was." She looked off toward the horizon. "Too many people would love to see me dead." She glanced at me. "But I can tell you what I was."

I nodded, silent.

She stared up at the ceiling, her body rocking with the motion of the bus. "Started out as a prostitute." She held up her tiny fingers. "Got a lot of the weirdos. Then I got recruited by the cops for a sting operation. The whole thing flopped. Nothing like running naked through the streets while getting shot at by the cops, your pimp, and your john."

My hands did a nervous twiddle in my lap. I cleared my throat. "So how did you end up at Del Gloria?"

"I ran into a church, buck naked. Hid out behind some curtains until the coast was clear, but the cleaning woman spotted me." Portia's eyes misted. "Instead of screaming at me and condemning me and calling the cops, she wrapped me in a towel from her supply cart and drove me to the pastor's house. They gave me food and clothes, then talked to me and prayed with me. By the time I left, I knew Jesus. It's like he'd been waiting for me to run into that church that day. Later, the pastor gave me a referral to the college, and here I am." Her voice dropped off as she stared at some point in space.

Then she held my gaze, conscious again. "The truth will set you free. I believe that, Alisha."

She reached out and touched me. I pulled away.

"Hey," she said in a gentle voice. "We're your team. Why don't you tell us what you've got going on in your life? Level with us. You'll feel better."

Koby stared with seeming disinterest out the window. Celia watched me with curious eyes.

I gave a big sigh. Level with them. I couldn't do that. Too much was at stake. My identity had to be kept secret until the man responsible for my mother's death and my father's exile was behind bars. I planned to be alive when it came time to marry Brad. And that meant the lie had to continue for now.

The bus jerked as it took the corner.

I looked my teammates square in the eyes and got ready to tell a whopper. "I got in a fight with my, ummm . . ." Parents? Boyfriend? Husband? I opted for ". . . landlord, and he kicked me out. Uncle Denton is letting me live with him until things die down."

The three of them stayed quiet as if waiting for more details.

I shrugged. "That's all there is to it. End of story."

The bus slowed and pulled up to the main stop on campus.

"See you tomorrow," I said with a smile and wave as I escaped to my next class. My heart pounded in my ears. That had been too close. Farther down the sidewalk, I thumped the heel of my hand to my forehead. As if anyone believed that lame story.

I wasn't cut out for a double life.

12

That night I made my way to the parlor to corner Denton like I'd promised. I lingered at the threshold a moment, my book tucked under one arm, hesitant to interrupt his ritual quiet time.

The professor relaxed on the settee. Blue cotton jammy bottoms poked out beneath a fastidious white terry robe. The man seemed so content with life. There he sat, reading the evening news, sipping a cup of steaming tea, surrounded by fine possessions in a beautifully renovated home.

I sighed with envy. How could he maintain such order on a daily basis when my life was one perpetual tailspin?

He looked up. "Alisha." His voice smiled though his face remained passive. "Make yourself at home."

"Thanks." I took a velvet-upholstered chair across from him.

"What's on your mind tonight?" He closed his paper, rolling it and placing it on the sofa.

"I know you said there was no changing your mind about the teams in the Revamp Program. But," I put out

a hand to keep him from interrupting me, "something has gone really wrong with Team A and I want you to be aware of it."

At his blank look, I told him the results of our spy mission.

". . . so I really think you need to reconsider the whole competition thing, or at least get some teamwork going over there."

I thought I saw a gleam in his eye, like he was laughing at the situation.

"It's out of my hands," he said. "This is a senior level program. I will not hand-feed adults who have the capacity to solve their own problems. This is part of the test, Alisha. If they don't pass here, they'll probably fail in the real world too. Let's hope they figure out how to put pride behind them and get to work."

His answer was a little too coldhearted for me. I had to speak up. "I'm not sure you really understand the scope of the project or what has to go into each of these renovations. It's hard labor and requires forethought, planning, and teamwork. Lots and lots of teamwork." My finger pointed in emphasis.

"Look around you." He glanced at the coved ceiling, the curved staircase, the moldings, the fireplace, the sparkling hardwood floor. "Don't tell me I don't know the scope of the project. I did this work myself."

Before my eyes, the professor morphed from a spoiled only child to a contributing member of society. "Wow. I'm impressed. How long did it take?"

His eyes followed the arch of the ceiling. "I've been at it on and off for about thirty-five years."

I straightened. "What about the exterior? Everything's done but that. Maybe once we've finished on Rios Buena Suerta, we can come here and get that done—"

"No."

The sharp word cut me off.

The professor leaned back and sighed. "Each aspect of this home is done as a reward for accomplishing a goal in some other area of my life. I haven't yet succeeded in the particular facet that would allow for an exterior restoration."

"Oh. What would you have to do for that?" I asked.

"It's personal." His tone put an end to the line of questioning.

Denton seemed more touchy than usual tonight. I ignored his attitude. "Hmmm. I wonder why Brad never mentioned you renovated homes?"

He picked up his newspaper and snapped it straight. "I'm not sure Brad knew."

Following his example, I flipped my legs up on my chair and opened my book. "Hope you don't mind. I borrowed your copy of *The Count of Monte Cristo*."

"Not at all. Excellent story," he said, "if you don't mind witnessing mankind at his lowest."

—ꟽ—

The next morning, I woke up feeling like a bag of cement had been dropped on my head. No sleep last night, just crazy dreams interspersed with tossing and turning. When I first arrived in Del Gloria, I'd had my prescription painkillers to help me rest. But now, with only the over-the-counter variety, I barely got a wink.

The alarm hadn't gone off yet, but I got up anyway, showered, and dressed. Then I did what Dr. Vandenberg suggested: I wrote down everything I'd done since the day of the accident. I tried to be as complete as possible, challenging myself to remember all I'd experienced.

I scanned my work. Memory loss, phooey. I recalled every detail since the moment I impacted the back end of that minivan.

In the lonely stretch between Salt Lake City and Sacramento, Denton had elaborated on the stress-induced memory loss theory the doctor in Minneapolis had proposed.

"Tell me about your childhood. What things do you remember?" Professor Braddock's voice blended with the soothing hum of the tires.

I glanced at him. His comic Einstein-wear had me wondering how Brad could think so highly of him. "I had a great childhood. Right up until my mom died."

"What great things do you remember?"

I kept it vague. "Oh, I don't know. We'd visit my grandparents on weekends and in the summer. That was always nice."

"Always?"

I scrunched my brows together, picking up a memory of a picnic here, a trip to the beach there. "Yeah. Pretty much."

"What bad things do you remember?"

I gave a shrug to hide the emotion crashing over me. "I remember my mom dying. I remember her funeral."

"Before that?"

"Nothing. It was all good."

The professor kept his eyes on the road. "It's never all good, Patricia."

"It was for me."

He cleared his throat. "Sometimes, in cases of child abuse, sexual molestation, or other traumatic situations, people lose the ability to recall specific events. If the circumstances are bad enough, people can forget entire years of their lives." He looked at me.

"That's awful."

"Actually, it's merciful." He pointed to the front of his head. "Our memories are kept up here, in the hippocampus. During times of stress, our bodies produce a hormone called *cortisol*. God designed the chemical to help us deal with danger—the fight-or-flight response. But when too much cortisol is present in our brains, it damages the connection between our memories and their recall buttons. The memory is still available, we just can't access it."

At that point, we'd been in the car too many hours. I could barely follow his logic.

He kept talking. "Sometimes it's good that we can't recall something too horrible to deal with at the time. But the problem occurs when stress becomes our normal state of mind. The hormone is released inappropriately. After a while, our thinking becomes muddled. We forget the simplest things, like where we parked our car and what item we'd gone into a room to retrieve. We forget useful and happy memories along with the bad ones."

Now, perched on the edge of the bed, I tapped my

pen against the journal. Professor Braddock had gotten my attention with the muddled-thinking comment. Maybe my brain was overproducing cortisol. And that's why I would sometimes forget stuff from day to day. Like Brad sharing his most intimate thoughts with me. Five minutes later I'd wonder if he even cared I was alive. Or when I'd make up my mind to be grateful in any circumstance. Five minutes later I'd wonder if God even cared I was alive. If living like that annoyed me so much, I could only imagine how Brad and God felt about living with me.

My pen retraced some words on the page. Denton implied that I'd been reacting to life by continually pressing some internal panic button that kept the cortisol flowing. It became my body's defense mechanism to cope with situations my mind couldn't handle, basically a self-induced memory block that allowed me to get through a rough stretch without having to deal with the actual events, because in essence, I'd forgotten them. But at the same time, I'd forgotten a lot of the good stuff too.

The million-dollar question was, what was my mind protecting me from now? What happened between the time Candice pulled the trigger and the moment of impact on I-35?

Yes, I'd been shot in the arm. But was that so traumatic that I'd blocked out the next twelve hours? With the events of the previous night, when I'd been run off the road and barely escaped death at the bottom of a quarry, and later held hostage at gunpoint by some fool who thought I knew where my dad was holed up, I suppose the cortisol had been flowing at top levels. Probably no amount of mental concentration could track down those hours missing from my memory.

I'd just have to let it go and convince Professor Braddock to do the same.

I took another ten minutes to write down the discombobulated images from my dreams, then went downstairs to catch the professor at breakfast.

"Good morning, Alisha," he said as I entered the dining room. His voice had a cold tinge to it.

"Morning." I scooted my chair up to the table.

Ms. Rigg poured my coffee, keeping track of me out of the corner of her eye.

I took a sip. "Mmm. Delicious. Thank you."

"Aye," was her best shot at being cordial.

"Did your daughter make it safely back to the city?" I asked her. Now that I knew Portia wasn't the looter responsible for taking my signature page, I wanted to explore the Jane equation.

Next to me, Professor Braddock blinked and turned to me, as if wondering what I had up my sleeve.

"Aye," Ms. Rigg countered, offering nothing more. She took a step to go.

"Does Jane come often to visit?" I held her with my question.

Ms. Rigg looked at Denton. Then her gaze swung back in my direction. "Only when she can afford to. Poor dear struggles for her bread. And her poor mum can't very well help."

The woman's comments were likely more directed at Denton than me. Fishing for a raise, I figured, remembering how Jane had focused on money the other day.

I took a sip of my coffee. "Oh. I was hoping Jane would be back soon. There was something missing from my tote the other day and I wanted to ask her about it."

The matriarch squirmed.

Denton looked back and forth between the two of us, nibbling on his bagel like popcorn at a movie theater.

Steam collected around Ms. Rigg's ears as she came to her daughter's defense. "I hope you're not calling my Jane a thief. She only opened the notebook to see who the tote belonged to."

I suppressed an "ah ha!" So, Jane was the guilty party after all. How else would Ms. Rigg have known about the notebook? What kind of scam was Jane running now? Her schmaltzy, overzealous smile reminded me of a con man I once knew. No doubt Jane was sweet as pie to my face but would gladly hold a knife to my back. No doubt she'd written the note and knew my true identity. The question was, what would she do with that information?

13

Ms. Rigg dashed out of the dining room as soon as I looked down at my plate. I supposed Jane could tell key people who I really was, putting my life in terrible danger.

"Don't worry about Jane. I've already spoken to her. She doesn't suspect anything," Denton said, with a terse wipe of crumbs from his moustache.

"Really?" I said it with a touch of sarcasm. "She certainly looked guilty the day she found my tote on the cliff."

Denton's eyes narrowed. "Jane fancies herself one of the family. Even if she knew who you were, she wouldn't have any use for the information."

My fingers tapped on the table. Was he talking about the same Jane I met in the kitchen? The woman was a leech. A leech with a plan. She must be a fine actress after all to pull the wool over Denton's eyes like she had. "I suppose you came right out and asked her if she snatched the page with my real name out of my notebook?"

"You wrote your real name in your notebook?" Denton

shook his head like he couldn't believe it. "What were you thinking? You should have told me."

"How was I supposed to know someone would snoop? Anyway, I crossed it out." I kept my voice low.

He leaned toward me. "Did you write your name so you would be discovered? Is there something in you that can't bear to live in peace and serenity?"

I looked at him, flabbergasted. "No. Of course I want peace and serenity."

"You're acting like you have a death wish."

Frustration surged through me. "I do not have a death wish. I just want to get home to Brad."

At the mention of Brad's name, Denton gave me a look that resembled hatred. "That is a death wish." Stony features underlined his derision.

I stood and slowly backed away, wondering how he could transform from the pleasant man in the parlor last night to this hardened stranger.

"I'm sorry, Alisha," he said. "I received some difficult news this morning. I don't mean to take it out on you." He cleared his throat. "I'll be leaving town for a few days. Ms. Rigg will be here for your needs."

I stared at him, frightened by the pain in his eyes. Where was the pillar, the rock I had come to depend on? I didn't want to see the swell of emotion on Denton's face. He was supposed to be the strong one, the protector. I was the weak one. As if to prove it, I grabbed my tote from beside my chair and whirled. "I've got to go."

I nearly ran over Ms. Rigg on my way out the door.

—‿‿—

Denton returned a few days later, the smile still missing from his voice. I avoided him. The way he looked at me, with something close to contempt, or at least anger, made me nervous. Brad had told me Denton would keep me safe. But with his recent change in attitude, I felt alone in enemy territory.

It seemed I wasn't the only one facing hostile forces. Portia had tracked down Gwen and discovered that Team A couldn't agree on anything. Dagger had dropped the class, citing "Too lame for me." The pencil-twirling brunette couldn't remember to show up without a personal phone call and an escort. And Simon Scroll still wouldn't lift a hammer.

"Gwen couldn't stop crying," Portia said. "If she quits the class now, it'll show up on her transcript—a big 'D' for Dropped. You'd think it was going to kill her. But if they can't finish the project and she gets less than a 4.0 for the class, I swear she'll kill herself. That girl is headed over the edge. Sheesh. I remember feeling that way. I'm really worried."

We talked as we peeled wallpaper in the one room that escaped our diagnosis for total demolition. I scooped up a pile of shredded remains and dumped them in a bag.

"Professor Braddock insisted that they're on their own. He refuses to get involved." A shake of my head. "I wish there was something we could do to help." I gave a discouraged sigh. "But we couldn't if we wanted to. We'll barely finish on time as it is." I hated to tell her I could bail out at any moment myself, the instant Brad called me to come home.

Portia kept scraping. "I've been thinking about it. What if Gwen helped us finish our side of the street, then we went over and helped her finish their side of the street? Our team would still finish first and qualify for the award, but the other homes would be completed for the families that are waiting."

I gave her a raised eyebrow. "Humanly impossible. Maybe if her entire team hadn't ditched her . . . but the way it is, I say no." I shook my head for emphasis.

"What if we can talk Dagger back in? The professor can reinstate him if he wants. And I can always walk over and get Maize Martin when her ADD is in overdrive. As for Simon, well, I don't suppose we'll get much out of him." She shrugged. "So what? Not everybody is handy with a hammer."

Portia seemed far too generous. I wasn't about to work my behind off while Simon Scroll lounged from porch to porch just so we could have even teams.

I soaked a new section with solution. "Why should we help them at all? With their team out of the running, we've got a better chance at the Covenant Award. Isn't that what you wanted?"

Her brows scrunched. "I don't know. I feel sorry for them now. It's not even fun winning when the teams are so unevenly matched."

"Weird, huh? Denton said he put a lot of consideration into the teams. I don't know. We definitely got the best members."

Portia brooded a moment. "Maybe the professor knew we'd all have to work together if the houses were going to get finished on time. The team thing was just to throw us off, make the project seem real-world. But there's only one way to earn the Covenant Award."

"What are you talking about?"

She paced the room as she explained. "The Covenant is all about serving others. Yes, we're helping people in the community by fixing up houses. But it's more than that. Gwen, Maize, Simon, and Dagger can't do the project alone. They need us. Professor Braddock knows that. And we need them. If we all work together, we'll get the whole block done on schedule. It's an exercise in teamwork, not competition."

I shook my head. "I don't know. I've never met a more helpless group of people in my life. They really don't deserve to finish if they're not willing to do any work themselves."

"Of course they're helpless. They've probably been told their whole lives that they couldn't do anything right. Let's give them a chance to find out that they can."

I thought for a minute, then nodded. "Okay. But Celia and Koby both have to agree or there's no deal."

We shook on it and headed downstairs. As my foot touched the bottom step, I realized that for the first time in weeks, I'd gone two entire hours without thinking of Brad.

Over the course of the morning, Portia and I convinced Celia and Koby to go along with our scheme. They agreed to take a shot at accomplishing more than any reasonable human being should even consider. Somewhere in my gut, little doubts screamed in protest. But I shut them down, knowing the busier I stayed, the quicker time would pass—and the less I'd mope about Brad's continuing silence. He wouldn't want me piddling away my life in a depression. He'd want me accomplishing great things, in preparation of our new life together.

I put in extra hours on Rios Buena Suerta over the weekend, happy to work in solitude once again. The rest of the time, I avoided Denton by staying in my room and catching up on my novel.

Sunday morning I consented to attend church with the professor. I couldn't explain it, but ever since he came back from that trip, he gave me the heebie-jeebies, like he was mad at me for something. His attitude had to stem from more than just me writing my real name in a notebook, and some sneak finding it. But I certainly wasn't going to ask him. And apparently, he didn't plan to clue me in. I tried to quash the feeling while sitting in the quaint, semi-modern sanctuary close to campus. But the sermon, which centered on Abraham's near-sacrifice of Isaac, seemed only to heighten Denton's aversion toward me. It was as if a thick, stone wall had been erected between us. I had no idea how it had gotten there, and no idea how to pull it down.

That week, Gwen and Maize from Team A joined our renovation squad. Portia gave the two women specific tasks and checked their progress throughout the morning. I watched and learned from her leadership skills, grateful she was in the Revamp Program.

By Thursday, Portia had talked Dagger into rejoining

the crew in time to unload the drywall delivery. And the next day, Simon finally caved and picked up a trowel.

With the two teams working together, the first property was ready for its finishing touches.

It wasn't until we'd finished painting the interior that I realized I'd gone an entire day without thinking of Brad.

—∿—

The heat of mid-July became stifling as we strove to keep to our schedule. The ocean breezes that kept us comfortable in early summer had departed, leaving a pall of humidity over Del Gloria's rocky promontory. I couldn't help but dwell on the fact that I'd been away from home more than a month and still hadn't heard from Brad. Things couldn't possibly be taking this long to wrap up, could they? Back in Michigan, my old log cabin would be cool in its woodland hidey-hole by the lake. What I wouldn't give to spend the blistering summer there in the shade. I knew it was impossible, but my fingers itched to pick up the phone, if only to remind Puppa to pay the electric bill. I calmed myself, certain I'd be home any day now.

Then came August. Still in Del Gloria. Still shriveling in the heat. I'd gotten in the habit of arriving at the project before dawn, while the air was somewhat bearable. The rest of the gang generally arrived around seven, allowing me treasured hours to work in solitude.

Before I knew it, September came without fanfare, and without a phone call from Brad. With each passing month, it got harder and harder to keep faith that he'd ever contact me.

Every morning I'd wake up and pretend everything was still okay. To work, to school, then back to Cliffhouse, like that was how things were supposed to be. I would put Brad out of my mind and get through each day, imagining that I could keep it up until the Old Town project was finished and I had my college degree.

Still, I couldn't shake the feeling that my life was like a balloon about to land in a field of needles. I'd aced my exams, the team was on track for completion of house number four, and the longed-for rain showers were holding off until the roof repairs got done. I should have felt blessed. But somehow I knew better.

I threw on my work clothes, put my hair in a ponytail, and headed to the curb for my date with Dogpatch.

Headlights came up the road, pulling over to let me board. I took my usual seat one row behind the driver. A few other sleepy riders looked toward me, then back out the window.

"How are you this morning, Miss Braddock?" the driver asked in his Chinese accent. He put the bus in gear.

"Could have used a cup of coffee," I answered, yawning.

"You and me both." His slight frame was made smaller by the immensity of the vehicle he drove.

"Have you heard the weather?" I set my tote on the floor next to my feet.

"Old Chinese proverb says when everybody wants rain, nobody gets it."

"I don't want rain. We still have to tar the chimney before it's allowed to rain."

"Good. Then it rains tonight." He looked in his mirror at me. "Better hurry with that chimney."

Daylight sifted slowly over the landscape. Brown lawns and shriveled plants made their plea for water.

The bus stopped in front of the old depot. The driver opened the door for unloading.

"Thanks, Mr. Kim. See you later." I made my walk toward Rios Buena Suerta. The other passengers stayed in the station, waiting to make their daily commute to the city via the Amtrak.

I shuffled along dim streets thinking about my latest stab at college. I was holding steady with a 3.5 GPA. The four-point in my Non-profit Organizations class was dragged down by the three-point on the Revamp Project.

I had asked Denton first chance I got why he gave me a B instead of an A.

"I assigned you to be the leader," he'd replied. "You're letting others do your job. You're skating through. You're lucky I didn't give you a C."

I paused at the intersection, smiling to myself. Despite Denton's rebuff, I was proud of my accomplishment. I almost wished I could complete my degree here at Del Gloria. It would reverse the fact that I'd had to drop out of Michigan State. But Brad's phone call would come any day. I just knew it. And as soon as I hit the disconnect button, I'd be on the first flight out of here and back in Brad's arms.

Guilt hit me at the thought of walking out on my

teammates. They were counting on me to be here 'til the end. But once I explained the whole situation, they'd understand and wish me the best.

I turned the corner onto Rios Buena Suerta and covered the distance to our mostly completed House Number Four. I grabbed the hidden key and climbed the ramp that covered the front steps. A swift turn of the handle, and I was in.

The dining and living rooms still needed paint before the project was complete. And, we were waiting for a friend of a friend of Dagger's to drop off his extension ladder so we could finish plugging the leak near the chimney. But with no rain in the forecast, there was no hurry.

I flipped on the lights and stooped over the paint cans. We'd gone with my favorite neutral, a pale ivory, to keep the rooms bright and warm. Rubbery paint separated as I pried the top off and poured a stream into the tray. The roller made a slurping sound as I wet it with color. I stood and turned toward my target wall.

I froze, staring at the wall and gasping for air.

PATRICIA AMBLE WAS HERE. The words were sprayed in huge black letters across the smooth surface.

14

The letters blurred as I shrank to the floor, instinctively holding the roller away from my clothes. I gave myself a mental kick. Whoever had written it knew I worked alone every morning. That meant they could be watching me right now. Waiting for me.

Caring more about protecting my secret than avoiding bodily harm, I dragged the roller across the words, painting them out. But the black showed through and I raced to get a fresh supply of paint to blot the letters.

By the time I was satisfied, tears and sweat had made a mess of my face.

Outside, the porch creaked.

I whirled as someone entered the room.

"Celia! Thank goodness it's you." My heart thudded out of control.

Her chair made a quiet whirring as she steered to me. "Are you okay?"

I nodded, still gasping.

"You shouldn't work so hard this early in the morning.

You look like you're ready to pass out." She took the roller from my grip. "Put your head between your knees."

She wheeled over to the wall, emptied the roller over its surface, then maneuvered to the tray for a refill. "When the rest of them get here, we should have these two rooms done in no time." She painted a patch of drywall.

"Yeah." I kept up my pattern of breathing, feeling my brain connections coming back on line. "Who was the last one to leave last night? Do you remember?"

"Uh oh. Did someone forget to lock the door? Usually I'm the last one out. But Maize, Koby, and Portia were still here when I left." She finished a lower section and went for more paint.

We'd started hitting the night shift pretty hard when some of the team members took jobs in addition to classes. Dagger and Simon showed up in the mornings. The rest arrived after supper and stayed until dark. I managed to cover both shifts.

The chaotic schedules didn't make it any easier to weed out my antagonist.

Today, Dagger and Simon pulled in around ten. I watched their behavior to see if either one acted strange around me. They both seemed normal, if they could be called that.

"Why do you keep staring at me?" Simon asked as we taped off the trim in a back bedroom.

I figured if I told him his birthmark was fading again, he'd think I was loony. I gave him a shrug of apology and went in search of Dagger.

"When's your buddy bringing his ladder?" I found him on the porch, flipping his cell phone closed.

"Said he'd drop it off tonight. I'm working late at the pizzeria, so I won't be here. Can you meet him?" When he wasn't speaking the lingo of his 'hood, Dagger sounded like any other surfer dude.

I glanced down the street. The heat of a California autumn rose in waves from the pavement. Birds in tree branches sang at the top of their voices. Perhaps they were praying for rain.

I nodded in Dagger's direction. "Yeah. I'll be around."

Inside, I took a last look. One more coat of paint later that afternoon and we'd be done. I tidied up the supplies and went to class, doodling while the youngish prof jotted his points on the whiteboard.

Godly Decisions in the Secular Corporation had a double underline. Eight steps followed. I dutifully copied them in my notebook, knowing I'd be able to memorize them later and ace a test. As for putting them into action . . . it seemed too monumental a task for real life. I figured I'd probably keep living the way I always had: react to the slightest situation as if an atom bomb was about to detonate in my hands. That worked well for me as the CEO of Tish International.

My pen slid to a halt. According to Denton, my atom bomb lifestyle is what had put my mind into cortisol-overdrive in the first place. Maybe I needed to take the processes being presented in class more seriously. More than my grades depended on it.

The instructor launched into a lecture. As I listened, I tried to imagine life without daily drama. Even in all the years I'd lived completely alone, I'd spent my energy rehashing the past, feeling guilty for the smallest mistakes, and crucifying myself over and over for the big ones. I didn't need an audience to be a drama queen.

Then when I met Brad . . . At the very hint that things could ease into a comfortable, long-term relationship, I was running for cover, ramping up the drama, determined to escape a ho-hum, albeit peaceful, existence as Brad's wife.

And I'd nearly succeeded at ruining things for myself. Brad's patience and forbearance had kept intact the ties that bound us.

Then just when everything was about to go right . . .

I rubbed at the ache in my arm that flared up every time I thought of Brad. I hadn't asked for Frank Majestic's drama in my life. It wasn't fair that other people's baggage kept showing up and wrecking things for me.

Tuning in to the man at the podium, I wrote down the details that would help me take a deep breath and make better decisions next time around.

After class, I grabbed a salad at the cafeteria, then took the bus back to Rios Buena Suerta. The team had polished off most of the painting by the time I arrived.

"Wow. It looks great." I marveled at the transformation the once-dilapidated house had undergone. "Some family is going to be proud to call this place home."

I helped Koby and Portia with the cleanup, rinsing the last of the brushes and laying them on the counter. "Why don't you two go ahead and take off? I'll shine the sink while I wait for the ladder."

Roofs were technically off-limits to students in the Revamp Program. For safety's sake, the department required the work to be contracted by professionals. But due to a localized construction boom, it was another week before the block of homes would be sealed from the elements. While House Numbers One, Two, and Three would hold up in bad weather, House Number Four wouldn't be so lucky. The metal flashing around the chimney had peeled away in previous years, leaving easy access for the rain. To protect the work we'd done so far, we planned to plug the leak ourselves, at least temporarily.

"I'll wait with you," Celia said. "No one should be here alone past dark."

I shook my head. "It won't be long. Anyway, don't you work in Dean Lester's office tomorrow morning?"

She groaned. "And I've got a test to study for."

"You go study. I can handle it." I shooed them out the door and wiped the new stainless steel sink and fixtures until they shone. The wood floors were worn, but we'd taken out the squeak and put on a new coat of finish, which gave off a lustrous glow even in the dimming light. A good sweeping and the place would be ready for its new occupants.

I poked my head out the screen door. No ladder guys yet. I sat on the porch surround, dangling my feet as I waited. In the distance, over open water, lightning bolted across the sky.

I straightened. Maybe Mr. Kim was right. It only rained when you didn't want it to. My thumbs twiddled with nervous energy. If the ladder would just get here, I could climb the roof and patch the leak before the downpour.

Lightning flashed again, followed by the rumble of

thunder. My feet thudded impatiently. I'd almost given up hope when a pickup with a ladder strapped to its rack pealed around the corner and screeched to a halt at the curb.

Two swarthy men in blue jeans and tank tops got out, their skin darkly tanned. "You the one who needs the ladder?" the tallest of the two asked.

I gave a relieved smile. "You're at the right place."

"Where do you want it?"

I turned toward the house. "Right there on the side. I have to get up to the chimney."

"Not tonight, I hope. There's a storm coming." The tall man unfastened the rope and slid the ladder down. The other caught one end, and between them, they moved it into place.

"Thank you so much," I said over the crank of the engine. An arm waved out the window as the truck did a U-turn and headed toward the main road.

I checked the western sky. Giant black clouds blotted out the last rays of sun, bringing on night like the drop of a curtain.

The chimney made a desperate sentinel alone in the center of the roof. There would never be enough time to seal the leak now. But if I draped the stones with a drop cloth, there might be enough protection to keep out the storm. I grabbed duct tape and the plastic and climbed the first rung . . . then the second . . . Halfway up, the ladder shifted. I leaned in the other direction to compensate. The ladder stabilized. Heart pounding, I took another step. My stomach knotted as I reached the top rung and the steep incline of the roof. Earlier, the guys had cast a rope over the peak, then thrown it back over, looping it around the chimney. The theory had been to provide a handhold for Dagger, who'd volunteered to make the climb. Too bad for me the rain decided to show up earlier than expected. Finding the twin lengths that dangled all the way to the ground, I hoisted myself toward the bricks like a mountain climber conquering Mt. Everest. At the top, I pressed my cheeks to the chimney, praying God would overlook my stupidity in tackling this project alone.

Lightning flashed directly above me. I cringed at my decision to climb a rooftop in a thunderstorm. If Denton could see me now, he'd throw me off the project. If Brad could see me now . . .

I didn't want to go that route. At the moment I could only hope to live to see Brad.

Straddling the peak, I tossed a corner of plastic over the chimney. The wind caught the edge, blowing it back in my face. I stood and tried again, legs shaky beneath me. I managed to get the sheeting over the stones. With a pull, the material tightened. I stuck tape to the plastic and wound it around. By the time I was done, the chimney looked like I'd taken it hostage.

Satisfied, I took a breather with my back against the stones. A raindrop landed on my cheek. Then the plastic beneath me crinkled. Surprised, I twisted to find the source of the movement.

The rope.

In the near blackness, one side sped up toward the chimney, while the other rushed down toward the ledge.

I gave a shout as I realized my sole means of getting off the roof safely was quickly disappearing. I made a grab for it, but the plastic interfered and the fibers slipped through my grasp.

What was happening? It was as if someone on the ground was trying to strand me on the roof.

"Hey, stop! I'm up here!" I screamed, my voice billowing in a thousand directions in the storm.

The end of the rope slid past. I instinctively made a grab for it, clenching the final three inches in my hands for less than a second as it continued with force on its way to the ground.

"Hey!" I screamed again, hoping for mercy. "Help! I'm up here!"

In desperation, I calculated the trajectory of my body in a slide down the roof. With friction, wind direction, and speed taken into consideration, the chances of landing at the top rung of the ladder without toppling to the ground were basically nil.

And yet at this point, with rain about to ruin my chance of escape, a good dose of lunacy was my only hope.

I laid on my stomach, clinging to the peak, angling for the best course. Visions of broken legs, punctured lungs, and shattered vertebrae, followed by a lengthy confinement, kept me frozen in place.

I looked behind me, down the slope of the roof. It could be possible . . . I might actually pull it off . . .

I watched in horror as the top of the ladder jiggled and pulled away from the roof. A moment later, it keeled sideways out of view. A muffled cry floated up from the ground along with the clatter of metal.

Someone stole my ladder.

"Whoa! Hey! That's my ladder!" I climbed, straddling the peak once more, praying I'd see the top rung come back into view. "Help! Help!"

Rain splattered my cheeks. The *tap tap tap* around me as drops landed on the shingles soon turned to a deafening roar. In seconds I was soaked, the heat of September exchanged for icy wetness.

Shivers streaked through my body. A numbness swept over my mind. Why was I up on a rooftop in a rainstorm? No amount of reason could justify my circumstances. And yet it had seemed so logical a few hours earlier, when the storm lingered over the Pacific and daylight had illuminated my path.

I took a deep breath. How could I know some thief would come after my ladder? I wasn't irresponsible, just jinxed.

Unable to save myself, I pulled up a section of tape and climbed under the plastic, leaving myself an air tunnel. At least I'd have some protection while I waited to be rescued.

15

The rain poured down around me, the pattering on the roof of my garden shed enough to drive me crazy. I played around with an assortment of tools, displaying them in a way that would catch the interest of a prospective buyer. I hummed as I worked, a song Brad's sister had written for their father.

> Then will come that dawn,
> When all around the angels sing,
> Christ Jesus takes my hand,
> And I feel it touching yours again . . .

Something flashed past the tiny shed window. I jumped, my heart racing.

It could have been my friendly doe, the one that always visited my neck of the woods here at my log home on the lake.

But through the sound of rain crackling on trees and grass and shingles, there came a knock on the shed door.

I jerked back at the unexpected noise.

"Who's there?" I moved with baby steps toward the door.

"It's me." The voice was so familiar. Soft and deep, saying "I love you" with its very tone.

Oh my. Brad. It was Brad.

I raced to the door, throwing it open.

He stood there looking at me with his corny grin.

"You're here!" I jumped at him, landing against his body, hugging him to me. We stood in the open, me squealing in glee to see him, and Brad making that wonderful chuckling in his chest.

"I missed you so much," I whispered in his ear.

"I miss you too," he said.

I laughed, then almost cried to see the crinkles I loved so much around his sparkling brown eyes.

"My goodness." I touched his cheek. "I was getting worried that I'd never see you again." I smiled at him, vaguely wondering why we weren't getting wet though rain still fell around us.

"Come home, Tish. It's okay to come home."

I felt giddy at his words, thrilled that we'd get to be together all the time now.

But . . . I was home. The garden shed was just a few yards from my house. I turned around to look at the shed, getting the strangest feeling that something wasn't right.

I gasped at the sight of only smoldering ashes behind me. There was no garden shed. It had burned down in the spring.

Twirling, I grabbed for Brad, knowing even as I did that he would slip through my grasp. He became pale as I watched him. My eyes pleaded with him to stay. I squeezed his hands tighter, willing him to remain with me. But my fingers turned wet and Brad slipped away, disappearing into swirling smoke.

When he was out of sight, I looked at my hands.

They were covered in blood.

I woke up screaming, tangled in the plastic that protected me from the rain pummeling my perch. I wiped something sharp and grainy from my cheek. Sandpaper would have made a better pillow than asphalt shingles. I rested my head on the back of my hands and hoped the terrible nightmare would fade with the storm.

—w—

After my bad dream, sleep eluded me. So when I woke to the chirping of birds and the faint glow of dawn, I nearly rolled off the roof in surprise. I estimated the time to be around six or so. Only an hour more and Celia would arrive.

I slapped the shingles in frustration. No, Celia wouldn't arrive. She was working this morning. My next hope wouldn't come around until ten o'clock, with Simon and Dagger.

"Help! Somebody help me!" Where was my mysterious bodyguard when I needed him?

I put out the call every few minutes, hoping someone would respond. But I was stuck on a roof in the back section of a deserted subdivision. What were the chances?

Trapped alone with my mind, I tried to stay calm and

not obsess over the extreme amounts of cortisol that could be flooding my brain at that very moment. I wanted to beg God for angels and a helicopter, but couldn't help feeling I deserved whatever consequences resulted from my foolishness.

A few hours later, I begged him anyway.

"Please, God, I know I'm stupid and I'm trying really hard to quit being that way, but could you please, please, please just get me off this roof in one piece?" My forehead scrunched tight as I concentrated. "And if you really love me, no one will ever find out I was stranded up here all night long in a rainstorm."

It had to be at least ten thirty before Dagger showed up. He walked down the street with his gangsta swagger.

"Hey! Up here!" I waved my arms.

He stared at me as he moved closer to the house.

"Yo. Alisha. What's up?"

"I'm so glad you're here." I swallowed all pride. "Can you see if there's a ladder lying at the side of the house?"

He disappeared from view. He was back in sight a few seconds later, squinting up at me. "No ladder. Ray said he dropped it here last night. What'd you do? Fly?" He hummed a laugh.

"No joke, Dagger. Please help me get down."

"Don't tell me someone stole it with you up there." He flipped open his cell phone and dialed three digits.

I tensed, every muscle aching. "What are you doing?"

"Getting you down." He turned away and spoke in soft tones. Then he disappeared. Moments later came the sound of feet up the front steps and the slam of the screen door.

"Hey! Get back here! You can't just leave me!"

The minutes ticked by. In the distance, the blare of sirens drifted to my rooftop, drawing closer by the second.

He didn't.

With a deafening drone, a fire rig turned onto Rios Buena Suerta, lights flashing. A police car and several civilian vehicles followed.

He did.

I put my face to the rough shingles and groaned. Why did stuff like this always happen to me?

The rig pulled over the curb and onto the lawn. In a few swift moves, men in full gear had a ladder in place and were climbing to my rescue. On the ground, cameras flashed.

Another car pulled up.

A black Jaguar.

Denton.

I was so dead.

Helping hands guided me to the ground. Safe once more, I hid behind strands of sopping hair and made a beeline for the bungalow, where I could hang out in a closet until the crowd dispersed.

But the group of ambulance chasers—or were they reporters?—photographed my every move. Some angled their long lenses for close-ups.

"Can you tell us what happened?" A woman's voice carried over the crowd.

"How did you end up on the roof?"

"Were you there all night?"

The questions fired at me as I faltered alone on the

porch. I must have looked like a fish out of water the way my mouth just opened and closed . . . opened and closed.

The scene was beyond nightmarish—this time I was really awake. It was really happening.

Denton brushed through the crowd and up the ramp.

His hand grabbed my elbow and he led me inside. "I suggest you get out of view, Alisha."

Back on the porch, Denton fed the crowd a glorified version of my adventure.

In the middle of it, Portia arrived, hustling past the paparazzi and inside. "Alisha. Are you alright? Dagger said you were stuck on the roof all night. What happened?"

I kept to the main points as I shared my adventure.

"I'm worried about you." She kept her voice low. "Who would steal a ladder around here? Especially when someone is still using it?" She gave a worried scrunch of her forehead. "Maybe your landlord knows you're here."

"My landlord?" At Portia's look of concern, I caught on. "Oh. Yeah. My landlord. Right."

A snort of disbelief. "You are so full of baloney, Alisha. Landlord, my foot. What's really going on here?"

Gawkers gone and the ladder truck driving away, Denton came back inside. The screen door slammed like a gavel behind him.

Denton sashayed in our direction. Portia touched my arm. "We'll talk later, okay?"

I nodded as she scurried off, leaving me to face my fate alone.

"I don't have to tell you how foolish your behavior was." Denton's voice came low and even.

"Of course it was foolish."

His hands swished through the air. "Besides putting yourself in great bodily harm—didn't your father ever teach you not to climb a ladder alone?—your face will now be on every major paper on the West Coast. Don't you care about staying alive?"

His two-point speech expanded into a ten-pointer.

". . . do you realize how much it will cost me to keep your photo under wraps . . ."

I watched in silence as he ranted. I dove in at the first pause.

"Hey. You can save your breath, really. I appreciate everything you've done for me. It's been great being out here. I'm grateful for your hospitality. But," I took a deep breath before continuing, "I think it's time I go home. This arrangement isn't working anymore. I'm used to being independent. I'll face whatever's waiting for me. I can't keep living like this."

I brushed his hand from my arm and stalked out the door.

16

He followed me out. "Killers are hunting you as we speak. The moment you return to Michigan, you are as good as dead."

I twirled to face him on the sidewalk. "It's apparent they've already found me. I don't understand why they're playing with me like a half-dead mouse. But the way things are going, I won't survive long in California. Michigan may be my best option."

"Michigan is not an option. You will stay here and you will be safe." His finger pointed with emphasis at the concrete beneath us.

I leaned my head on one hand to combat the confusion. Logically, Denton was right. Returning to Michigan too soon could be a fatal error. But emotionally, I wasn't sure I could survive out here much longer. I needed to see Brad. I couldn't shake that nagging feeling that he should have called me by now—if he could. Had something happened to him?

"I'm sorry. I have to go back."

Denton looked like his blood pressure was ratcheting

into the red zone. "A person I love very much asked me to watch out for you. 'Keep her alive,' he said. I am not going to let you make some spontaneous, rash decision that puts you back in danger."

"Hey. I'm already in danger." My own temper was beginning to flare. "And I get to make the choices about my life."

"You're not ready for the consequences." Denton's voice dropped to a low rumble. "Give it three more months."

Trapped in Alisha Braddock's life. I wanted out. Out of Del Gloria, out of California, and back to me. Back to the life of Tish Amble.

I crossed my arms, debating. Maybe it was too soon for me to handle the consequences of leaving the coast.

I nodded. "Okay. But only three more months. Then I'm going back. I have to go back."

He gave a nod. "All right then. Let's get you home to Cliffhouse."

—w—

The months wore on. Since that day on the ladder, Denton seemed to soften toward me, his previous anger now a gentleness, which I interpreted as pity. But again, I didn't understand what caused the attitude shift and didn't care to ask.

It wasn't long before Thanksgiving arrived, with skies overcast and a stiff west wind. My attitude was as glum as the weather. I tried not to think of last Thanksgiving, and Brad, and his generous invitation to share the holiday with him when I was still new to Rawlings.

This year I was a thousand miles from Brad. It didn't matter that later today there'd be guests. None of them were Brad. A forlorn sigh escaped my chest. My arms ached from missing him.

The silky floral comforter on my borrowed four-poster brushed against my wrists as I lay on the bed, flipping through the binder of mementos I'd put together to keep my time in Del Gloria from fading into the mist like Brigadoon. Outside, rain began to fall.

I paused at an article I'd cut out. "Ladder Stolen from Rooftop Heroine," the headline read. The photo showed a vague shape climbing to the ground surrounded by rescue workers. How Denton had kept Tish Amble's face from the front page, I'd never know. But he'd also managed to put in a pitch for the college's Revamp Program and plug the dedicated students who were part of the life-changing course of study, making me appear more like a champion for saving some drywall than a nut for being up on a roof in a lightning storm. The stolen ladder had been found several days later beside the railroad tracks, the theft chalked up to practical jokers.

I rubbed a finger against the newsprint. Things hadn't been so bad here. I had a crowd of friends for the first time in my life. And my studies had improved my mind and my outlook on life. I was even getting into the whole Christian swing of things, and felt better about myself now than ever before. But with only a few weeks until the end of the semester, I was faced with a gut-wrenching decision. Would I stay or would I go?

I looked around my little piece of heaven. The beautifully furnished room with its view of the Pacific had begun to feel like home. I had barely a care here at Cliffhouse. With Denton footing my bills, no job was required. Three squares a day and even housekeeping services were provided, freeing me to focus on my classes and the Rios Buena Suerta project. It was better than being a kid again—and I didn't even have a curfew.

I turned the page to a collage of the earlier photographs. Koby, Celia, Portia, and I. We looked like the Four Musketeers, showing off for the camera at each victory.

I leaned on one elbow. How could I even contemplate leaving my team? We were making good progress. Five more families had a place to call home. Besides, Brad hadn't even contacted me. He must have a very good reason for wanting me to stay in Del Gloria. And if I showed up unannounced back in Michigan, he might be less than thrilled to see me.

Over the past months, the ache that shot up my arm at any thought of Brad had become little more than a twinge. I squeezed a hand to the scar. My injury was barely visible, the hurt a mere memory.

My eyes wandered to a rain-splattered window. Isn't that what I wanted? Isn't that what I'd hoped for—to forget?

But why? The question nagged at me. Why would I want to forget? I closed my eyes, concentrating on my last moments in Port Silvan. Candice LeJeune lifted her pistol—but no, before that . . . what had she said before that? She'd said, "Remember, I'll always love you." Then there'd been the blast of the gun and then . . . the flash of white dropped over the past.

I sighed and closed my scrapbook. It seemed useless to even try remembering.

My fingers beat a rhythm on the cover. Think . . . what had happened just before? Candice came into the room and grabbed Frank Majestic from behind, gun to his head. Then Brad came in the room.

I grabbed my temples, massaging them against the building pressure. Why couldn't the synapses in my mind link up so I could remember whatever it was I was trying so hard to forget?

Brad. He was in the room when the gun went off. He came in right after Candice did. So why couldn't I remember anything about Brad afterward? He must have helped me after I'd been shot. He wouldn't have just left me there, bleeding, all alone. I knocked my knuckles against my skull. Think, think . . . but nothing came to me beyond the glaring whiteness.

I glanced at the bedside clock. Already 9:30. I'd slept in and lounged long enough. I dressed and wandered downstairs, making myself available in case Ms. Rigg broke down and wanted help for once.

She didn't.

I snuggled on a chair in the parlor, catching up on my reading as I waited for our dinner guests to arrive. Around me, the gilded walls became stone, and I was in the deepest, darkest dungeon beside Edmond Dantès. With the help of his prison mate, he planned his escape. Soon he would be back in France, back to his old life, which he would reclaim at the expense of his enemies. Best of all, he would have a great treasure at his disposal with which to exact his revenge.

The doorbell rang, tearing me from Edmond's discovery on the Isle of Monte Cristo. Book aside, I opened the door to greet six members of the Revamp Program. Only Celia had nearby family to visit with over the Thanksgiving holiday. The rest took advantage of the professor's invitation to a traditional feast served in the formal dining room at Cliffhouse.

We enjoyed hors d'oeuvres and rousing conversation, followed by the unexpected arrival of Ms. Rigg's daughter Jane.

The room quieted as the pseudo-sophisticate entered, laying on her Hollywood poise and charm.

"Hello, all. What a perfectly miserable day to give thanks." Her svelte figure, draped in a loose white satin pantsuit, captured every eye.

"Jane. What a surprise," Denton said. He turned his back to the party crasher, focusing his attention on Maize Martin, who commenced babbling at her usual rate of five hundred words a minute.

"Denton, dear brother. Where else would I be but home for the holiday?" She touched his shoulder.

He flinched away.

The elder Ms. Rigg scooped up an empty bowl of dip and slinked out of the room.

Beside me near the buffet, Portia raised an eyebrow. "What's that woman doing here? Is that really his sister?" she asked under her breath.

I dabbed a carrot in ranch dip and crunched. "Mm mm mm," I said to the tune of "I don't know." I waited until I was done chewing. "Her mom's the housekeeper. I guess she grew up with the Braddocks. Apparently she's like family to the professor."

"Maybe the black sheep of the family," Portia said.

I chewed and watched Jane work the room. She started with Simon, practically purring as she laughed at something he said. Having conquered her first victim, she meandered seductively toward Koby.

Portia tensed. "She's such a parasite." She glared knives in Jane's direction.

"Simon doesn't look too upset about it." I couldn't help but grin at the way his eyes followed her shape.

"She is twisted and evil. You can almost see it in her eyes." Portia's venom grew.

I touched her arm. "Stay calm. She's just making the rounds. She's not hurting anybody."

Portia gestured toward Denton, who kept his back directed at Jane as if calculating her every movement. "I'm not so sure. The doc seems pretty upset. That woman shouldn't be here. And she knows it." Portia took a sip of punch.

I shrugged. "Last time I had a run-in with Jane, Uncle Denton made her seem harmless."

"Harmless as a jellyfish. Just don't get wrapped in her tentacles."

"Uh oh," I whispered. "Human jellyfish headed our way."

Jane sauntered toward the food, plucked a square of orange cheese from a platter, and plopped it in her mouth.

"Hello, Alisha. And you are . . . ?" She nodded her head in Portia's direction, waiting for an introduction.

"Miss Romero. How do you do?" Portia's voice was cool.

"I'm good. Thanks for asking." Jane turned toward me. "So. How are you surviving Del Gloria?"

I refused to read a deeper meaning into her words. "Great. Loving it."

"Not antsy to be getting home to . . . where is it . . . Galveston, right?"

I slanted my head. What was she up to?

"Yes, Galveston," I said. "And no, I'm not antsy to get back there."

"Can't say I blame you. What is it? Hurricane season right now?"

I nodded, no clue about the weather in Galveston.

"Of course," she went on, "I hear Michigan just had its first big blizzard of the year. I guess things could always be worse."

Her tongue slithered behind her lips, I was sure of it.

Next to me, Portia's fingers twiddled against her pant leg, as if fighting the urge to punch Jane in the mouth. In the background, Denton peered over his shoulder, checking on the rogue actress. If he had a move up his sleeve, I wished he'd make it and spare me the woman's line of questioning.

"So, Alisha"—Jane's eyes scooped me back into her net—"what do you think of that whole drug drama going on in northern Michigan? Have you been keeping up?"

I gave her a blank look and shook my head, praying she couldn't see the beads of sweat breaking out on my temples.

"Some big drug lord got nabbed in a sting operation. Big shoot-out, bodies everywhere . . . It's so LA. Who would think that kind of thing happens in those teeny little backwoods towns?"

My throat constricted. Was she talking about Frank Majestic and the morning at my log cabin?

Her hands swooped the air as she prattled on. "It's all gone to trial now—thank heaven the fiend lived to face a jury. Too bad some of the others weren't as lucky."

I drew in a strangled breath. Why was she telling me this? What did this have to do with me?

I blinked and stared at the food. Movement in the corner of my eye. Denton grabbed Jane by the wrist and swooped her toward the kitchen. Her mock protest sounded more like laughter.

The only thing in focus was a ring of ice floating in frothy pink punch. Cold, hard ice.

I gasped. Had anyone winterized my cottage? If it was really as cold in Michigan as Jane said, there could be ice in the pipes right now. I should get on a plane and take care of the place myself instead of frittering away my life fixing up houses for other people while my own fell to ruin.

A hand touched my arm. Through tears swimming in my eyes, I saw Portia, her face squinched in concern.

"You okay?" Her raisin-colored satin blouse caught my tear as she leaned to hug me. "I don't know what just happened," she said, "but I'm guessing it has something to do with your landlord?"

I glanced at her with a sheepish look. "I guess you could say that."

She kept her voice low as we gathered onlookers. "Don't let her get to you. It's a holiday. Relax and have some fun."

I nodded and wiped my eyes. "I'll try."

Muscles popped from her neck. "And if that witch so much as looks at you the rest of the day—well, you'll think you're watching tryouts for *Catfight, The Movie*."

I smiled at the vision of Jane's white slacks flapping in the wind as Portia swung her around by the hair. "Thanks. You're a good friend."

To pass the time before the big meal, we broke out a trivia game and set it up in the parlor. Dagger dazzled us with his sports aptitude, Gwen with her grasp of science, and Maize with her capacity for little-known Bible facts.

Koby read a psychology question that had us stumped.

"Where's the professor?" he asked. "He'd know the name of the surgeon who performed the first lobotomy."

Just then Simon joined us, slicking back his dark hair with one hand. "Can you imagine letting some guy take out part of your brain?" He made a casual flop onto the settee.

I wondered where he'd been. I hadn't even noticed he'd left the room.

With the crowd stumped, Koby put the card back in its box and went on to the next question.

A few minutes later, Ms. Rigg invited us to be seated for dinner. There was no sign of Jane, though a place had been set for her. I sat next to Denton, wondering what he'd done with the derelict diva. I watched his hands reach for his cloth napkin. No signs of gunpowder residue on the skin. A quick glance under the table revealed clean shoes. No grave digging before supper. Jane had obviously escaped murder.

"Shall we pray?" Denton bowed his head and the rest of us followed suit.

At his "amen," the chatting and laughter resumed. Steaming veggies and sliced turkey made the rounds. Afterward, dessert found an eager lineup at the buffet. I chose a slice of blueberry pie. Portia went with pumpkin. Maize and Gwen turned their sundaes into works of art topped with a cherry. The guys gravitated toward the apple pie. I was already planning a covert mission to the kitchen for leftovers later that night.

I watched the happy group. Even with voices all around me, I could only think about Jane's untimely revelation of the drug trials in Michigan and what that meant for me . . . and Brad.

Mindlessly, I chopped at my blueberry pie. The same old questions came to mind. Was I really safe in Del Gloria anymore? Were those around me safe? Who knew what someone like Jane would do with information on my background. She hardly seemed like the type to keep it to herself. In fact, the way she flaunted her secret, with Portia standing right there, I figured most of LA, Beverly Hills, and Hollywood already knew Patricia Louise Amble was hiding out somewhere on the coast. It wasn't that the information would mean anything to most people, but in the right hands it could mean cash, drugs, or death. I wondered which payment plan Jane had chosen.

"Hey. You going to eat that pie or turn it to mush?" Portia nudged me out of my daze.

I put the fork to my lips, shocked by the sweetly sour blueberries laced with flaky chunks of crust.

Portia angled next to me at the table. "You ready to talk about it?"

I shook my head, then went ahead and told her anyway. "You know, that landlord thing. I'm having trouble remembering all the details. When Jane mocked me like that, it made me wonder what really happened. Maybe something bad, something worse than I thought, and I forgot about it." I shrugged. "I don't know. I just can't seem to remember."

"Like I said before, 'The truth shall set you free.' Why don't you Google it? Or ask Koby for help? He's an ex-hacker. He can find anything. What's the worst that can happen?"

"No." I clenched my jaw. "No. I'm just going to wait for my phone call. And when I get back home, I'll know what's going on. It'll be fine. Nothing bad happened."

The clanking of dishes, pleasant voices, and laughter swirled around us.

Portia rested her hand on mine. "I waited for that phone call once. You know what? It never came."

I tried to pull away, but she gripped my fingers in hers.

"It was a good thing too, Alisha. Look at my life now. I've got an education, good friends, good food, and a roof over my head. And I don't have to sleep with men to get it. If a special man comes along someday, great. If not, I'm happy. My life wouldn't be this awesome if I'd gotten that phone call. The life at the other end of that phone line wasn't anywhere as good as the life at this end."

"That's not going to happen to me." My voice rose in defense. "The person at the other end of my phone line loves me. He wants me home with him. And that's where I want to be."

At the look on Portia's face, I explained. "Don't get me wrong. I love you guys. This has been a really good experience for me. I'm like a whole new person since I came to Del Gloria. But there's someone waiting for me . . . that special someone. We were meant to be together. And nothing can stop us." My words started to sound desperate and I petered off.

Portia stared at me, jaw set. "You better find out what's going on back there. It doesn't sound to me like you're going to get that phone call. Why set yourself up for devastation? Find out what happened, face it, deal with it, and move on. Life flows in one direction, honey. Once you leave a place, there ain't no going back." Her face hardened into that of the Portia I'd first met.

"I'm sorry you never got your phone call, Portia."

I stood, ready to excuse myself from the gathering.

A scream from the kitchen.

"Professor! Professor, come quick." Ms. Rigg appeared at the dining room arch. Wet hair from a bun gone asunder clung to her cheeks. Water dripped from her dress, puddling on the floor. "It's Jane, sir. I think she's dead!"

17

Denton sighed and pushed back his chair, as if refusing to get drawn into Ms. Rigg's drama. He crossed the room, moving with the speed of a man who suspected he was already too late. We practically ran him over as we herded behind him on the way to the portico, morbidly curious, if not mournful of Jane's demise.

Ms. Rigg pointed to the end of the driveway. "Look. She's down there! That's her purse—there on the edge of the cliff. I went to get it and I saw my Jane, dead on the sand below." She gave a wail of horror.

Portia, Simon, Dagger, and I stepped into the weather, following Denton down the concrete slope. Behind us from the comfort of the covered porch came offers of help if we should need it.

I shielded my face from the relentless rain as we strode toward the red purse abandoned beneath the guardrail across the road.

I waited on the curb with the weeping Ms. Rigg, watching as Denton stepped over the metal and peered with caution over the rain-soaked rocks to the ground below.

A shake of his head. "Simon. Call 9-1-1."

Simon nodded and hurried up the drive.

"Oh, Professor! Is she dead? Is she really dead?"

Ms. Rigg's hysterical sobs broke through my cold-hearted observation. I put an arm around her. "Come on, let's get back indoors."

"Oh, my Jane! My Jane!"

I shushed her with soothing tones as we made the climb to Cliffhouse. Portia stayed below with Denton and Dagger. Gwen, Maize, and Koby consoled us as we stepped into the house.

"Come on, let's get you to the parlor," I said and helped Ms. Rigg get situated on the settee. "Gwen, please grab a blanket from the linen closet upstairs. Maize, put on hot water for tea, if you would. And Koby," I patted the spot next to Ms. Rigg, "would you sit with her while I try to find out what's happened?"

Koby took a seat and Ms. Rigg leaned on his shoulder as if she were accustomed to leaning on others. I knew better.

"Jane. My Jane," she murmured.

I stood, ready for my mission.

"I didn't know Jane except for today," Koby said softly to Ms. Rigg, "but I really liked her smile."

I paused at the door, looking back.

"My Jane knew how to smile. That she did." Ms. Rigg burst into a new round of sobs.

I hurried away, somehow feeling that I should be mourning as well—but not for Jane. I shook my head to clear my thoughts and walked down the hill in the drizzle. A police cruiser was parked at the base of the drive, a burgundy-and-cream City of Del Gloria logo on the doors.

I met Portia and Dagger on their way back up to the house.

"I wouldn't go down there if I were you," Portia warned with a shake of her head.

"Thanks," I said and kept walking.

Denton and a uniformed officer stood near the guard-rail. Passing cars slowed to gawk in curiosity. A sedan arrived, angling next to the cruiser. A man in a trench coat stepped out and joined the men on the opposite side of the rail. I paused at the curb, not certain I wanted to involve myself in another death. At least this one couldn't be blamed on me.

I made the approach, picking up Denton's flustered voice.

"Maybe I was too hard on her. I don't know. I couldn't have her stay for supper when she was being rude to my other guests."

The newest arrival nodded his head, but didn't sound convinced. "Could have been her last straw, I suppose. But why set the purse down, then jump? Wouldn't a woman take her purse with her when she goes?" He studied the scene, moving like the victim prior to her fall. "What do you think? Would you leave your purse?" The man turned to me, as if he'd sensed my arrival.

Flustered by his question, I stared down the cliff, watching a vehicle cross the sand toward the body, which was still hidden from my view by the ledge. A few more steps and the corpse would be in full, gory sight. I stayed rooted to the spot. "Umm . . . I guess if I was going to jump off a cliff, I wouldn't even have brought a purse with me. I would have left it in my car or—" I swallowed at the whole gruesome thing, "—or whatever." My voice trailed off.

"That's what I was thinking." He stretched out a hand toward me. "Detective Larson. And who are you?"

My eyes grew wide. "Uhhh, Alisha Braddock."

"I thought you looked familiar. The Rooftop Heroine." He gave a snort. "Well, Ms. Braddock. What do you think happened here?"

The question took me by surprise. "Well . . ." I made it up as I went along. "Maybe she was just getting in her car to leave when she saw someone she knew, and, I don't know, came down the hill to talk to them. Then they pushed her over."

"Good theory."

I hated to tell him that dead bodies and I went back a long way.

Detective Larson looked at the uniformed officer. "Why don't you go in and get statements from the others." The detective turned to Denton. "I'm calling this one a murder. Don't leave town."

He hoisted a sturdy leg over the guardrail. He was at the double yellow line down the center of the blacktop when he stopped and looked back at me. "Same goes for you, Ms. Heroine. Don't plan any trips 'til I figure out what a stolen ladder and a dead blackmailer have in common."

Blackmailer? It sounded like Jane had figured out

an easy way to get a raise in her allowance. But as a wealthy benefactor who'd already doled out money to cover my tracks, Denton probably considered Jane a mere nuisance, not a threat to my safety.

Rain trickled down my face as I watched the detective's bulky shape cross to the lawn. A car pulled off the road and parked next to him, marring the wet grass with its tracks. A woman got out of the white midsize. As the detective talked with her, she bent inside the vehicle and emerged with an umbrella and a camera outfitted with a monster lens.

I swung around and caught Denton's gaze. Maybe I was mistaken, but he looked as busted as I felt. Sherlock Holmes over there was on to us.

I stepped toward my host uncle. "What are we going to do?"

He pulled me to him and held on to me like he'd be sorry to ever let me go. "You heard him. You have to stay here."

I nodded into his shoulder, an ache climbing from my chest to my throat. "What did he mean about Jane being a blackmailer?"

He pulled me tighter. His chest heaved and I thought for a minute he might be crying.

"She found out that you're really Patricia Amble. From your notebook, as you suspected. She looked into your background, then held the information over my head." He lowered his voice as the detective and his aide looked our way. "I paid her to keep it quiet."

I pushed away and searched his eyes. "Why would you do that?"

"I didn't have a choice. She threatened to expose you . . . and she had other information that would have disgraced my family."

"Oh. You mean that thing about being your half sister? So what if she was? You could survive it."

He shook his head. "She's always wanted DNA testing to prove she was blood . . . that meant exhuming my father's body. Based on the results, I might have been forced to turn over half my inheritance. So to let my father—and his good name—rest in peace, I've been paying her a healthy sum every month. But when she found out about you, she claimed grounds for a raise."

"When I first met Jane, Ms. Rigg denied the ambassador was Jane's father."

"Knowing Ms. Rigg's background, I'm not sure she can accurately say who Jane's father was. But she saw in my father an opportunity to raise her child in America, and she convinced him he was the responsible party. When I was growing up, Ms. Rigg lived in my house and rubbed my father's mistake in my mother's face day after day. My mother was gracious. She took pity on the Irishwoman and her child and allowed them to stay, despite the torment she lived with every moment."

"But you did have a choice. We always have choices. There had to be a better option than feeding Jane's greed. Why not just do the testing?"

"That's not what I chose. Perhaps you would have handled it differently." His eyes squeezed closed for a brief moment. "I wanted to give her time to change her mind. But it's too late to change things for Jane now."

I nodded and watched a drop of rain roll down his face.

The investigators crossed to us. We stayed back as the camerawoman snapped photos of the red leather pocketbook and area around it. She leaned near the cliff's edge for aerial views of the body.

The detective bagged the purse. "My wife's tells her life story." He dangled the clear plastic in the air. "I wonder what I'll find inside this one."

"Thank you, Detective. Anything you can turn up will be a great comfort to Ms. Rigg." Denton touched the back of my elbow and steered me gently up the hill toward the house.

With a damper thrown on our holiday, I expressed my condolences to Ms. Rigg, bid my teammates goodbye, and headed up to my room. I tried to read, but the plight of Edmond Dantès only depressed me. Now that he had his treasure, he was bent on seeking revenge against those who stole his life from him. Somehow his transformation from victim to perpetrator grated on me.

I put the book down and picked up my journal. I wrote down the events from the past several days as well as outlining today's tragedy. Finished, I set my pen on the bedside table.

The pages made a fluttering noise as I flipped through them in review. I couldn't imagine ever looking back and having my life make sense to me. It seemed more like a spoof on a Three Stooges episode than a story with a plot. As much as I'd been going to church, attending Christian-based courses, hanging out with good people, and tossing up prayers now and then, I still lacked the faith that God could actually take this warped, wretched human being and make her life count. If God's intent was to use me as an instrument to attract slugs from beneath rocks, then things were right on track. Maybe I just had to accept the humble role I'd been assigned.

My thumbs twiddled. I flipped onto my back, and stared at the canopy above. Maybe it was time I faced facts. Portia was right. There wasn't going to be a phone call. It was practically December. I'd been in Del Gloria six months. In Rawlings, two towns ago, I'd only lasted a little over four months. And Port Silvan, the last town, was only a notch more than three. That made Del Gloria more home to me than either of the others. So, the question wasn't really would Brad ever call. The question was, did I really want Brad to call?

I blew at a speck of dust floating over my head. The most honest answer I could come up with was no. No, I didn't want Brad to call. I wanted to stay right where I was. Finish the project. Finish college. Start appreciating life just the way it was, however messed up. Start being grateful for those who cared about me and wanted me in their lives. Denton, Portia, Celia, Maize—there was a whole list of them.

But even as I named off those closest to me here in Del Gloria, I couldn't shut out the faces of those I'd left behind in Port Silvan. My grandfather and Great-Grandmother Olivia, my cousins Joel and Gerard, Melissa Belmont and her kids. Even Samantha, Brad's sister. And—my heart did a flip-flop before resuming its natural rhythm—Brad. Especially Brad. Tears crept from my eyes as I tried to block his face from my mind. But there it stayed, etched forever in my memory. Today, instead of the jovial Brad with his crinkly eyes, his face seemed sad. I imagined myself holding his head in my arms, as if to say goodbye. He opened his lips to whisper something to me . . .

The world flashed white. I sat up, stricken. What had I just seen? Was it memory or imagination?

Brad's face burned itself to the back of my lids. Even with my eyes open, no matter where I looked, his face was just a blink away. His eyes followed mine, as if to accuse me.

Why did he look at me like that? He sent me away. I should be angry with him, not the other way around.

I raced out of the bedroom, seeking a distraction. Anything to get away from the guilt that washed over me at the thought of Brad.

Downstairs, Denton sat in the parlor, alone. A single lamp lit the room, the daylight long gone. I tiptoed to a chair beside him. He glanced up, acknowledging my arrival, then stared at the floor again.

"You okay?" I asked, shaken that the Unshakeable Professor Braddock might actually have felt a speed bump on his smooth road.

He gave a deep sigh. "It's so hard when you can look at someone else's life and know exactly what they should do. Then they don't do it. And they wind up dead."

I nodded in agreement. "But it's not your fault. Jane was going to do what Jane was going to do."

His eyes blazed into mine. "I was thinking of you, Patricia."

So I was Patricia tonight. Not the obedient Alisha. "I

don't get it. What exactly should I be doing that I'm not already?"

"Put the past behind you. Stay here with me."

"I've been doing that. I did that."

He glanced at my hands in my lap. "Look at your fingers. They want to go. They want to run. Don't let them. Make them stay."

I stilled my fidgeting. "I saw something tonight. A memory, I think. Of Brad."

He stared without saying anything.

"I was holding Brad's head in my arms. He looked so sad. He was whispering something to me. And then—" I closed my eyes in concentration. "That's all I can remember."

"How did seeing his face make you feel?"

"Guilty. Like I'd left him." I gave a sigh of exasperation. "But he's the one who wanted me to come here."

Denton nodded. "You did the right thing coming here. Now carry it through."

"I used to be so angry with Brad for sending me away. Now I feel guilty because I left him. What changed? Why do I feel differently today?"

Denton's palms turned up as he explained. "Whether you realize it or not, Jane's death has had a profound effect on your mental state. It's bound to bring up memories of another episode."

My throat constricted. "What do you mean, another episode?" My voice was barely a whisper.

He shook his head, almost in annoyance. "Remember for yourself. It's not my place to tell you things your mind isn't ready to handle."

"Tell me. I can handle it."

"No. Don't ask me again."

I raised my arms in frustration. "I hope torturing your patients isn't something they taught in your doctoral program."

"You're not my patient. You're my niece."

"I'm not your niece. I'm nothing to you. I'm a boarder, a housemate, an acquaintance. That's all."

He breathed out, staring at the floor. "You've become so much more to me these past months. So much more."

I panicked at the sincerity in his voice. What did he mean? More like a real niece? More like a daughter? More like . . . what?

I stood. "Where's Ms. Rigg?"

"Resting." He got to his feet. "I hope you'll be willing to help with her duties until she's able to work again."

"Of course." I gave a nod. "I'm calling it a night."

"Sleep well, Patricia." His voice haunted me as I dashed up the staircase.

18

I paced my room the next morning. Denton had asked me to help with Ms. Rigg's duties. But that meant I'd have to face him again. My feet tapped a rhythm across the wood floor, onto the plush rug, then again on the wood floor as I mulled the matter.

Something had changed between Denton and me. Lately, he'd seemed somewhat possessive. I felt the bite of an invisible chain around my ankle. He wanted me to stay. He insisted I stay. And somehow that made me want to go. Made me want to find the truth behind the questions he refused to answer.

Only two more weeks left in the semester. Then a few weeks off before the next semester began. What could it hurt to take a quick trip back to Michigan and just see for myself what was going on? Then I'd zip back in time to start the next round of classes.

I met up with Denton in the kitchen as he fumbled to make a pot of coffee.

"Let me help," I offered and poured water into the brewer. With a glance in his direction, I seized the opportunity to

chat openly. "I've been thinking about going home. For a short visit." I set the carafe on the burner and pressed the power button. "Just a week or so to see how everyone is doing." I swallowed hard at the thought of Brad.

Denton pounded a fist on the counter. "Are you out of your mind?"

Water dribbled into the decanter, its gurgling filling the momentary silence between us.

"Why do you think I paid Jane to keep quiet? One word of your whereabouts and you might have been the one at the bottom of the cliff."

"But Frank Majestic must be behind bars by now." Majestic was the drug pin I'd accidentally crossed when I helped my friend Candice LeJeune try to make a clean break from her past. Unfortunately, I'd been somewhat responsible for the death of one of Majestic's leading distributors, who also happened to be his son-in-law, and ended up hiding his daughter and grandkids at my log home in the woods. Needless to say, the man didn't like me much.

"Even if they'd caught him, metal bars don't stop men like him." Denton's eyes blazed red.

"So how long does a contract last? It's been almost six months. They must have forgotten about me by now."

"Until you're dead, Patricia."

My skin crawled. I glanced around the kitchen for eavesdroppers. "No offense, but when you call me Patricia, I feel uncomfortable. Could you just stick to calling me Alisha, even in private?"

"Perhaps now you're beginning to understand the threat to your life."

"Define life. If it means hiding out 'til I'm ninety years old and pretending to be someone I'm not, then I'm not impressed. Life and freedom should go hand in hand. This is America."

"Perhaps you'd think otherwise if life meant a bullet lodged in your spine and paralysis from the neck down."

I weighed the option. "I suppose there are worse things than death."

"If you take my advice, you'll never have to find that out for yourself."

I put my fingers to my temples and took a deep breath. "You're right." Another breath. "It's not so bad here. I've actually got it pretty good." I looked at Denton's strong chin and determined brown eyes.

He smiled, victorious, eyes crinkling in the corners, kind of like Brad's.

"Good girl," he said. "You'll make it just fine."

I stared at him, the steam from my coffee swirled in the shape of a question mark.

"Coming from you, that's a high compliment." I took my coffee with me and walked out.

Maybe it was just my gypsy blood churning, but I was suddenly sick of Cliffhouse. I was sick of Del Gloria. While my surroundings might imply I was a princess in a castle, the truth was, I'd failed here just like everywhere else. I was done letting Denton or anyone else have power over my emotions and my life. I'd make my own choices from here on out. I didn't owe him any explanation. I could do what I wanted. What I felt was best for me.

And that meant going home. But Denton didn't have to know that. I'd finish out the semester, then hop on a bus and be home in time for Christmas. Six months' exile was long enough. I'd take two weeks' vacation in Michigan, then head back to California in time to start classes and keep working on our renovation project. It would be like I never left.

—ɷ—

The next week passed uneventfully. Denton's eyes followed me more than usual, as if trying to read my mind. But I kept a relaxed look on my face, enjoying the peaceful days before my road trip, comforted in knowing that he couldn't possibly guess my plans.

Two days remained in the countdown. I waited for the opportune moment to share my plans with Portia and Celia.

"Hey, guys," I said, scraping stain remover goo from the floor planks, "Just wanted to let you know I'm taking a short trip. I'll be back right after break."

"Where are you going?" Celia's clear voice asked from over by the front windows. She held her scraping tool, filled with slimy gook from the sills, suspended for a moment.

I looked away. "Back to Galveston for Christmas."

"Got your phone call, huh?" Portia asked without pausing her work.

"Kind of. It doesn't matter anyway. I'm going."

"Does the doc know?" This time Portia stared me down.

"No. And you're not going to tell him."

"Hmmm." Portia's body took on a "we'll see about that" attitude.

"I mean it, Portia. Please don't say anything. He'd be really upset."

"Why? 'Cause you lied to him?"

"I didn't lie."

"You just didn't tell him the truth."

"He can't handle it."

"Because he knows it's not safe. If you didn't get the phone call, then it's not safe."

"What's going on here?" Celia tried to keep up with us.

I shook my head. "Nothing a few days in Mi—" I stopped before I said the word, "—Texas won't solve."

Portia stood, hands on hips. "Come here. We have to talk." She grabbed me by the arm and hauled me to the tiny back bedroom. The door crashed closed behind us.

She practically pinned my arms to the wall. "I know who you are."

19

My heart skipped a beat. "Alisha Braddock. I'm Alisha Braddock." I hoped the more I said the name, the more convinced Portia would become.

She squinted in accusation, shaking her head. "Your name is Patricia Louise Amble. You're from Walled Lake, Michigan. You were the first ever convicted of assisted suicide in the state. You were a suspect in the murder of some guy named Martin something, but they let you go without charges. And the cops in Michigan want you for murder one, grand theft auto, and leaving the scene of a crime. Did I forget anything?"

My eyes felt like saucers in my head. "How do you know all that?"

"Come on, Alisha, Patricia, whoever you are. It's the information age. You just have to know where to look." She put her hands on her hips. "Okay, I confess I had Koby check into it. And if he got the info that easily, so could anyone else. Am I right?"

"So—," I gulped, "what do you want? Money or something?"

She turned away in frustration. "I can't believe you'd think that. I'm your friend. I want you to be safe. Believe me, if it was money I was after, I could have sold the information a month ago."

I looked around, dazed. "I guess so. Didn't know there were warrants out for my arrest. Denton said he took care of everything for me. Covered my tracks. I figured he must have explained what happened and everyone understood and let it go."

"You'll be surprised to hear that you're also dead. Funeral and everything. Maybe that cancels out the warrants."

"Dead? Are you serious?" I giggled, then sobered as I digested the information. "If you and Jane both know who I am, other people probably know too. How safe am I here?"

Her face was blank. "I don't have an answer for that. But I have a few ideas how you can get off that hit list."

From the other room came the sound of glass breaking. Then a scream.

"Oh no." Portia raced into the hallway.

I followed behind. Air rushed past as we staggered down the hall toward the sound. Then came the whoosh of an explosion.

"Celia!" Portia's voice came from just ahead, but flames and smoke blinded me. I kept one hand on the wall as a guide.

Celia's cries came shrill from across the room. "Help! I'm on fire!"

Orange blazed over the floor and up the windows, fueled by the chemicals we'd been using. Through eyes burning with heat and smoke, I watched Portia make a dive toward Celia's chair. But flames drove her back, gasping and slapping fire from her own clothing.

"The tarp! Grab the tarp!" Portia crouched to the floor and crawled through the thick haze toward the kitchen. Right behind her, I snatched a corner of the cotton painter's cloth she thrust toward me and scooted back into the mayhem.

Celia's screams of agony and fear filled our ears, mixed with the deafening roar of the inferno.

"Hurry!" Portia pulled the fabric out of my hands as she made the rush toward Celia and threw the cloth over her frail body, crouched and burning in the wheelchair. Portia patted out flames where she could, even while her own clothing caught fire. She grabbed the handles of the chair and pulled it toward the hallway and the back of the house.

Another crash of glass as a second bomb, what looked like a bottle stuffed with burning gauze, hurled through the back door and exploded, blocking our escape.

"We're trapped. Get to the bedroom, quick!" Portia's orders kept me from dropping into a useless heap on the floor.

We pushed through the blinding smoke toward the tiny space.

Portia jammed Celia's chair against the threshold. "It won't go through."

A moan came from beneath the charred tarp.

"Thank God she's still alive."

I heard Portia, though I couldn't see her through the smoke. I dropped to the floor for a breath of air. Through heat-singed lids, I caught a glimpse of Portia. Hair had melted like a helmet to her head. One cheek was black and oozing. Her palms were blistered from the heat of the chair handles. Smoke came in puffs from her clothing.

Portia's burns spurred me to action. "We have to get out of here."

I yanked the wheelchair from the doorway and squeezed through, pulling Portia behind me. Her vacant eyes told me she was heading into shock. I left her on the floor by the window and went back for Celia, still wrapped in the smoking tarp. I dragged her by the feet onto the floor. Her head made a thud as it hit the wood.

"Sorry," I muttered, tugging her dead weight across the planks. My lungs were at the bursting point. I stretched out a leg and kicked the door closed, hoping to conserve oxygen. I crawled across the room and felt around for the window latch. A twist, then a push as I tried lifting the sash. But the years had left it swollen in place, like so many of the others we'd already repaired. I tore off my ragged cardigan and wrapped a fist in the cloth. My face instinctively turned away as my arm smashed the glass.

Smoke rushed outside as fresh air streamed in. I gasped for oxygen, feeling new energy with the momentary gust. But behind me, flames snuck through the gap beneath the door and spread up its panels, engulfing the corner of the room. I grabbed at Portia and nudged her toward the window. Her body seemed to move in slow motion as she lifted herself onto the sash. With a push of her toes, she was outside. Now it was Celia's turn, but the lump beneath the tarp didn't budge. I wrapped my arms around her bulk and tried lifting her through the window, but my arms were made more of jelly than sinew.

Lying on my back, I worked my feet underneath her chest and hoisted her headfirst toward the sash, using the same kind of airplane ride my mother used to give.

My legs were ready to give out when Celia jerked forward as someone pulled her swaddled body through the window to safety.

The fire had spread to the floor nearby. Above me, only choking black smoke. I tried to breathe, but my chest wouldn't move. I closed my eyes and focused on the pinpricks of light that danced behind my lids. Soon the dots formed a face—a crinkly-eyed, laughing Brad. As blistering heat pressed against my skin, sadness swept through me. I'd never see that happy face in this world again. The dots moved and a light took shape. I relaxed, knowing that the pain to come would be fleeting. In a moment I'd be through the veil, meeting my maker, dancing for Jesus. The world spun beneath me, hurtling through the blackness of space, and I felt every revolution. Blood rushed through my ears, a steady *whoosh whoosh*. I waited for the sound to slow and eventually stop. Instead it grew more intense, gradually becoming a shrill *beep beep beep*.

I opened my eyes. Through white haze, I realized I was in a hospital room. As my senses checked back in one by one, I detected an oxygen mask over my nose and mouth. The beeping must be a heart-rate monitor, and the tender area on my arm must be the needle for an IV drip. But the oxygen—I took another deep breath—the oxygen tasted so wonderful and pure. It tasted like . . . life.

I was alive. I'd made it through. Somehow I hadn't died in the fire.

A figure sat in a corner of the room. "Welcome back, Ms. Amble." A man approached me.

Detective Larson wasn't exactly the first person I'd wanted to see after my brush with death. But stuck in a hospital bed, I didn't have much say in the matter.

I peered at him through lazy lids and let the oxygen mask do its thing. He'd obviously figured out my identity and was about to hammer the fact into my smoke-damaged brain.

His lumbering form towered over the bed. "Lucky for you I put the pieces together in time. If I hadn't ordered personal protection for you when I did, you'd probably be taking up space at Del Gloria Mausoleum instead of Del Gloria Memorial." He chuckled like he'd just told a funny joke.

"See," he continued, taking advantage of the fact I had a muzzle on, "in this day and age of computers, the human mind is still the smartest kid on the block. Computers can match faces and fingerprints, determine DNA, and look up criminal records. But it takes a real live person to noodle through the information and come up with four."

His body shifted and his voice sped up. "Back in the fall, I had a good laugh when I read the report on the rooftop heroine and her stolen ladder. Never thought another thing about it. But when I saw the same girl at the scene of a murder, I couldn't help but wonder, why her? What made Alisha Braddock the common denominator between the two crimes?"

The detective's voice droned on like background music to my heart monitor.

"If this was LA, I'd have never linked the two events. But here in Del Gloria, we pride ourselves on being The Town Crime Forgot."

He chuckled again, this time almost dousing me with a stray spitball. I cringed, shrinking deeper into my pillow.

"So I did my detective thing. Fed the computer your picture, your name, and whatever else I could come up with, made a few phone calls, checked a few sources, called in a couple favors, made some hypotheses. And last night, I ordered personal protection on a woman named Patricia Louise Amble. The officers tracked you to the same block. But instead of a missing ladder, they found a raging inferno." He shook his head in awe. "I gotta hand it to you, kid, whatever guardian angels you got looking out for you, they're doing a pretty good job."

I thought of Portia and her single-mindedness in saving Celia and getting us out of the building.

"How's Celia? Is Portia alright?" My mouth spoke the words, but only a muffled sound made it through the mask.

His eyes watered. "Ms. Romero will be fine after a few surgeries." He choked and looked to one side. "They're not sure about Ms. Long. Her health was fragile as it was. She might not pull through."

A deep moan filtered through my mask. I squeezed my eyes closed and felt a stream of tears burn down my cheeks.

"It's like this." Detective Larson leaned toward me. "I'm

the captain of the Good Ship Del Gloria. When a Jonah sneaks on board, I find him and throw him into the sea before any more of my passengers get hurt."

I should have known better than to stay here. What made me think I could escape a well-oiled drug machine? The day I got involved with Candice LeJeune was the day I signed my own death warrant—along with Jane's and maybe even Celia's.

Detective Larson was right. I was a Jonah in this town. I could wait for the cops to throw me overboard, or I could jump ship myself. Either way, the sharks were circling.

"We've got an idea who's behind the bombs," Detective Larson was saying over the beep of the monitor. "Your classmate Simon Scroll seems to have skipped town. I'm guessing it was his job to make sure you never left Del Gloria alive. And as far as he's concerned, he succeeded."

"What do you mean?" I asked, my words barely legible through the mask covering my mouth.

"Mr. Scroll has been employed by Professor Braddock as your bodyguard."

I groaned. Simon was so useless . . . I would get him for a bodyguard.

The detective continued. "We think he got a better offer from someone else to make sure you turned up dead. We're hoping to get the feds to step in this time with a little more sophisticated version of witness protection now that there's proof your life is on the line. Professor Braddock had good intentions, but it's obvious you need another fresh start."

I squeezed my eyes shut. My throat hurt from trying not to cry. I didn't want another fresh start. I didn't want any of this to be happening. If I couldn't stay here in Del Gloria, then I wanted to go home to Port Silvan. I didn't want another name, another town, another life. I just wanted to be Tish Amble again, whatever that entailed.

But something in the back of my mind warned that if I ever remembered what it was I'd forgotten, I might not be so excited to get back to my old life.

I told that something to shut up.

20

I was released from the hospital with nothing worse than an irritating cough, curling eyebrows, and a section of singed hair, which Maize agreed to shape into a spunky layered style.

"You are so lucky to be alive," she said while I holed up at her apartment a day later.

I watched more and more hair drop to the ground as she snipped and talked, snipped and talked. "I think that's enough off the ends," I told her before I ended up bald. "It looks really good just like that."

"Sure. Whatever." She put the scissors down and picked up a yo-yo, performing a bevy of tricks as she kept her hands occupied. "So you're taking off for a while?"

"Yeah. I hate to abandon Celia and Portia at a time like this, but I really have to check into things back home."

"Do what you have to. We'll keep plugging away at things until you get back. Probably won't get very far without someone telling us what to do and how to do it, but we'll give it a shot—"

I touched her arm, interrupting her nervous prattling. "You guys will do great."

"Listen," Maize said, "if there's anything you need while you're on vacation, just call Koby. The guy's a magician when it comes to getting flights out of thin air.

He can probably hook you up with a ride home. I know you have to take the bus there since you don't have any identification, but he could probably even get you a fake ID if you're desperate . . ."

I didn't even want to know how she knew all that. With a nudge from my hand, I stopped her monologue. "Thanks. I'll keep his number handy. You guys have been so understanding. Thanks for not being mad at me for misleading you about my name and stuff up front. Just, you know, try to keep it a secret until I can figure out how to make it all go away."

"No problem there. I never tell secrets. And even if I did, no one would listen to me anyway, since I'm always talking so much. They barely hear a word I say as it is, unless it's something really juicy like the time I found out about the college president . . ."

I smiled, letting her ramble on, tuning out the gossip as I focused on plans that would get me safely home to Brad.

—w—

The Sacramento station was hopping at four thirty in the afternoon. The cab driver stopped across the street in the dimming light. "Watch yourself in there. And don't use the bathroom."

I thanked him and stepped into the cool December air. On the way downtown, we'd passed a towering Christmas tree—the only indication it was time to deck the halls. I wrapped my black slicker close. No snow, just chilling, damp air so close to dusk.

I stepped toward blinking neon lights and pushed through the glass entry door. Bodies milled aimlessly through the overly bright interior. I couldn't tell if they were homeless folks or passengers restless for a getaway driver. I sat on a plastic seat defaced with ink and carvings. A smell like ripe baby diapers permeated the air. I kept my nose tucked close to my collar. As the 4:50 departure time neared, more passengers trickled in, waiting for the only cross-country transportation that eluded Big Brother's radar.

I adjusted the black flapper-style wig on my head and pushed my sunglasses a notch higher on my nose, hoping to avoid eye contact with my fellow travelers, who looked as directionless and despairing as I felt. I kept my luggage on my lap and both eyes peeled for trouble.

I'd planned the perfect escape—so far. I knew I couldn't leave from the Del Gloria station without Denton or Detective Larson tracking me down. So I'd hired a cab to drive from the nearest big city and pick me up at the Del Gloria McDonald's, then drop me here. With so many cab drivers in this city, what were the chances they'd question some guy named Ferdinand Olivares? And it had been easy enough walking into the fast-food restaurant as Alisha Braddock, and exiting the bathroom a few minutes later as the temporary me, Tasha Stewart. The name seemed both mysterious and boring, and hopefully would never have to be uttered before my arrival in Michigan.

A loudspeaker announced the bus's arrival. Passengers filed past the driver, handing him their tickets and boarding.

I hovered at the back of the line, contemplating if I really wanted to be in an enclosed area with the fellow up ahead who kept mumbling to himself and waving his arms. Or the woman with the cleft chin and Adam's apple.

"Watch your step," the blue-jacketed driver muttered as I nudged by, passed him my ticket, and climbed the three stairs inside.

I took a seat as close to the driver as I could manage, whispered a prayer for protection, and geared up for a trip scheduled to last two days, ten hours, and forty minutes. If I didn't jump out a window first.

—w—

Somehow I'd misread the itinerary. Had they really meant I'd be arriving at 4:30 in the morning Manistique, Michigan, time? The bus pulled away and I stood outside the twenty-four-hour gas station, wondering how I'd managed to mess that up.

The sign of a major hotel chain glowed in the distance. I started walking. Snow melted in my sneakers as I cut along US-2 toward shelter.

The clerk gave me a strange look when I told her I didn't have a credit card. But I flipped enough bills on the counter to satisfy her need for a security deposit while I slept the next four hours. During my stay at Cliffhouse, Denton had provided a monthly stipend to cover my day-to-day expenses. My frugal nature meant I had enough set aside to make a run for it.

I stuck the plastic hotel key into its reader, got the green light, and pushed in. A shower before bed. The thought of sleeping in sheets contaminated with whatever germs I'd picked up over the last two and a half days didn't sound appetizing.

While steam cleared the grime from my nose, I scrubbed with soap and a washcloth, hoping some plan would form before I turned the water off. Warmed through and squeaky clean, I slid beneath the sheets and pondered my next move. Sleep came before any strategy.

I woke up rested some time later.

A glance at the clock told me I'd slept past ten.

"Uhh." I'd better get moving before the maids came knocking at my door. I stared at the phone, knowing I'd have to pick it up sooner or later if I were ever going to get to Port Silvan.

I grabbed the handset. Dial tone blared long and loud as I hesitated.

"If you'd like to make a call . . . ," the recorded voice kicked on.

I pressed the disconnect and waited. The phone dangled by its cord from my hand. Calling Brad was out of the question. Even if I knew where he was right now, I couldn't call him. He'd be so mad at me for . . . something. Coming back before he gave me the green light. Leaving when I should have stayed. Something.

I swung the phone back and forth in a gentle motion. Who would be most understanding? My cousin Joel? My grandfather? Maybe I should call the snowplow guy. No one would suspect I'd contact him.

The handpiece banged my shin. I scooped it up and dialed my grandfather. My heart thumped like crazy as the phone rang.

He answered. "Hello?"

I almost burst into tears at the sound of his voice.

"Hello?" he said again.

I cleared my throat. "Um, hi. I heard you helped women who are in trouble."

Silence at the other end.

Tears streamed down my face. I tried to keep my voice steady. "Can you come get me?"

"Who is this?" His voice held a note of panic.

I evened out my breathing before answering. "Ti—" I almost said my real name. "Tasha . . . Stewart."

More silence. I prayed he knew from my voice that it was me.

"You're at the Econolodge?"

I nodded, knowing he had caller ID. "Yes," I spoke into the handset.

"I'll be right there."

I hung up the phone and broke into loud sobbing. My chest heaved and my back shook and tears and snot got everywhere. I hadn't realized how much I missed my family. How much I missed my life. I was so grateful to be back. Puppa would help me work through the hurdles facing my return. I was so glad to be home.

A little while later at the sink, I splashed cold water over my face hoping to bring the redness and swelling down. I pulled the wig over my hair, packed my luggage, put on my sunglasses and slicker, and waited at the window, watching for Puppa through sheer curtains.

An eternity passed before his black truck arrived. The vehicle hesitated, finally pulling slowly down the row of motel units. I opened the door and stepped into the parking lot. His brake lights blinked red as he stopped and backed up. I pulled open the truck door and climbed into the passenger seat. I kept my eyes straight ahead so I wouldn't look at him and start crying again.

"Thank you," I whispered, afraid to say more.

The truck made a circle and headed west on US-2. The road curved toward the lake. Out in the harbor, waves washed over thick ice already covering the jetty. The lighthouse stood lonely and cold, bleeding red against gray water and white snow.

A sorrowful sense of déjà vu crept over me as we passed places it seemed I'd only just left. But it had been nearly a year since I'd first returned home. Perhaps the scenery hadn't changed much, with ice and snow and cold being the same from year to year. But the people would be different now, having lived through another year of experiences. I knew I was different.

Sneaking a glance toward my grandfather, I wondered if he'd be happy for the changes I'd made in my life or if he'd be angry at me for continuing to make the same mistakes over and over. Life could be so frustrating when the old adage "the more things change, the more they stay the same" came into play.

Puppa's hair had whitened in the last ten months. And from my angle, his face looked weary and sad.

"How have you been?" I couldn't stop myself from asking the question, though I wasn't sure I could bear the answer.

He stared at the road ahead, driving another mile or so in silence. I fidgeted, worried he was passing judgment on me.

At the passing lane, he swung his eyes in my direction, staring at my profile. I pulled off my sunglasses and returned his look.

So much sadness in his eyes. What had happened while I was gone?

"Where have you been?" He croaked the words.

It never occurred to me that he had no idea where I'd been all this time. I just assumed Brad had let him in on the plan. Or Denton had contacted him so he wouldn't worry. But what good would disappearing from the face of the earth do if everybody knew where you were?

I bit my lip. "Puppa. I'm so sorry. I hope you weren't worried. I thought Brad would have told you."

At Brad's name, he snapped his head in my direction and blinked hard. "Brad? How could he tell me?" He looked straight ahead. "We've all thought you've been dead since June. They told us you died in a car crash in Minneapolis. We had a funeral."

I shook my head. "No. I was in a car crash, but I'm fine. I got away to California, where Brad told me to go so I'd be safe from Frank Majestic."

He gave a little nod of his head. "A faked death." He hummed in disgust. "And we all fell for it." He glanced at me. "You were safe as long as you were dead. Now here you are, back in the thick of things." His eyes watered up. "And you're alive. You're alive."

I laughed in spite of myself. "Yes, I'm alive. And I'm home. But I wasn't safe in Del Gloria. Someone's been trying to kill me. I'm not sure there is anyplace safe for me." I looked in his eyes. "I might as well be home."

A mile of pines passed by the window before he spoke.

"Patricia, things have changed. Things happened . . . You were dead, for crying out loud."

I nodded in agreement, still smiling to be home. "I know. I've been gone a long time. I kept waiting for Brad to call." I gave a little laugh. "I guess if he thought I was dead, that was a pretty good reason not to call . . ."

My brow scrunched. Something wasn't right. Denton assured me Brad would call when it was time. They must have been in touch. Denton should have told Brad I was still alive. I put a hand to my forehead. Brad must know and was just keeping it a secret. Because if Denton hadn't told him the truth, and Brad really thought I was dead, Brad might have moved on with his life. He could have met someone new. He might be engaged to some other future Mrs. Walters instead of me.

I gave a ferocious shake of my head. It wasn't possible. Brad knew I was alive. He had to know.

We turned onto the Silvan Peninsula. Just a few more miles to my log home on the lake. I looked at Puppa. "I'm sure there's no heat or anything, but I'd like to stop at my house and see if I can get things going."

I'd lived a few places in my life, but none felt as much like home as the lodge. I'd spent summers there as a girl, wandering through half-pint pines that now towered skyward. And after I'd been ripped from the secluded safety of the lodge by well-meaning grandparents, I dreamed of the day I would return to Port Silvan and buy the log cabin and make it my own. And I'd done just that. Now that I was back from my leave of absence, I could finish the renovations and get the yard ready for an outdoor wedding, sometime next summer.

Puppa stared straight ahead, not responding.

The miles flew past in snow-covered splendor.

"Looks like we'll be having a white Christmas this year." The closer we drew to home, the more the goose bumps raced up and down my arms. Three days 'til Christmas. I was home just in time.

My driveway was around the next bend. My right leg pressed against the floorboard as I willed Puppa to slow down for the turn.

He turned in. The drive was plowed, the banks pushed back in tidy order. Tracks from multiple cars covered the surface, and strangely, a large wooden sign was posted to a tree. VALENTINE'S BAY LODGE, it said in burgundy and cream, with a phone number and website address beneath it.

"What's going on? Who's been down here?" I was used to my house being off the beaten path and my drive only lightly traveled. Who would post a sign?

"Patricia, this isn't a good idea." Puppa stepped on the brakes. "Stay at the lake house with me. We'll come back another day."

"Keep going." I got a sick feeling in my gut. "I need to know what's happening here."

The vehicle slowed. "You've been dead since June. Things have changed."

"Obviously my house is one of them. Keep going." I pressed my Tasha Stewart sunglasses onto my face and set my mouth in a tight line.

Puppa accelerated, though I could tell by the set of his jaw it was only against his will.

We crossed the creek and came around the corner. And there it was. My log cabin. Or was it mine? The logs were newly stained, the door was painted a welcoming shade of red to match the new shutters, and Christmas lights and garland hung in joyous celebration of the holiday. I took a jagged breath. I hadn't expected this. A dilapidated cottage in need of repair, yes. But this pristine building with a perky sign announcing Guest Parking where my shed once stood had never entered my mind.

I did a double-take as we passed. My Explorer—there it was in new condition, as if it had never been crunched by a murderous truck.

But the lodge . . . What if they'd sold it? What if it didn't belong to me anymore? Could they do that? Maybe they thought I was dead, but now that I was alive again, it was still mine. Right?

Grandfather pulled close to the entry. Welcome to Va-entine's Bay arched over the door. Window boxes filled with cedar boughs, pinecones, and red bows garnished the porch.

The car doors slammed as I stepped into the crunching snow. A woman came to the door as we approached. She smiled, her dark hair and eyes sparkling even in the dingy gray light of early afternoon.

"Hi, Bernard. It's great to see you. Who's your friend?" she asked, holding the door wide.

I came to a dead stop. Samantha Walters. Brad's sister. What was she still doing here? She'd been scheduled to return to Rawlings and her Coney Island diner back in September. It was now December and there she was. Standing at the door to my home like she owned it. And didn't she realize that frumpy blouse made it look like she was pregnant?

21

I stood on the porch, speechless, my feet glued to the boards.

"Come on in," the happy-as-ever Sam said, gesturing her welcome.

I looked past her into the kitchen, made warm and inviting by red accents against the black and tan floor tiles and gold-speckled countertops. Naturally, Sam was in her element with the '50s décor.

I stepped closer for a peek at the ceiling. The asbestos tiles were gone. Soaring walls gave a spacious feel to the room. My eyes narrowed and my jaw set. That had been my idea. I was going to do that. Who did she think she was, stealing my house and my decorating ideas?

Behind me, I sensed Puppa's hesitation. His hand nudged my arm, but not to prompt me forward. I could tell he wanted to pull me by the elbow back to the truck and fly down the drive at high speed. And if it weren't for the anger that kept my attention on the woman before me, I would have gratefully complied.

But seeing Sam in my home, at my place at the door,

just didn't set right with me. No. So what if the last time we'd been together she'd saved my life?

A white flash shot through my brain and I was back in the great room of the lodge that terrible morning. One of the gunmen pointed his weapon my way, I heard a growl like a mother tiger, then Sam pounced the guy, his weapon discharging into my arm instead of my heart.

A cold wind rushed around me, permeating my California slicker and sending shivers through my body. If that flicker of memory was accurate, I'd been shot by one of Majestic's cronies, not Candice LeJeune like I'd thought all these months.

But I could still see Candice with her weapon raised, hear the blast of the gun . . . If she hadn't shot me, then who?

I swayed, my legs turning to jelly beneath me.

"Hey, you don't look so good." Sam reached for me, wrapping her arms around my shoulders and guiding me into the house. The tiles passed strobelike beneath my feet, then we were through the arch and in the great room. She stood me in front of a recliner near the crackling fire. I collapsed into the soft leather, my eyes inundated by the towering Christmas tree, the draping garland, the twinkling lights. My ears flooded with the voice of Bing Crosby, ". . . may your days be merry and bright . . ."

I couldn't take it. This was so wrong.

Sam passed me a glass of water. My hand automatically reached for it, but my mouth refused her hospitality.

She gave Puppa a worried look. "Is your friend okay?"

"Samantha . . . ," he began.

I set the glass on a coaster and stood, my anger giving me strength.

"Samantha Walters, isn't it?" I held out my hand, forcing it to hold steady.

She nodded, a confused look on her face. "Russo now," she said.

Don't tell me Puppa adopted her. Maybe that's why she thought she owned this place.

I gave a tight smile. "I'm Tasha Stewart."

Samantha met my hand in a loose grip.

"Mr. Russo there," I smiled in Puppa's direction, "promised I could have a tour of the lodge. But now probably isn't a good time. We'll just be going."

At Sam's questioning glance, Puppa shrugged. I made it two steps toward the arch when a man clomped down the open staircase, humming along with Bing.

"Hello, Papa B." He smiled at my grandfather and shook his hand. "And you are . . . ?" He turned toward me, hand extended, like he was Mr. Congeniality or something.

I made no move, instead just stared at my cousin Joel. His hand hovered a moment, then returned to his side at my rebuff. His eyes squinted as he studied my face.

Samantha still wasn't getting it. She jumped in to fill the awkward silence. "Tasha, this is my husband, Joel Russo. Joel, this is Tasha Stewart. Bernard brought her by for a tour."

Complete silence.

If that didn't just beat all. Sam and Joel—married. And with his arm around her shoulders like that, pulling her tight like he was trying to protect her from me, why, didn't they just make the cutest couple? And a baby on the way too.

Joel gave an extended sigh. "Tish. Welcome home. Again."

"Thanks, cuz." Buried rage kept the tears at bay. "Try to act happy I'm actually alive."

Samantha's eyes grew huge. "Tish? Tish!"

Her stammering came off as a stalling ploy. I could just hear the thoughts running through her head. *What would be the best way to react?* she was probably asking herself. *Should I be excited, like* "Oh my goodness, you're still alive!" *or should I be sad, like* "Oh my goodness. You're still alive."

Her face continued to waver.

A smirk crept over my features as I watched. If I were in her shoes, I'd be mad as a rabid rat. Because what she thought was hers all this time really belonged to me. How dare she take my house, my car, my life?

Her face crumpled and she burst into sobs. Her arms flung around my neck. Long black hair stuck to my cheek, plastered there by tears. "You're not dead. You're not dead." She said it over and over like a chant, swaying back and forth, rocking me with her.

I lifted my arms, at first trying to push her away. The firm bump of her stomach pressed against me, the fullness of her womb somehow emphasizing the emptiness of mine. But stuck in Sam's iron grip, I felt myself relaxing, succumbing to her love. After a minute, with my sunglasses digging into my nose, I managed to slide out of the hug and take them off.

She stared me in the eyes. "It's you. It's really you."

I nodded, not daring to speak.

Behind Samantha, Joel looked at me stone-faced.

What softening I'd felt a moment ago evaporated and I seethed in his direction. There was the guy who had torn my mother's picture in two because he didn't want his long-lost cousin moving in on his turf.

But tearing up photos and burying empty caskets didn't change the facts. This place—this house, this land—belonged to me, not him. I bought it from Puppa fair and square. It was mine, and mine alone.

"I love what you've done with the place." I sounded husky, like Cruella de Vil.

Samantha snuggled into Joel. "Thanks. It's exactly the way you described it to Joel last spring. He wanted to—" she paused and swallowed, "—honor your memory by sticking to your ideas."

"How sweet of you, Joel." Evil dripped from my voice.

Grandfather's hand grabbed my elbow again, as if ready to escort me out at the first sign of violence.

So what if I was a little sarcastic, a little snippy? Who wouldn't be in these circumstances? Sam and Joel were lucky I didn't throw them out right now. Maybe if she weren't pregnant, I would.

"So, Samantha, when's the little whippersnapper due?" Bitterness, hatred . . . all the negative emotions welled up in my voice. It was as if the past seven months hadn't even happened. Everything I'd learned in the Revamp Program, all the classes, the journaling, the working with others, the learning to live together, the improving my attitude, the changing my outlook . . . I might as well have spared myself the agony. Because when it came down to it, I was just plain jealous. I was just plain mean. And the worst part was, I didn't even care how bad anyone else got hurt.

"March ninth," she whispered.

Joel wrapped his arms around her.

"You two didn't waste any time." I glanced around. "I suppose you figured you had a lot of rooms to fill."

Sam looked at Joel, as if begging him to make me stop.

Puppa stepped to the plate. "It's time to go, Patricia. Put your sunglasses on and meet me in the truck."

A final nasty glare and off I stomped. The moment the kitchen door slammed behind me, I burst into tears. It was good that Puppa stopped my downward spiral. Who knew what had been about to come out of my mouth next?

I scrunched down in the front seat of the truck. What was my problem, anyway? Joel had bent over backward for me last spring, and almost been killed in the showdown at the lodge that morning. No wonder he and Sam got married right away. Life was too short to dilly-dally.

And what had I been thinking? Their new baby would be blood to me, a second cousin twice removed or some such thing. I'd better have an apology ready next time I saw the new parents if I wanted to watch the little sweety grow up.

My grandfather climbed into the driver's seat and turned the key. The diesel roared to life. He backed up and started out the driveway.

The last time I'd been here, summer was just around

the corner. Green grass, green leaves, a comfy seventy degrees. Now everything was white again. Snow on the ground, snow in the pines, snow in the clouds.

And last time, I'd been driving Brad's SUV. I'd taken it right down this driveway, past the emergency vehicles, and onto the highway. I'd driven and driven and driven west, hoping to get to Del Gloria. But there'd been the pain in my arm, some blood on my sleeve, and a heavy fog in my mind. I must have been hanging on by a thread when I smashed into the back of that minivan somewhere in Minnesota.

I gave Puppa a sidelong glance. "So how'd Brad's car do? Did it get fixed up okay?" Maybe I should have started with an apology for my earlier behavior, but I couldn't even deal with it yet.

"Brad's vehicle pulled through just fine." No inflection in his voice.

"Sheesh." I laughed in embarrassment. "Brad must have been so mad."

"When you're dead, the condition of the car doesn't matter much."

"That's right. I supposedly died in that crash." I met Puppa's eyes. "Was Brad really torn up? I mean, he was sad, right? But he's good now? He's okay? And he doesn't have a girlfriend or anything like that, right?"

Puppa stared at the road straight ahead. He sniffled and his words came out all scratchy. "I'm glad you're alive, Patricia. It's so good you're alive."

I left him alone the rest of the way, not wanting to see my grandfather cry.

22

Puppa's home overlooking Silvan Bay appeared about the same in December as it had last March. It was too early for fishing shanties on the bay beyond the house, but another week or two of cold and they'd spring up like a village on the ice.

Unlike the warm aura of Christmas we'd found at my lodge, Puppa's house looked cold and lonely. Two stories of gray shakes and white trim on the wraparound porch seemed dingy in the dull afternoon light. Not even the red steps and colorful stained-glass panels surrounding the front door could offset the home's dismal spirit.

Puppa pulled the truck into the detached garage and turned off the engine. Neither of us moved. Perhaps we both dreaded the inevitable conversation to come. With a sigh for strength, I pushed open my door. He did the same. He closed the garage door behind us and we started toward the house.

A whinny from the barnyard stopped me in my tracks.

I faced the corral. "Goldilocks!"

In a moment I was hurdling the snowdrifts toward the horse Puppa had given me that spring. At the fence, I clung to her furry head, breathing against her soft muzzle.

"There's my pretty pony. How are you, my Heaven Hills Gold?"

My grandfather joined me. "She recognized you. Even in that ridiculous wig."

"You know who loves you, don't you, girl?" I said in baby talk as I rubbed Goldie's ear. I rested my face against hers. "It's so good to be back. I missed my pony." I laughed. "And Puppa. And Great-gram. And Gerard. What's he up to these days, anyway?"

Puppa just kept looking at me like he couldn't believe I was standing in his barnyard, cootchy-cooing my horse.

I went to him and wrapped my arms around his neck. "I love you. Wow, is it good to be home."

He squeezed me to him like he wouldn't let me go. "I thought I'd lost you. I thought I'd lost you."

The pain in his voice triggered more tears from my eyes. I'd driven out of the driveway in Brad's SUV seven months ago to avoid my own personal pain . . . what pain? Nothing could have hurt back then as bad as the pain of seeing my grandfather crying today.

His shoulders heaved in silent misery. I held on to him, not sure who was comforting whom. My socks were wet with melted snow and my bare hands were turning numb. I pulled away.

"Come on. Let's get inside. I'll make you and Grandma Olivia a cup of tea."

He followed me into the mudroom. We hung our coats and stacked our shoes in a neat row. I couldn't help but notice ours were the only two pair. Joel must have taken the overload of coats and boots with him to my lodge.

I walked up the steps to the kitchen. The house felt abandoned. A pile of dirty dishes sat to one side of the sink, waiting for attention. I scurried to fill the teapot with water. I set it on the stove and turned the burner to high. Blue flames shot out from beneath the silver container.

"There. Let's go visit with Great-gram while that's brewing." I walked the length of the dining area to the living room. Water spots smudged the view of the lake, the film lending a haze to the already monotone landscape. Great-gram's knitting basket sat by her rocking chair, the yarn neatly balled. Needles poked like chopsticks from the host of colors. I wondered what she was working on this month. Probably a blanket for her new great-great-grandbaby-to-be. At the thought of the new generation, my hand went to my stomach. Why couldn't I be the one having the child?

I ran down the list of why-nots as I headed to Great-gram's room to track her down. First, I wasn't married. Second, I was on the run from the backwoods mob, and that was no time to start a family. Third, I was just starting to creep out of emotional adolescence. Fourth . . .

I turned the corner to Grandma Olivia's room. I gave a quiet knock at the half-closed door. When there was no answer, I pushed it open. The resulting breeze twisted the mobile that hung from the ceiling's center, sending the perpetually hungry lion chasing after the giraffes.

I smiled and looked toward the other end of the room, expecting to see Great-gram. But the hospital-style bed was neatly made, covered with her favorite afghan. The straight-back chair I'd once sat in to hold her hand as she slept was tucked against the wall.

My hands gripped the doorway. With Puppa standing a mere six feet away, watching my reaction, I couldn't pretend I didn't understand what the empty bed meant. My fingers pressed against my mouth, sealing in the moan that would have gushed out.

I blinked and hot tears squeezed out. "When did she die?"

"August."

I nodded, sniffling. I'd left this place so that I could be safe in Del Gloria. And while I'd been hiding out, my ninety-three-year-old great-grandmother had died. Such a high price I'd paid for serenity. Only to discover now that there was no such thing. The pain I'd hoped to avoid had multiplied . . . and multiplied. How could I survive this news? And what else happened while I was gone?

Puppa took me in his arms and cried with me.

"I thought . . . I thought I'd get to know her better before . . . she died." My voice shook with emotion.

Puppa shook his head. "She was so glad for the time you had together. You brought her hope she'd never had. You loved her even though she acted unlovable. That's what she said about you at your funeral."

A huge sniffle. "I can't believe she spoke at my funeral. And now she's gone . . ." A shuddering sigh.

"She'd be thrilled to know you're still alive." Puppa wiped tears from his face.

"I only wish I'd been here for her in August. What happened? She was so healthy."

From the kitchen, the teapot announced its boiling point.

I followed Puppa through the swinging door.

"Heart, lungs, kidneys. Everything gave way at once." Puppa poured hot water into two mugs.

"I wish I could have been here. I feel terrible."

"She was ninety-three years old. She was ready."

I nodded, dipping a tea bag. "Still, I had so much I wanted to ask her. Things about her life, her childhood."

We took our hot drinks into the living room and settled into the comfy, mismatched furniture.

"Be content with the time you had with her. There's no going back now. And you don't want to beat yourself up over something you can't change."

Hot tea soothed my throat. "I missed a lot while I was gone. But I learned a few things too. Not trying to change the past is one of them."

"I'm glad to hear you're learning to let go. That's a hard task. Some people never master it, and their days are filled with regrets." Puppa leaned back in his recliner.

"Exactly. And that's something I'm determined not to suffer from anymore." I raised my tea in emphasis.

"Go easy on yourself. Nobody's perfect. Expect an occasional relapse."

"Pshaw. Who me?" I smiled. "At least I'm aware of my thought patterns now." I reached out and touched his arm playfully. "I'm not perfect yet, but I'm making progress."

He held on to my hand. "You're perfect to me."

"Thanks. I like hearing it."

We sipped in silence, enjoying our close proximity.

I twirled my tea, watching a stray flake twist in the tiny whirlpool in the center. I couldn't put off the question forever. I had to ask at some point. It might as well be now. My arms crossed my chest, as if to protect me from the answer.

"How's Brad?" The words, husky and raw, sounded as if they came from some other throat.

Puppa stared at the braided rug like it could help him weave the right answer. His head moved slowly from side to side. "He didn't make out good that day. I'd say it pretty much killed him."

I gasped, sucking tea down the wrong pipe. Brad—dead?

In a flash I was back in the lodge, cowering as Candice LeJeune hauled Frank Majestic out of the room. But before she left, she had a final message for me: "Remember, Tish. I'll always love you."

Then her gun swung from her captive's head toward . . . not me, but Brad standing across the room. The sound of the explosion . . .

"No! . . ." Breath sputtered out of me. My lungs froze in an exhale. An electric jolt blazed across my brain. After a moment, the synapses connected and I watched in horror as the scene replayed in my mind. *Candice aims her gun at Brad. Then those horrible words. A blast cuts through the air. Screams and chaos, but all I can do is stare as Brad sways and then drops to the floor. I go to him, close enough to hear him whisper my name. There's a salty smell. Hot, sticky blood everywhere on his chest.*

Then paramedics, endless CPR, a stretcher . . . and the back of the ambulance driving away from the lodge.

Air raked down my throat. "She shot him, didn't she?"

Grandfather raised a brow. "I assumed you knew. You were there."

I let out a moan. "I was there, but . . . I didn't know . . . I couldn't remember." I pounded knuckles against my temples, wishing I could put the knowledge back into that dark space in my brain, or rip it out of my head altogether.

Denton had known Brad was dead, hadn't he? He'd avoided talking about Brad. I'd assumed that was because he hoped I'd forget about Brad, me being an unsuitable match for his favorite protégé.

Perhaps deep down I'd known the truth and couldn't face it. Look at me now, I was a blubbering mess, runoff dripping down my face and onto Puppa's sweater. Yeah. I couldn't handle it. I wanted to go back to Del Gloria, back in time, when, if only in my mind, Brad was still alive and well and watching out for me, waiting until the coast was clear to call me home.

I wiped my face and took a breath. Portia was right. There would never have been a phone call. I'd been dead to these people. And Brad, the only person who knew where to find me, was dead too. Only Denton had known what was really happening. He knew the phone call would never come.

Squeaks and hiccups lingered. Everything I'd wanted, everything I'd hoped for, everything that was good and happy and right was dead. It all died with Brad. The man who loved me, the one I loved. No wonder I'd driven off and never looked back. My life, my future, was over. And I'd known it, I just couldn't face it.

The facts kept seeping through some protective barrier in my brain, forcing me to ask questions to which I didn't want to know the answers.

Anger shot through my chest, but I pushed it back. Denton's job was to keep me safe. What better way than convince the people after me that I was dead? The unfortunate side effect was that the people who loved me also believed I was dead.

No wonder Denton was so angry with me for being careless with my identity. I'd been utterly safe until someone had figured out I wasn't Alisha Braddock. I smoothed the wig on my head. It wouldn't be long before others saw through my Tasha Stewart disguise. And I'd be back in the crosshairs.

But I was home now. I didn't want to keep running.

Grandfather touched my cheek, but the tears kept flowing. If I couldn't have Brad back, and I couldn't have the future children and the love and the laughter that disappeared with him, then I at least wanted my bed and my bedroom and my house back. I wanted what was left of Patricia Amble back.

I sighed with exhaustion. My brain ceased to function.

Puppa must have noticed. "Come on. Let's get you in a hot bath. There's nothing a pair of warm pajamas, a hot meal, and a good night's rest can't cure."

He seemed oblivious to the sound of my heart breaking.

23

"Feeling better this morning?" Puppa asked, slathering cream cheese on a bagel.

I gave a shrug and sifted through the fridge, not really sure what I was looking for. I squinted to see through my dark sunglasses. It would take more than ice to bring down the swelling around my eyes. Especially since I hadn't really even stopped crying yet. I'd even cried in my sleep. At this rate, I'd have to wear sunglasses the rest of my life.

"I talked to Sam this morning and we decided it wouldn't be a good idea for you to see him yet," Puppa said between bites.

I shut the fridge door. "See who?"

"Brad."

I crossed my arms and pursed my lips. Tears squeezed out from behind my glasses. I didn't feel like tromping through six inches of snow to see a headstone. That would make it too real. "I agree."

"We'll have to bring the idea up slowly. Let him get

used to the possibility that his Tish is still alive. Otherwise it could be too much of a shock."

I'd been going for the coffeepot, but my arm hung in mid-reach as his words sunk in. I swung around. "What are you saying? Brad's not dead?"

He got a startled look on his face. "No. Brad's . . . alive. Did you think he was . . ." He stopped and shook his head. "I'm sorry. I thought you realized. But, of course. You must have left before they revived him."

"Brad's alive." I repeated the words. "Brad's alive." My heart launched into wild thumping. Black prickles danced before my eyes.

"Sit down." Puppa led me to the dining room and into a chair. "Take it easy. Just breathe."

I cast the sunglasses away and cradled my head in my arms. *Whoosh, whoosh, whoosh.* Could I take any more of this emotional turmoil? First he was dead, then he's alive. Brad was alive!

The room swam when I lifted my head. "Take me to him. I want to see Brad."

Puppa patted my back. "Let's give it more time. Sam can drop by there today and see how he's doing. It could be awhile before he gets used to the idea and agrees to see you."

"What?" I laughed in disbelief. "Of course he wants to see me. He'll be so happy. He'll be ecstatic. Come on, let's go." I ignored the ringing in my ears and pulled Puppa toward the back door.

He dragged behind, then grabbed my arm and stopped me. "Patricia. Wait. Things are . . . different for Brad now."

"You're right. We're not dead, either one of us. We're both still alive." My voice was giddy. I was breathless with joy.

"Brad's body is still alive, yes. And his mind. But his spirit . . ." Grandfather squeezed my hands. "He's given up on life. He has no will to live. He's dying, Patricia."

"What do you mean, he's dying?" I blinked in confusion.

"His injuries . . . your supposed death . . . it was all too much for him. He's barely hanging on."

"Then I'm here just in time. When he sees me, sees that I'm still alive, he'll want to live again. He'll want to live so we can be together."

Puppa gave a weary sigh. "No. It's not that simple. Having you see him in his condition may just set off a downward spiral he'll never pull out of. Physically, emotionally, he's not the Brad you remember. I don't know how else to put it."

I batted his arm. "Not my Brad? Of course he is. And knowing that he's not well makes me want to see him more."

A swift shake of his head. "Things didn't look good for Brad the day he got shot. But they managed to revive him on the way to the hospital. Thank God for modern medicine. Surgery saved him, but his spinal cord was nicked by the bullet. He should have experienced paralysis only to the lower half of his body. That would have been enough of a hurdle to overcome. But once he found out you were dead, he was adamant there was feeling only from the neck up. Tests showed everything should have worked down to his hips, but you can't make a man want to live. We tried for a while. Samantha tried, Joel tried, I tried. The hospital finally discharged him, suggesting we provide hospice care. So there he lies at River's Edge, wasting away. Waiting to die."

"I don't believe it. That doesn't sound like Brad. I mean, Brad's the guy who got me going to church. Seeking God. Trusting Jesus. He can't just give up on life."

"No one could have predicted this. But good health was important to Brad. He worked out, ate right. That bullet changed everything. Even the best of us can suffer depression after a blow like that. And then to lose your fiancée too."

"Not fiancée. Girlfriend. It wasn't official."

"I think it was official in his mind."

I sniffled. "It's good to hear that." I cleared my throat. "So what can I do to fix the situation? As his former wife-to-be, I'm not going to sit by and watch him languish."

"We can't predict how he'll react. We just have to take it slow. I'm sorry."

I clung to him. "Take me to see him. Please. If I can't be Tish, then I'll be Tasha. I don't care. I have to see him. Please let me see him."

He scratched his head, thinking. "I don't know. Sam wouldn't be happy about it."

"What is she, his keeper? I have as much right to Brad as she does. Brad loves me. He wants to marry me. We're going to be together the rest of our lives and raise kids together and sit in our rockers on the front porch when we're old."

My voice rose along with my level of desperation. I

shook Puppa by the arms. "I have the right to see him. You take me to see him!"

He wrapped me in a calming embrace. "Shhh. Everything's going to be okay. I'll take you to see him."

I nodded into his shoulder, filled with relief. But behind the calm, a tinge of uncertainty crept in. If Brad was really the way Puppa described him, would I be enough to make him want to live again?

What if I wasn't? My heart skipped a beat. Of course I'd be enough. Of course I would.

—∾—

The road meandered through a residential area. Large two-stories and sprawling ranch homes were arranged in spacious order along the edge of the Manistique River. Puppa slowed as we crossed a snow-covered bridge. Below, swift-moving water flowed black against white banks.

Around the next curve, we came to a newer one-story institutional building disguised as a Georgian manor home.

River's Edge Assisted Living, the sign read.

I bit my lip, gearing up for my first glimpse of Brad.

"Don't talk to him or get too close," Puppa told me on the way over. "Just take a good look at him and come out. We'll talk more then."

We passed through a central gathering room with cathedral ceilings and tasteful décor in mint and mauve. Long hallways led off on two sides. Puppa followed plush carpeting down one hall to the last door on the left. He knocked.

A twenty-something man wearing blue scrubs and a buzz cut came to the door.

"Mr. Russo. Welcome. And who is your guest?" He ushered us into a small private living room and gestured toward two chairs. "Please have a seat."

"Thanks, Austin." Puppa sat.

I took the other chair.

A kitchenette was built into one corner of the room. Austin sat on the edge of the counter.

Puppa spoke. "This is Tasha Stewart. She'd like to observe Brad for a few moments."

"Oh? A student at Bay?"

"Yeah." I nodded, going along with his theory that I attended Bay de Noc Community College in Escanaba. "Physical therapy."

"I'm afraid Mr. Walters will be a disappointment for you," Austin said. "He's refused therapy. He may never regain his strength."

I gasped, then quickly composed myself. I nudged the sunglasses up on my nose. "Just have to take a few notes, make a couple observations. I'll only stay a moment."

"I'm sorry, he's sleeping right now and doesn't care for company. If you'd like to come back later, I can see if he's willing to help you with your project."

"No." The word popped out more quickly than I'd planned. "I'd rather make my observations while he's sleeping if that's okay. He doesn't even have to know I was here."

Austin hesitated. "It's probably not a good idea. You know how he can be, Mr. Russo." He looked at Puppa as if hoping he'd take the hint and get me out of there.

Puppa gave him a determined look. "If he's sleeping, what can it hurt? Go ahead in, Tasha."

I stepped toward the door. Austin made a move to follow me.

"Let her go alone, Austin. She doesn't bite," Puppa said.

Austin looked panicked, like he'd be held accountable if he let a stranger in to see his client without proper escort.

But at Puppa's smile of reassurance, Austin calmed down and gave me the sign to go in.

Puppa gave me a stern glance. "Remember what I told you."

I nodded and turned the doorknob. Stepping inside, I removed my sunglasses, clutching them in one hand. My eyes took a moment to adjust. Dim light filtered in where the blackout shade gapped from the window. I pressed the door closed behind me, careful not to make noise. A bed, a chair, and a dresser took shape in the darkness. I moved a step toward the lump under the covers and stopped, recalling Puppa's warning.

I stood and listened to the sound of Brad's breathing. Eyes closed, I basked in the gentle rhythm. I hadn't heard that sound in seven months. And if he'd died that day, I would never have heard it again. Now to think he'd lost his will to live and wanted to die . . . I felt like racing to the bed and shaking him. Life was too short. Life was too precious to waste like that.

Another step closer. What could it hurt? His breathing hitched and I half expected Brad to sit up. But the rhythm resumed and I bent my face close to his, studying the sight that had kept me going during my exile. The promise of seeing those eyes crinkled in laughter once more had brought me through the long months of separation.

His face took shape in the gloom. Black lashes lay in soft slumber along his lower lid. How often had I pictured those same full lashes surrounding the eyes of my imaginary daughter? And there was that broad forehead I loved to press against my cheek. The strong arch of his brow led to a staunch nose and gentle lips . . . while I stared, his mouth twitched, as if begging to be reunited with mine.

Oh, Brad, I whispered in my mind. *Wake up and love me and everything will be okay.*

He was so close. Right there in front of me, only a breath away. My love, my groom, the father of my children yet to come . . .

I leaned forward and softly pressed my lips against his, nearly fainting at the rush of emotion. His skin felt exactly as I remembered, smelled of the same subtle musk. I was with him again. I was with Brad, touching his lips, feeling the heat of his body.

A tear coursed down my cheek, making a *tink* as it landed on his pillow.

A sharp breath sounded in my ear. I gasped and pulled back, horrified to see Brad's eyes open, looking at me in outrage.

"Who are you?"

My eardrums echoed with the bellowing words. I went scuttling to the far wall.

The door flew open and Austin dashed in. "Everything okay, Mr. Walters?"

"Who is she?" Brad thundered again. He made no move to get up, instead allowing his writhing face muscles to express fury.

Austin shooed me out the door. "Just some pesky student working on a report. Sorry she disturbed you, sir."

The door slammed closed behind me, Austin remaining inside to calm his client.

In the living room, still seated in his chair, Puppa smiled and wagged his finger at me. "I told you not to get close to him."

I blushed at my own audacity. "I thought he was sleeping."

"You kissed him, didn't you?"

I gave him a frown. "You say that like you knew I would." I wagged a finger back in his direction. "Dirty old man."

"It's good for him. Let him start thinking about the good stuff in life. That'll give him a reason to live." Puppa chuckled.

"I'd probably be okay with it if I'd gone in there as myself. But I don't want him fantasizing about some chick with black hair."

"Come on," Puppa said, grabbing my hand and practically skipping out the door with me. "We did enough damage for one day."

24

Safe in the truck, Puppa and I shared a laugh attack bordering on hysterics. Brad. I was so happy to see him again—even kissed him—but at the same time, so devastated at his condition.

Puppa wiped a tear from the corner of his eye. "Good grief. I haven't had this much fun since . . . well, since last time you were here. You sure know how to show a guy a good time."

"It's great to be back. Gosh, I missed you . . . and Brad." I used the edge of my coat to dry my face.

"I tell you what," Puppa said, shaking his head, "I could never have predicted the amazing things that have happened this year. When you turned up last February," he gulped with emotion, "I had no idea the blessings that would be showered on our lives."

I squeezed my eyes closed, thinking of Brad's fate. "I think I brought only darkness."

"You are one of those people who bring light to the darkness."

"Please. I can't see how stumbling into a drug ring,

stumbling over a dead body, almost getting my boyfriend killed, then stumbling out of here in four months or less could be considered bringing light to the darkness."

"It's that journey you're on. Somehow you allow others to see their own darkness. Once they're aware of it, they can't ignore it anymore. They have to embrace it, or step into the light."

"Well, I'm no Gospel Queen if that's what you're getting at."

"Not at all. People see you seeking God and that gives them hope that maybe God can love them too."

I crossed my arms and humphed. "I'm not sure that's a compliment."

Puppa gave a chuckle. "Yeah, that didn't exactly come out right." He gripped the steering wheel with enthusiasm. "Patricia, you have no idea how those few short months changed all our lives. I thanked God every day when you were with us." He glanced over at me. "I guess I shouldn't be surprised he brought you back from the dead. Obviously you have more good works up your sleeve."

I snorted. "Where do you come up with this stuff? I'm totally useless as a Christian. I've broken every commandment and then some."

"That kind of honesty is what makes you so priceless. You accept that God loves you just the way you are. Flaws and all."

"Sheesh. Do I have a choice? How do you point out to your creator that he made a piece of junk? I don't think he wants to hear that. Sounds like an insult to me. I mean, I once had a guy walk through one of my renovation projects and point out all the bumps in the drywall, as if those minor flaws somehow negated the incredible beauty of the home. I don't even want to tell you what I did to him."

Puppa swung his face my way, eyes bulging.

"Oh, my gosh," I said quickly. "Nothing like that. I just gave him a piece of my mind and threw him out."

I leaned back and looked at the passing scenery. The sun poked out from behind thick white clouds, giving the woods a dusting of diamonds as the rays hit ice on branches.

"There's nothing like winter in the U.P.," I said, caught up in the view.

"Too warm for you in California, was it?" Puppa asked.

"Too warm in lots of ways."

The sun disappeared behind the clouds, returning the world to dull gray. I wondered how Celia was faring. And Portia. For a moment I wished there could be two of me.

I stared at my hands. I hadn't brought light to Del Gloria. I'd brought darkness to that world. It would take time to get over the guilt. If Celia died, maybe I'd never get over it.

I swallowed hard and aimed my misery at a new topic. "So what am I supposed to do about Samantha and Joel in my house? I can't see throwing them out with a baby on the way. But, come on, it's my home."

"Let's keep the return of Patricia Amble under wraps awhile longer until we can weed out any threats on your life." He gave me a look. "Now that you're alive again, someone might actually try to kill you."

Puppa turned toward Port Silvan. "If we could keep it quiet, the deed could be reversed, and maybe Samantha and Joel can rent it from you. They love it there. They've turned it into a happy home for themselves."

I bit my lip and squelched a tear with my fist. "Yeah. They seem happy. I guess I'll have to think about it."

We passed the driveway. VALENTINE'S BAY LODGE, the sign said. Wish I'd have thought of turning the place into a bed-and-breakfast.

Puppa kept his focus on the road, somehow knowing I'd lost the mood for fun and games.

The truck slowed to take the curve at Cupids Creek.

"Tell me more about Brad," I said. "He used to love life. What happened?"

"You died."

"Then it makes sense he'll be fine now that I'm not dead anymore." Through hovering tears, farmhouses drifted past like ghosts.

"Let's take it slow. I liked his reaction today. That's the most life I've seen in him since the accident."

"Yeah," I said in a wry voice, "there's nothing wrong with his lungs."

"But, Patricia," Puppa said, serious, "I'll warn you right now. Don't get your hopes up. If Brad decides not to pull out of this, you may have to accept that choice and move on."

I shook my head in stubborn denial. "That's not going to happen."

Puppa turned down the drive to the lake house. "I hope not. I really hope not."

—ɯ—

That night, in the upstairs bedroom farthest from the stairs, I snuggled under a pink ruffled bedspread and tried to focus on the downward spiraling days of Edmond Dantès, now the vengeful Count of Monte Cristo. I scarcely felt sorry for him as he finagled an invitation to see his lovely Mercedes, now married to another man. But when the envious Count conjured up a despicable plot against Mercedes' son, I slammed the book closed, going for my journal instead.

On paper, I relived the day's events, wiping away tears as I wrote of Brad's shattered life. Reading over the account, I became more determined than ever to be an instrument of change for Brad. He had done the same for me. He had loved me when I'd loathed myself. He'd had faith in me even though I acted untrustworthy. Now it was my turn to demonstrate unfaltering love.

I yawned. The words blurred in my sleep-deprived eyes. I set the journal on the bedside table and turned out the light. But my mind fought the solace of dreams, instead lingering in Brad's bedroom at River's Edge, tracing the lines of his face and revisiting the touch of his lips. I drifted to sleep, imagining I was safe in his arms.

25

I woke the next morning excited to talk strategy with Puppa and pin down our plans to revive Brad to the land of the living. I dressed in layers to combat the nippy temperature in the drafty old house, then raced downstairs for a cup of hot coffee.

The sun rose bright over the icy bay, splashing light the color of hope against the walls. Puppa took a sip of coffee. "Don't forget what we talked about," he said, caution in his voice. "I've been dealing with this situation a long time. We've tried everything. Brad may not be as happy as you think to find out you're alive . . . and that you've seen him in that condition. In fact, it may just put him over the edge."

"I know—you said that before. But that's worst-case. He's going to be so happy to see me. Just wait. When he realizes his physical condition doesn't have anything to do with my love for him, he'll work toward recovery. He'll want to get better so we can be together."

Puppa tapped fingers to his lips. "This isn't some fairy tale where you kiss the prince and he magically comes

back to life. It's real. Real tragedy. Real heartache. You need to accept the fact that Brad may never recover. He may never be part of your happily ever after. I'm already sorry I brought you over there."

I shook my head. "You're right. Life's not a fairy tale. It's real. Real love. Real hope. Real miracles. Those are the facts I'm going to accept."

"Then you're setting yourself up for real disappointment."

"I'm willing to take that chance. I have to take that chance, because if I give up on Brad, I give up on myself. Then I'll die too."

Puppa stared at some distant place. Then with an abrupt humph, he stood. "I just don't want to see you get hurt. I've been where you're at. Love isn't always enough to save someone." He stomped toward the kitchen.

I shrugged it off and drank my coffee. There would be no tears, only laughter this time around for me and Brad.

Later that morning, Puppa presented me with a box of stuff salvaged from the lodge.

"Sam thought I'd want this. It's all the stuff you left behind when you died."

I fished through the oversized bin, which contained my purse, complete with wallet, checkbook, and credit card; the passport I'd gotten years ago for the day when I could finally take that trip to a remote beach in the Fiji Islands; an album of before-and-after shots of my various projects; a couple keepsakes from my youth; and Konrad the Clown, my seventh grade sewing project. The poor guy was showing his age, with one button-eye missing and worn patches on the tube socks that formed his legs and arms.

I raised my arms in a questioning shrug. "So where are my tax records and receipts?"

He looked at the floor. "Sam figured you couldn't be audited if you were dead, so she shredded them."

"Great."

"I think you have a pretty good excuse. Don't fret over it. Here," he said, throwing me a set of keys.

I caught them in one hand. "What are these for?"

"Thought you might want to take the truck for a ride."

I smiled. "I like the way you think. Thank you."

—∞—

I checked my wispy black wig in the rearview mirror as I drove toward Valentine's Bay and my pilfered lodge. I figured I needed Sam and Joel's support if I were ever going to wake my sleeping prince.

I slowed coming around the final corner, frowning. Cars were everywhere, cramming the drive and the extra lot that now stood where my shed used to be. What on earth?

I parked behind a yellow Volkswagen, not surprised that one of Samantha's retro friends would drive the throwback.

I snuck between cars to the entry deck. My hand hovered a moment before I gave an insistent knock on the door. Guilt sparked when I realized I was probably about to crash a Bible study or a praise group or something.

But I stifled the feeling and reminded myself that the lodge was really mine. It wasn't as if Sam could throw me out.

Nobody answered. I gave the handle a turn and pushed the door open a crack.

"Hello?" I called softly.

Through the slim opening, I saw Sam stirring something at the stove. Her white apron did nothing to hide the bulge in her belly, giving her the amazing glow of a mother-to-be. How could I have been so rude and unfeeling toward her yesterday? She was as much a victim as I was in the whole situation.

I pushed in and stood near the door.

A young woman came alongside me. "Hi. I'll be right with you." The same white apron as Sam's draped the woman's slim form. The tray in her hand bore an assortment of tall mugs, the kind you drink root beer from, like she'd just bussed a table at a restaurant.

The woman dropped the tray off on the counter, the noisy *clink* of glass adding to the cacophony of voices and clatter of silverware that drifted through the arch from the great room. A round of laughter floated in.

"Just one today?" the young brunette asked, returning to my side.

A group of three or four people came through the arch, smiling as they filtered past the counter toward the door behind me.

"Thank you, Sam. It was delicious again today," one said.

"I want the recipe for that chili," another called, moving my direction.

"Sorry, family secret," Samantha teased, wooden spoon held high in a goodbye gesture.

They passed through the door and were gone.

"Follow me," my hostess said with a smile.

Samantha turned back to her task, oblivious to my presence as she scooped sauce onto Coney dogs lined up on the counter.

"Order up," Sam said as we passed.

My hackles rose—again—at the sight in my great room. I'd obviously gotten here before the lunch rush yesterday, before the folding tables and chairs, packed with talking, laughing people, crowded the area. The young woman sat me at a table for two. A dark green napkin was folded like a tent in front of me, the merry color standing out against a crisp white tablecloth. Water from a carafe was poured into a stemmed glass to my right. A menu appeared in my hand.

"Would you care for a beverage to get started?" the voice beside me asked.

I shook my head, dazed at the title on the menu. *Sam and Joel's on the Bay.* My house was now Samantha Walters' latest food service establishment. Why'd she have to bring her stupid diner to the U.P.? Why didn't she just get out of my house and go back downstate where she came from?

I opened the booklet and perused the list of selections. Lunch choices ranged from traditional coneys, to reubens on rye. For supper, guests could choose from a variety of fresh fish, prime rib, and even chicken parmigiana. Served, of course, with fresh-baked homemade rolls and spinach salad drizzled with bacon dressing. A separate insert announced the festive Christmas buffet that would be served from noon to six just two days from now. And all for just $19.99 per person.

I curled an edge of the laminated menu, ruining the seal. Right now I hated Sam. Was there anything she couldn't do? Did she have any ideas that were lame instead of brilliant? Was there anything she owned that she hadn't stolen from me?

I glanced through the dark tint of my sunglasses at the others in the room. I supposed she knew each of her customers by name and they were all completely taken in by her charm.

Christmas lights twinkled around the perimeter. I glared at the tree crammed in the corner, picturing the room as it had been before Sam got a hold of it: tatty furniture, dim lighting, no decorations . . . I seethed inwardly. What had she done with my stuff, anyway? The couch that once sat in the same place as this table had been a family heirloom. It was the same one I'd bounced on when I was a kid. I closed my eyes.

Boing, boing, boing.

"Patricia Louise Amble!" my mother would yell from the kitchen. "Get off that sofa!"

"Have you decided?" The woman had returned, order pad in hand.

I jerked my mind from the past. "I'll take two Coney Deluxes to go, please."

"Fries or chips?" she asked.

"Chili-cheese fries. Thanks."

She was gone. I stared past the crowd to the lake. A slash of gray water ran between slabs of white ice.

If Doomsday hadn't happened last May, how far would I have gotten on this place? I looked up at the cedar beams that crossed the ceiling. Someone had given the whole soaring room a coat of glossy polyurethane, allowing the light to gleam off each surface. That colossal project hadn't even been in my plans. And after my excitement in Del Gloria, I was almost ready to swear off ladders. The most I would have done to improve the great room was duct tape a dust mop to an extension pole and sweep down the cobwebs. But this . . . this was awe-inspiring.

The burgundy, green, and cream accents Sam had splashed throughout the room made the space feel elegant, yet still like a woodsy lodge. And her idea to have every piece of décor for sale, tied with a tiny white price tag, made me want to retch. On the wall above me, a clock chimed the hour to the tune of "Somewhere Over the Rainbow." Without knowing why, I craned for a look at the tag.

A few minutes later, the waitress brought my order, bagged in paper and fastened with a red raffia bow.

She laid the bill upside down on the table. "I can take that when you're ready."

"How about right now? And," I gestured at the wall clock, "I'll take that too."

She disappeared with the clock and a few minutes later returned it wrapped in recycled paper and tied with green ribbon. I counted out enough bills to cover the check and tip and hightailed it out of my own house.

Sam caught a glimpse of me halfway across the kitchen.

"Oh, my gosh. Tish?" She slapped a hand over her mouth and checked for spies. "I mean Sasha."

"It's Tasha."

She looked at my excess baggage. "So you're the one who bought the clock."

I nodded, sidestepping toward the door.

"Is that a Christmas present for your grandfather?"

I shook my head, mute.

She stared at me, her eyes turning hard. "Listen. Stay away from Brad. I heard about that stunt you pulled yesterday. He's not ready to see you. I'll let you know when he is."

I was sorry she couldn't see the scorn in my eyes. With a spin, I took off out the back door.

Packages safe on the passenger seat next to me, I made the drive to Manistique. No former sister-in-law-to-be was going to scare me away from Brad.

26

Brad's personal bodyguard opened the door.

"Hi, Austin," I said, praying Brad hadn't told him about the kiss yesterday.

"The crazy college chick. What do you want?" Austin kept his fit and trim physique between me and my goal as he looked into the hall behind me. "No Mr. Russo today?"

I shook my head, struggling with my box and bag. "I'm about to drop this stuff. Can you get the door for me?"

"No can do. You can't come in."

Sighing, I put on a weary voice. "Look. I know I upset Brad yesterday. I brought him lunch to make it up."

Austin sniffed the air. "Sam's Coney Deluxe. That's Mr. Walters' favorite."

"I know." I took a step forward, edging into the opening.

He cut me off at the pass. "Sorry, no visitors."

"Come on. I'd like another chance to talk to Mr. Walters." I rocked the aromatic bag of Coneys under his nose and spoke in a singsong voice. "I brought him food."

Austin grabbed the bag off my larger package. "I'll tell him it's from you." He started to close the door.

"Give that back." I slapped at the paper, missing. "That's my lunch too."

"Sorry, no visitors." The bag disappeared and the door was almost closed.

"Who's here, Austin?" a voice boomed from the bedroom.

"Hey!" I yelled through the crack. "Brad! It's me! I brought you a Coney Deluxe."

Austin slammed the door in my face.

I stood there, the toe of one shoe wedged against the threshold. Brad had to realize it was me, Tish, come back to life. Any moment Austin would open the door and usher me inside. I waited, listening. When Austin didn't return, I rested the clock on one hip and stuck an ear to the door.

The rustling of a paper bag.

I jiggled the doorknob. Locked.

My fists hit the wood. "Hey! Open up! That's my lunch! Hey!" I kept pounding, determined not to stop until Austin opened the door.

Down the hall, a head poked out of a doorway.

"Excuse me, miss," an elderly gentleman said with a missing-denture lisp. "*M*A*S*H* is on. I can't watch it with all that racket. Makes a rumble in my hearing aid."

I held my hand suspended mid-thud. What was I doing? Standing in an old folks' home pounding on doors was definitely low-class.

"Sorry." I gave a little wave. The head disappeared.

I turned back to my task. I was not leaving here without seeing Brad.

Tapping a finger softly on the door, I spoke through the wood. "Come on. I promise I won't upset him today. Anyway, you have to open up. I have a present for him."

Silence. He probably couldn't answer because his mouth was full of that special sauce with meat and beans and topped with onions . . . My stomach growled.

"Fine. Give me back my lunch and I'll go away."

Still no answer. Maybe he was back sharing the spoils with Brad.

A building attendant passed by in the narrow hall. "Can I help you with something?" the man asked.

"Ahhh . . ." I wiped the guilty look off my face. I had every right to be here. More than every right. "I seem to have been locked out. Could you show me where I can find a phone?"

The man in navy coveralls walked me to the lounge and pointed to a phone on a decorative desk. "Local calls only unless you have a calling card."

"Thanks." I put the clock down and sat in the straight-back chair. I opened the long top drawer of the desk. A phone book. Just the thing.

I flipped through the *W*s. No Brad Walters. But one listing read Walters-Russo, Samantha. Instead of a Port Silvan prefix, it had the Manistique exchange. That had to be Brad's number at River's Edge.

I dialed it.

"This is Austin," came the voice.

"Austin. Hi. It's the crazy college chick. Open the door, okay? I really need to talk to Brad."

Click.

I dialed the number again. It rang once, picked up, and slammed in my ear.

I dialed again—and this time got a busy signal.

The receiver dangled from my hand, its *beep beep beep* audible throughout the lounge.

"What's the matter, dear, he's not taking your call?"

I looked toward the gentle voice. A woman with a wizened face sat in a corner by a window, the various shades of pink in her clothing allowing her to blend with the general décor. No wonder I hadn't noticed her earlier. Gray hair swirled in perfectly round curls atop her head. It had to be a wig. I touched my own masterpiece, suddenly conscious of how foolish I must look.

I smiled and turned away, avoiding conversation. The pages of the phone book fluttered under my fingers as I delved for the secret to visiting Brad.

The voice interrupted my thoughts again. "Perhaps I could help."

The sweet old lady apparently couldn't take a hint.

I waved a hand and nodded. "I'm fine, really. Thanks anyway."

Back to the pages of phone numbers. I could call Puppa and get him to come out. Or call Sam and bawl her out. No. There had to be a better, faster way of getting in there.

Movement in the corner of my eye. I glanced up. The old gal had moved to the chair closest to me.

She leaned forward and spoke in a scheming voice. "I happen to know Austin runs errands for that Walters fellow between two and three o'clock."

My brows shot up. "Really." How did the spry old gal know what I was up to?

She gave my leg a firm pat. "They keep him locked up in there like a prisoner. No visitors outside of family, they tell us. And he never comes out. Never." She *tsk*ed her show of disapproval. "Not even for Bingo. I say that poor young man needs some excitement." She looked me up and down. "And you seem like the exciting type."

Good heavens. Was the old woman trying to set Brad up on a date? As Brad's onetime almost-bride-to-be, I was mortified that Ms. Matchmaker was on the job in the lobby. Brad did not need excitement. He needed me.

That being the case, how could I pass up this opportunity to see Brad? All I needed was a way to get inside once Austin left.

Another pat on the leg. "I have a plan," the old gal whispered and crooked her finger. "Follow me."

—∾—

The clock in the box chimed and sang its soulful melody from its place on the table in the woman's apartment, two doors down from Brad's.

"Patience," my cohort advised. "Give Austin a few minutes to get out the door."

The saucy gal's name was Ruby Callahan and she'd been a resident of the building for some time, she'd told me.

"Not often we get youngsters like that Mr. Walters in here. Shame about him, isn't it?" She leaned toward me on the plain ivory sofa and checked her watch. "It's time." She gave a nod toward her adjoining bedroom.

I snuck into the room and hid behind the door, listening for my cue.

The sound of humming . . . the main door to the hallway opening . . . Ruby's voice of fake surprise.

"Why, Austin. Just the man I'm looking for. Remember that magazine I lent you? With the article about finding the perfect mate? I have someone else in need of it and I must have it back, please. Snip snap."

"Just heading out, Mrs. C. How about I grab that for you when I get back and drop it by?"

"That'll never do. You promised to return it last week."

A sigh. "Fine. I'll be right back."

"Nonsense. I'll come with you."

A few minutes passed with no voices. Then a perky, "Thank you, thank you. The young woman will be thrilled. Thirty-four and she's never been married, poor dear."

"You're welcome. Talk to you later." Austin's exasperated voice disappeared down the hall.

"Coast is clear," Ruby said a moment later.

I stepped into the hall. "Now what?"

"Door's unlocked," she said with a sly grin. "Just make sure you fasten it when you leave."

"Thanks." My heart fluttered with excitement as I headed down the corridor, clock in hand, to Brad's apartment.

I gripped the knob, half expecting it wouldn't turn. It did. Tiptoeing, I closed the door behind me and locked it against the meddling Ruby Callahan.

The air inside felt oppressive. Through the partially open bedroom door came the canned laughter of a television show.

In my hand, the package ticked like a bomb as I stood,

hesitating. Austin could return at any moment. If I was going to do this thing, I'd better get to it.

I set the clock down on the counter, the paper scraping softly on the surface, and steeled myself.

"Austin? Is that you?" Brad's voice spoke tentatively from the direction of the bed.

I cleared my throat. "No, Brad. It's me. Tish."

The door swung back under my fingertips. I stepped into his sight, taking off my wig and sunglasses, holding them in one hand while I smoothed my snarled hair with the other.

His eyes were huge, as if he were seeing a ghost.

"Hey," I tossed my disguise on the coverlet over his feet and circled to the head of the bed. "It's okay. It's really me."

I touched his hand, which lay on top of the sheet, holding its warmth in my fingers as if holding a lost pearl, now found.

"You're . . . They told me you were dead." His voice tore from his chest.

I nodded, squeezing back tears from my smile. "I know. I heard. But turns out I'm still around to haunt you."

He looked up at the ceiling a moment, as if searching for an explanation. Then he shot a hard glance at me. "Who let you in here? I told them I didn't want to see anyone."

The words burned. I pulled my hand away. "I'm not just anyone."

He strained to look down over his body. "Look at me."

I crossed my arms, running my eyes from his face to his feet. "I heard most of this is your own doing."

"What?" His voice rumbled. "I was shot and almost

killed. Nothing works anymore. You think I wouldn't change that if I could?"

"Puppa told me you won't even try."

His face turned red and I could see rage build in his heaving chest. I welcomed the thought of him leaping from the bed and chasing me from the room. My mission would certainly be accomplished.

But no such miracle.

"Get out and don't come back!" His roar almost peeled the hair off my head.

I stood my ground. "Come on," I said in a soothing voice. "Don't chase me away. Do you know how much I love you? How much I've missed you?"

"I'm not that man. He's . . . dead. Gone." He turned his face away from me. "Nothing means anything to me anymore. Including you. Leave me alone."

The words hurt. I scrunched my face as a shield against them, but they crawled under my skin anyway and made a home somewhere a little right of my heart. The pain stole my breath.

I gasped and choked for air, trying to keep myself from melting into a pile of unwanted cells right at the foot of Brad's bed.

"You're all I thought about. You're all that kept me going in Del Gloria. And you just want me to walk out of here like we had nothing?"

He gave a wild look. His neck and shoulders moved slightly as if he were trying to sit. His head flopped back to the pillow and he closed his eyes, catching his breath.

From the other room came the sound of a key being inserted into the lock.

27

I controlled my sobbing long enough to know I'd better be out of sight when Austin entered the room. "Please . . . ," I whispered, followed by a hiccup, "don't tell him I was here."

I pulled back a curtain from the window, the sudden light blinding me. My hands scoured the panes for a locking mechanism.

In the living room, the door opened and Austin's voice filtered in as he conversed with a male visitor.

"I'll see if he's up for company. Just a minute."

My fingers fumbled, but the window wouldn't budge. I searched the room in a panic, my eyes darting to the closet. I grabbed my wig and sunglasses on the way past and stepped inside the tight square, sliding the louvered door closed and feeling ridiculous as I did so. What prevented Brad from telling Austin I was hanging with the shirts?

Inside, my cheek rubbed against fabric, fascinating my nose with the Brad-scent that had always messed with my hormones.

By some miracle, I held my breathing quiet and steady when Austin entered the room.

"Hey, Mr. Walters," Austin greeted. "I barely made it out of the building when I came across a friend of yours. Are you up for a visitor?"

Brad must have made some sign to the negative.

"He's come a long way to see you. It's Mr. Braddock. Says it's an emergency."

My jaw clenched. What if Denton was here to track me down? Once he figured out I'd flown the coop, he'd probably made some inquiries, then headed this way.

A sigh from Brad. "Go ahead and send him in."

At least Brad hadn't told on me.

Footsteps, a door opening. Then Denton's voice as he entered the room.

"Hey! How are you feeling?" Denton sounded more exuberant than usual, as if trying to compensate for something.

Brad remained silent.

A pause. "Everything okay?"

"You lied to me."

A longer pause. "What's this all about?" Denton asked.

"I saw her. I saw Tish. She isn't dead. She said she's been in Del Gloria. I assume that means she's been staying with you."

No answer.

Brad's voice again. "How could you? Do you know what you did to me? And now it's too late. Too late."

Denton went on the defensive. "You asked me to keep her safe. I did what I had to. Besides, you find strength in God. You find strength in hope. You don't obsess over flesh and blood. She's not the reason to wake up in the morning and do your therapy and move on with your life. You do it for God. And God alone."

Brad took in a seething breath. "I hate God."

I cringed at the words, stuffing a shirtsleeve against my mouth to keep from crying out as my heart ached for the man who'd introduced me to God's love.

"And I hate you," Brad told Denton. "Is that why you left Mom? You actually had to pay attention to something besides God in your life?" Brad emphasized each word. "You couldn't hack being a husband and father. That's the truth. It had nothing to do with God."

I pressed close to the louvers, reeling in the accusation. Denton Braddock was Brad's father? Brad . . . Braddock. Duh. It should have been obvious, but I'd been focused on surnames—and Brad's "mentor" baloney, not to mention he'd always implied Samuel Walters was his real dad.

Denton sighed. "I . . . barely knew your mother. What was I supposed to do, drop out of life because I'd slept with the banquet waitress?"

A choking sound. "Don't demean her. She was the finest woman who ever lived."

I strained for a peek at the two men, but could only see Denton's feet through the louvers. His dark slacks draped gracefully over salt-stained shoes.

The professor gave a deep sigh. "I know my shortcomings, my flaws. I admit I sometimes let things get between me and God. But I don't blame him for any of it. I just keep thanking him for the good that has come from my twisted mess of a life. How can I be sorry to have founded Del Gloria College—a safe haven and re-training ground for those whose compass hasn't always pointed true north? Don't hate a God that can take pain and turn it to love."

Brad's breathing sounded strained.

"Son—"

"Don't call me that. When I agreed to have a relationship with you—what's it been, twenty years now?—it was as a teacher and a student. Sam Walters was my father. The only man with the right to call me son."

"Brad, then." Denton's voice became intense. "Listen to me . . . I was wrong. Your Patricia . . . she was more than I thought. She was everything you said. So many times I wanted to send her to you, let her come to you and help snap you out of this self-destructive mind-set. But . . . how could I risk her life? I'd made a promise to you. I'm only sorry now that I wasn't able to keep it."

Through the louvers, I watched Denton's feet pace the room.

"I can't have you for my son. I know that. You've made me pay over and over for the mistakes of my past. But Patricia—she's like a daughter now. She loves me, she's grateful to me. It's in her eyes, on her face, in her smile when we're having coffee or talking about the day."

I bit my lip. Is that really how Denton felt? He'd been so good at staying distant. Perhaps he'd been afraid to show his affections, knowing I would leave him the moment I could find my way back to Brad.

The feet stopped at the head of the bed.

"You said Patricia had been here? She probably took one look at you, said something polite, and left, never to return. How could she choose you, lying in a bed wasting away? At least I can take care of her."

Puh-lease. Denton knew I was perfectly capable of taking care of myself. I was about as low maintenance as a woman could get.

"You're pathetic." Brad nearly spit the words. "You stole my wife and turned her into your child? And you have the gall to justify your actions?"

I snuck in a breath. There was that word . . . *wife*.

Denton's voice took on a cutting edge. "I thought you'd understand, since you've given up on life anyway. What do you need a wife for now? A few more months and she'd be your widow. The doctors tell me your kidneys are on the verge of shutting down, your staph infection is out of control, and you might as well forget about ever walking again. Your nerves and muscles don't even know your legs exist. Once you're gone, Patricia will be my heir."

Brad growled low in his throat. "You're nothing but a scheming, conniving—"

Denton interrupted, his voice sharp. "I'm not here to argue with you or explain myself. That's entirely unnecessary. I'm here because Paticia's life is in danger and I intend to make sure she returns to Del Gloria with me where I can keep her safe. There are others there who need her as well."

"I'm sure if she wants to go with you, she will." Silence hung in the air as if Brad was giving me a chance to come out of hiding.

I stayed put, my loyalty to Brad inflamed by Denton's harassment of the injured man.

Denton's voice broke the silence. "Now that she's seen your condition, I have no doubt she'll be ready to come back with me. If she stays, it will only be out of pity."

My jaw set as I fought the urge to blaze through the doors and knock Denton on his backside.

"Get out of here," Brad snarled. "Don't ever come back. I'm sorry I let you back in my life. I'm sorry I sent her to you."

The hurt behind his words stung my own heart. Brad blamed himself for so much, and none of it was his fault. He was a victim, imprisoned for life in his own failing body. None of Brad's misfortune had been of his own making. I had brought it all upon him. My own negligence had put Brad in the path of Candice LeJeune's bullet, sending him to the depths of his own dungeon.

Worse, Brad couldn't even lift a finger in the name of justice—or vengeance.

I watched from the closet as Denton's wingtips exited the room. The slam of the main door, then Austin came in, white tennis shoes under blue jeans.

"I couldn't help but overhear, Mr. Walters," the young man said. "Anything I can do?"

"Yes. There's a woman hiding in the closet. Please escort her out of here."

I drew in a breath of surprise. He'd turned me in.

With a push, I opened the doors and stepped into the room. "Brad . . . I'm going to stay. We're going to work through this together. I'm not giving you up again." I skirted the waiting Austin and walked to the bed, touching Brad's hand. A gentle pulse beat beneath my fingers.

"Tish." He said it slow, soft, like a guy might say, "I love you." He gave a lingering blink of his eyes in lieu of a squeeze with his hand. "We had something special, didn't we?"

I held on to him, afraid of his past tense.

He shook his head. "We were something." A tear escaped his eye. He couldn't wipe it away even if he wanted to.

My face collapsed at the sight and I threw myself over him, clinging to his chest and neck. Tears streamed down my face.

Brad heaved a sigh. "If only I would have known . . . I'd have asked you to marry me that first night I saw you. Things could have been so different for us."

I touched a fist to his heart, praying that he'd stop the torture, but my mind heard only the thump of Brad's fist against the hood of my Explorer that day in Rawlings. The day I'd left him to return to Port Silvan, the home of my childhood summers. Had finding out about my deceased mother really been more important than being with Brad? I'd put the car in reverse and backed up. Then Brad pounded on the hood. I'd shifted into park and he came around to my window. *Wait out the storm, Tish. The weather will be better tomorrow,* he'd said. Then he kissed me. My brain must have been suffering from electric shock, because when he stepped away, I put the car in drive. I don't even remember looking back.

Talk about defining moments. Talk about turning points. That was one moment in time I'd give anything to have a second shot at. Knowing what I knew today, would I have done it differently? I'd like to think so. The moment Brad's fist hit the hood, I would have slammed the car into park, leaped out, and tackled him to the ground, smothering him in passionate kisses. I would have gladly thrown my past to the wind and been ignorant of my heritage if I'd known how much every second counted, how little time there was to waste. Then, even if the same tragedy had happened to Brad in the line of duty back in Rawlings, perhaps he'd have had a child to smile him back to life, if smiles from me couldn't do the trick.

Instead, I'd driven away. And I'd lost everything.

28

In the glum bedroom, I cried a puddle all over Brad's chest. "It's not too late. It's not too late. There can still be us. We're together again, you'll be back on your feet in no time." I clung to him. We were together. God gave us back to each other. God would give him back his health.

"Austin," Brad said, his voice rumbling beneath my ear. "Please."

"Yes, sir."

Hands grabbed my arms, gently at first, then rough as I resisted.

"Time to go," Austin said, his voice straining with effort.

"Let go of me. I'm not leaving." I took Brad's cheeks in my hands. "I'm not leaving."

He closed his eyes and turned his head away.

"Brad. No. Don't do this."

Austin grabbed my wrists and wrenched them behind my back.

He lifted me off Brad's body and pointed me toward

the door. We stumbled through to the living room, his arms locked around my struggling wrists. He let go of one hand to open the main door. As soon as he did, I snapped my arm around and pushed against the doorframe. But I was no match for Austin's strong upper body, and in seconds I was headed out the door. I flipped my legs up on the way through, barring passage. With a mighty backward shove, I landed on top of Austin in the middle of the floor. As he recovered, I jumped to my feet and ran back to Brad's side. Behind me, I heard the tones of Austin dialing the phone.

"Brad. Look at me. Brad. Please."

But he kept his eyes closed tight and his head turned. Safe from Austin as he spoke on the phone, I walked to the window and pulled the curtains back. Daylight flooded the room.

"Gosh, it's stuffy in here." I studied the window and found the latch that would have meant my safe escape earlier. I twisted it and pushed the window wide.

Frigid air blew in, bringing the bright scent of the holidays with it.

"That reminds me. Christmas Day, Sam's dishing up a buffet. I'll stop and get us a couple takeouts. If Austin's going to be here, I can bring some for him too."

Brad's bedside table was covered with an assortment of over-the-counter meds, prescription bottles, and boxes of sterile pads. The trash bin next to the bed held a fresh liner. I scooped out the plastic sack, held it close to the table's edge, and swiped the whole contents into it.

That got Brad's attention.

"What are you doing?" His voice was panic-filled.

"Cleaning up. What a mess. Too many bottles." I gave the top of the bag a twist and tucked the whole thing into the top dresser drawer. "That's better," I said, dusting the newly revealed wood with my sleeve. "Not quite so dreary in here anymore."

A stiff knock sounded on the outer apartment door.

"She's in the bedroom," I heard Austin say.

I maneuvered to Brad's side, not sure who would be walking through the door.

A man in uniform entered.

"Mike. How are you?" I asked, greeting Officer Segerstrom, Brad's state cop buddy from his training camp days. I clung more tightly to Brad's hand as if that would somehow keep me from being hauled off.

The officer sighed and looked between Brad and me. "Samantha filled me in with the details. Heard there's a problem."

"No problem here." With my free hand, I pulled the light cotton blanket to Brad's chin, folded it back, and smoothed the wrinkles.

Brad wouldn't look at Mike, just kept staring at some point in the corner.

Mike cleared his throat. "It's pretty tough to get in here for a visit. Tried a couple times myself."

Brad stayed quiet.

I met Mike's gaze. He looked as torn up as I felt. I hoped he'd have the courage to defy Austin and Brad and let me stay.

"How are things going for you, Mike?" I asked, buying time.

"Good. The baby's a couple months old now. Sure is

cute. Don't know if you heard—his name is Brad Walter Segerstrom. Strong as an ox."

A funny sound came out of Brad's throat.

I looked at him. A tear ran down his cheek.

"Congratulations," Brad said finally.

Unable to bear the sight, my eyes flew back to Mike. "That's great news. We're so happy for you and your wife."

The officer nodded once in reply.

The room was silent for a moment. Then Austin spoke up from his place at the door. "How about it, Mr. Walters?"

Brad nodded his head.

"No." I grabbed on to Brad again, covering the top of his body with mine.

"Tish. Miss Amble." Officer Segerstrom spoke the words softly.

Still clinging to Brad, I glanced up at him.

He gave a gentle shake of his head and a shrug, as if to say "What's the use?" and reached a hand toward me.

I held back, burying my face in Brad's blanket, smelling him, hearing him, feeling his skin, his breathing, his heat.

"Tish. Go."

Brad's words crushed my heart. The sobbing started again, along with a headache that made me weaken my grip.

Officer Segerstrom's gentle touch nudged me away from Brad. I resisted. How could I do otherwise?

"Brad. Don't make me go. There's no reason. How can it be bad for us to be together?"

"Not bad for us," came his answer. "Bad for you. Go on. Get out of here. Live for both of us."

"This is stupid. I'm not leaving."

"Get out of my life. I don't want you here. Don't ever come here again." Brad's voice sounded ominous. "Get her out of here, Mike, and leave me alone. I just want to be left alone."

"I don't believe you," I whispered.

His answer was a roar. "Get her away from me! Get her out of here. Get her out of here!"

I jumped back in fright. As soon as I let go of Brad, Officer Segerstrom locked me in an embrace. In moments we were out of the bedroom and through the living room. Once in the hallway, he dropped one arm, still guiding me by the shoulders toward the parking lot. Mrs. Callahan's door was open and from the corner of my eye, I saw her watching my removal.

"Thanks, Mrs. C.," I called on the way past. "It was worth a try." My voice hitched.

By the time we got to the front door, Officer Segerstrom's hold had loosened to a mere hand in the center of my back. He knew I wouldn't run back in there to see Brad. I'd be an idiot not to take such a bold hint. The guy didn't want me around. That was that. It was over between us. When he'd given up on life, he'd given up on us.

Officer Segerstrom must have recognized Puppa's truck and led me that direction. At the driver's side door, he put his hands on my shoulders, sympathetic.

"I'd heard he was doing bad, but I had no idea how far things had gone. Nobody gets past his doorman." The officer gave a shrug. "I gave up trying awhile back."

I gave a loud sniffle.

"Hey." He squeezed my arms. "Have some dignity. You're a beautiful woman with a full life ahead of you. Do yourself a favor. Get over him and get on with it. Try to forget what you saw in there. I know that's not the Brad he wants us to remember."

My lips drew down in a pained gash and I fought back more tears. Dignity. Pride. Did I really care about any of that stuff anymore? How about if I was just a humble nobody who fixed up old houses and visited her boyfriend at River's Edge? That kind of life seemed like it should count as a decent one in God's eyes. Why should I care what anyone else thought? Why should Brad?

The officer pulled the door open for me and I slid behind the wheel.

"Probably better if you left town," he said. "They thought they had a conviction, but Majestic was acquitted. There's a price on your head. Not to mention I'd have to arrest you, seeing as you're no longer deceased. Don't worry. I won't file a report. Besides, I'm not sure killing that lowlife Drake Belmont counts as a crime, even though taking off that day in Brad's SUV made you seem like the prime suspect." His momentary smile gave way to a look of regret. "Take care of yourself." He slammed the door closed.

Everything about me was numb as I put the vehicle in gear and drove from the lot. From the road, I looked back. Officer Segerstrom gave a salute. My throat tightened and I stared ahead, concentrating on the curves along the river. Was I really driving away from Brad again? Was I really allowing him to send me away for a second time? Some wild impulse made me want to turn back, but the urge passed and despair settled into my bones. How did you make someone love you? You could only be yourself . . . and they either loved you or they didn't. Brad couldn't love . . . not me, not himself, not God. Forcing him to love again would be like Sisyphus pushing a rock uphill only to have it roll back down moments before reaching the pinnacle—and then repeating the futile task over and over for eternity. Could I withstand a curse of those proportions? I couldn't even handle peeling wallpaper for more than two days in a row.

I drove without even realizing where I was until I saw the sign for the lodge. I slowed, angling the truck down the driveway. Samantha could help. She'd understand. Maybe I hadn't done things her way so far, but she must have some idea how we could get Brad turned around.

29

I hiccupped on the way inside. I'd left my wig and sunglasses in Brad's closet. Without my disguise to hide behind, paranoia crept over me. My face was plastered all over the Yooper Mafia's Most Wanted list—what if somebody recognized me? Standing in the kitchen watching Sam ladle soup into bowls, I figured it was too late to turn back anyhow.

"Just one this evening?" The hostess, a different one for the supper hour, smiled as she greeted me.

"No. Thank you." I pointed in Sam's direction. "I'm just here to speak with Samantha a minute."

"I'll tell her you're waiting, but I'm not sure how long it will be before she can break away."

"No problem."

"Okay." She shrugged. "I'll seat you in the dining area until she can get to you."

She put me at a spot next to the window. The sun was just beginning to set over the lake, like a juicy grapefruit sinking into a red Jello parfait. My stomach growled. I wished I had placed an order. It had been a long time since coffee with Puppa this morning. And thanks to Austin, I never got one taste of Coney Deluxe at lunch.

The last bite of the golden fruit was consumed by the horizon when Sam finally appeared at my table.

"Now's a bad time, Tish. Why not come back around eight. I'll have things cleaned up and we can talk."

I planted my elbow on the table and leaned on my wrist. "No rush. I'm just making myself at home." Perhaps the words came out with a bite of sarcasm. But that was no excuse for her to get that snarl on her face.

She looked down on me from her almost six-foot height. "You've been making yourself at home in places you don't belong. Austin called and told me about your latest exploit. I asked you to stay away from Brad." She ground a fingertip on the tabletop. "Don't make me take out a restraining order."

I stood, looking eye to eye with her. "Considering you're standing in my great room, in my house, maybe I'm the one who should take out a restraining order."

"Let's not reduce this to a catfight. Joel and I got this place fair and square. You were dead, remember?"

"Pardon me for coming back to life and disturbing your thriving little enterprise and your cozy little family, while my fiancé lies dying in hospice care." I poked a finger toward her chest. "Yeah, you're going to have to get a restraining order to keep me away from Brad, because I'm not going to give up on him as easily as you did."

Her eyes were fierce. "Give the man the dignity of his own choices. You have no idea what he's been through. And thank God you're not his fiancée. Where were you when he needed you? Hiding out in some commune?" She shook her head, voice filled with disgust. "Deal with this: you walked out on us—all of us—when we could have used a little help around here. You couldn't handle things then. What makes you think it's any different now?"

I shook my head vehemently. "I didn't walk out. I did what Brad wanted me to do. He's the one who sent me to Del Gloria. He's the reason I'm still alive."

Sam looked around the room as if realizing for the first time that neither of us had lowered our voices. A blush crept over her cheeks as she met the glances of several diners.

Her voice was a livid whisper. "You have to leave. I'm working." She twirled and dodged tables on her way back to the kitchen.

I followed. "I need you to back me up, Sam. Please let me try to help Brad. If it's all my fault, at least give me a chance to fix it."

"The same way you fixed your grandmother's situation? Hmmm. Maybe you should get involved. You'd probably put Brad out of his misery in no time."

A quick inhale. How low could Sam get? "You're just waiting for him to be out of his misery? What is wrong with you?"

"Don't lecture me. I've been watching him go downhill the last six months, like a cancer patient who refuses chemo. It's just a matter of time. And you can only hope it ends quickly. Painlessly."

"What happened, Sam? You used to be the one painting the sky blue."

"That was before . . . all this. Now I'm about to be a mother. That's a pretty serious responsibility. I can't afford to be hanging out over the rainbow with you." She gave a wobble of her head. "Nice choice of clocks, by the way. Austin said Brad wanted it hung near the bed where he can hear it. Probably feels one hour closer to heaven every time it chimes." A wry voice. "Gotta hand it to you. You can sure pick 'em."

I crossed my arms. "You are not without blame, here, Samantha. If I recall, it was your idea to let Melissa Belmont and her kids hide out at the lodge. And between your ex-husband and her father, we're lucky we're still around to fight over the chimes on Brad's clock."

It had turned out that Melissa Belmont's father was Frank Majestic. I hadn't seen that slap in the face coming until the man's ugly mug was staring me in the eyes, demanding that I tell him where to find my AWOL father. Apparently, Dear Old Dad had turned in Majestic once before, a sin that fell in the "unforgivable" category. Samantha had been there with me on the couch that day. She'd made the leap that saved my life, tackling Majestic's crony to the ground before he could shoot me in a spot more serious than the arm.

I frowned at the breakthrough in my memory and shrank against the counter. "Sam. Let's not fight. We're on the same team. We want the same things."

"What is wrong with you? Everywhere you go, there's a dead body. And you want me to let you hang out with Brad? You know, it's just a matter of time before someone tracks you down and tries to kill you again. If not to get back at you for that whole drug thing, then to get back at your dad for whatever it was he did. It's like a plague."

"Well, doesn't that fit right in to your 'fast and painless' plans for Brad?"

"You know what? Why don't you take care of your family, and I'll take care of mine. I think Brad made it plain today that you two no longer have a relationship. I'm going to honor his decision. And if you have a compassionate bone in your body, you'll honor it too. Go find your father. But leave Brad alone."

Joel entered the room. "Everything okay in here, Hon?"

Samantha looked at me. "Well?"

I glared back and forth between the two of them with their haughty attitudes. *We're right and you're wrong,* their crossed arms and stiff lips said.

"Have it your way. I hope you can live with yourselves." I tromped toward the door, pivoting at the last moment. "By the way, you've got thirty days to vacate my property."

Out the door and into Puppa's truck. I peeled out, snow flying behind the vehicle as I raced up the drive. Just around the bend, a car came at me on the one-lane road. I slammed on the brakes and pulled to one side, letting the startled woman pass. Traffic on my backwoods driveway? I spun the wheels in anger. Uhhh. I hated Samantha and Joel for what they'd done to my once-private hideaway.

I fled to the lake house, the scenery passing in a blur of tears. Puppa was sitting in the living room, reading a newspaper, and looking lost in the empty space.

He lowered the pages as I entered. "How'd it go?"

I flopped forlorn onto the love seat, feet asunder, hands in my lap. I couldn't even talk, my throat was so full of pent-up anger and grief. Though I tried to stop them, tears kept dripping down my face. I wiped them on my hands, and wiped my hands on my pants, not caring if Puppa saw me at my crudest.

"Not good, eh?" he said. He folded the paper and set it on the floor by his chair. He walked over, snuggling me on the love seat, a little pat on my shoulder. My body gave an occasional shudder while I told him the day's events. As I talked, my emotional baggage gradually packed up and shipped out. By the time I got to the latest visit to the lodge and my argument with Sam, my stomach was gurgling.

"Hungry?" he asked.

I nodded, staring off.

"Come on. Food always helps." He got up and pulled me to my feet, dragging me, mute, into the kitchen. "What'll it be?" he asked, opening the freezer door. "Pizza, fish sticks, potpie, or TV dinner?"

I shrugged my ambivalence.

"Patricia," he said, pulling out two potpies, "don't take Samantha's overprotective attitude personally. She's been through a lot with this situation. She suffered a broken heart early on when Brad first threw in the towel. You can't expect her to get her hopes up now, when it seems he's bent on dying. She needs to take care of herself more than ever."

"I'm so angry." Grabbing the printed cardboard from Puppa, I tore open the boxes, digging out the delicate frozen pastry as Puppa set the oven. Chunks of crust fell on the counter. "Sam's not leaving me with any options here, short of kidnapping Brad and sneaking him off to Mexico."

Wordless, Puppa set a cookie sheet on the counter.

I slammed the pies onto the metal tray. "Gee, you think border patrol would be suspicious?"

Puppa slid supper in the oven and set the timer. "Don't get yourself worked up. You can't control what Sam or Brad does. Ask yourself what you can control, then focus on that."

I scooped crumbs into my hand and tossed them in the trash. What was my course now? Would I fight for the lodge? Would I fight for Brad? Would I disappear into hiding? Would I return to Del Gloria and finish my college education? I had loads of options, just no answers.

Opening the fridge, I fished for the cottage cheese. The stamp on the container promised it was fresh. I put it out, along with a bag of not-quite-stale bread and a slab of butter. "I haven't heard anything more about Melissa. What's she up to these days?"

"She cut ties with the area and relocated, forwarding address withheld. Said she'd love to be back in touch when the kids are older. Right now she's just lying low and working on getting her life in order."

I nodded. "So what'd she have? A boy or a girl?" Melissa had been expecting her third child at the time of the ordeal.

"Little boy. Named him Gerard Owen Russo." Puppa's face blushed with pride. "Your cousin Gerard married Melissa in July."

I slumped against the counter. Another Russo baby. So, both my bachelor cousins were married off. I'd missed two weddings and a funeral while I was dead.

I put on a smile. "I'm glad for Gerard. Seemed like he

and Melissa really respected one another, just from the little time I saw them together. And to be honest, I was getting worried he was one of the casualties this spring. Nobody's said a word about him."

"He took a bullet to the knee, so he has to take things easy now. But he and Melissa couldn't be happier. I sure miss them around here, but they're both glad to be on a new adventure. Justin Jones wasn't as lucky."

I'd never heard the name before. "Was that the skinny kid with the gun?" I'd called him Skuzz, loathing everything about him, right down to the waistband on the Hanes peeking out from his low-riders.

"He was one troubled kid. Shouldn't have been involved with Majestic to begin with. He met his match when he messed with Candice."

I bristled at the name. "I guess I've been reluctant to ask about her too. Tell me she's behind bars." At least if she were in jail, I'd feel better. She'd confessed murder to me and I'd closed my eyes to it, instead leaving it to the police to solve the case and arrest her. But things had snowballed and next thing I knew, she'd shot Brad. No wonder I'd blocked the event from my memory. How do you live with guilt like that?

"Candice left Frank with a head injury—too bad the guy's got a skull like a steel drum—then took off. Just vanished," Puppa said.

"She vanished?"

So Candice was still out there, on the loose, able to hurt anyone at any time for whatever reason. The two halves of my heart tugged in opposite directions. How could you love someone deeply on the one hand, but hate so much of what they've done on the other? And yet, wouldn't it be for the greater good if she was taken out of commission, after what she did to Brad . . . all because of me?

The timer dinged.

"Dinner is served," Puppa said, putting on oven mitts.

We ate the steaming potpies in the dining room, the two of us lost at one end of the twelve-seat table.

"So, whatever happened to you that night?" I asked. "The last I saw of you was at the Watering Hole honky-tonk. We were diving for cover out the back door. You went one way, Candice went the other." I shrugged. "And I almost took a plunge into Mead Quarry."

"That night just kept getting better and better," Puppa said. "I caught up to Candice and tried to get her to turn herself in. Told her she could cut a deal, get involved in the witness protection program, but—" he shook his head and gave a sigh of disgust—"talk about stubborn. She just waved her gun at me and threw me out of the car. She must have changed her mind about running when she realized Majestic would be on the warpath. Sounds like she got to the lodge just in time to save you."

"Just in time to shoot Brad, you mean."

Puppa cradled his head in his hands as if weary. "I think she's got problems with men."

"That's one way to put it. Plus she's got control issues, a cold-blooded streak—"

"Enough. She's suffered enough. You don't need to heap on more condemnation."

Humbled, I nodded. "You still love her, don't you?"

"Never stopped." He rubbed at a spot under his eye.

"I used to think she was a cancer in my brain, always there, always on my mind, growing over the years. I'd have done anything to have every memory, every thought of her surgically removed from my head. The idea of being with another woman turned my stomach. It was like she'd ruined me. It was Candice—or nobody. But after studying and praying and puzzling over it, I realized that I wasn't infected with a cancer. I was infected with love. I love that woman unconditionally. She's capable of murder, yet I still love her. When I realized she was involved with Majestic and the local drug trade, I wanted to be angry. I wanted to hate her. Maybe then I could stop wanting to be with her. Maybe then she'd be out of my head. But it made no difference. Since that night at the Watering Hole, I've tried to find her. I want to bring her home. Show her that I love her no matter what. If only she'd let me."

He broke into tears, and then so did I, weeping beside him, my cloth napkin soaked in the by-products of grief.

Was I crying because I was sympathetic to his plight? I knew better. I cried because the woman he loved unconditionally took from me the man I loved unconditionally.

My shoulders heaved and I struggled for air. My heart beat painfully, squeezed by some cruel hand inside my chest.

I loved my grandfather. I really did. But I couldn't ignore my own torment. There was only one way to ease the pain of my broken heart.

I took a calming breath. At least now I knew what course I would take.

30

With a final swipe of napkin against nose, I crossed my arms and leaned back.

"I saw Officer Segerstrom today," I said. "He suggested I lay low for a while."

Puppa adjusted in his chair. "Going back into hiding?" He sounded too tired to care.

I nodded. "Guess you could say that."

"Probably a good idea. There's nothing worth fighting for here."

I bit my tongue. Did he really think I was giving up on Brad? Did he really think I was giving up on the lodge? Maybe it was better to let him think that. He would certainly be more cooperative than if he knew what I actually had in mind.

Puppa scrunched his brow. "They found you in California. How about Cuba this time? I know a guy who keeps an apartment in Havana. Might be the perfect hangout for now." He shook his head and made a face of disgust. "You'd think Frank Majestic would get sick of revenge. But I guess that's all he knows."

"Not Cuba," I said. "I think I'll try Canada this time. Always wanted to go there."

Puppa got a startled look on his face. "What's so interesting about Canada? It's no different than here."

I gave a shrug. "This whole Brad thing, the lodge thing . . . I don't know. Makes me want to head to Canada."

Puppa was slow to respond. "I guess Canada is as good a place as any. You'll have to make sure you stay off the beaten track, though. Don't want to leave a trail."

"I'll just go where the trail leads me." I kept my voice nonchalant. Puppa didn't need to know that last time I saw Candice, she mentioned her escape plans to Canada. With a little help from some friends, I might be able to track her down—and bring her to justice.

Would that change Brad's mind about dying? Probably not. But it would help me stay focused on living. With my heart still crushed from my visit to River's Edge this afternoon, and nothing better to do, I figured hunting down Candice LeJeune would give a feeling of purpose to my otherwise aimless existence.

"So," I said, pushing my chair away from the table and clearing off my spot, "if you don't mind, I need to borrow your computer."

Puppa complied, a dazed look across his face as he set me up on his Internet connection.

"Thanks." I tapped the keys, typing a greeting to Koby. Puppa hovered over my shoulder a minute, then left the room.

"How are Celia and Portia doing?" I asked first thing in the email. Then I got right to the point. "I need a favor," I wrote. "I need help finding a missing person." I was sure my grandfather had already used the means at his disposal to find Candice, but maybe Koby had a fresh approach up his sleeve that would pin her down. I gave him the rundown on Candice: full name, where she lived, where she was born, approximate age, physical description, occupation, the car she owned, and a fairly accurate account of why I wanted to find her, minus the revenge bit.

"I really hope you can help me," I added. "She's the love of my grandfather's life. It's kind of my Christmas present to him." I cringed at my own duplicity even as I put grandfather's phone number on the bottom to speed the process. Then I hit the Send button. With any luck Koby would be at his computer, able to hear the *ding* of new mail.

I paced the length of the lake house, dining room to living room and back, watching dusk disappear into night.

Puppa had turned the television on low and was laughing at some oddball detective and his daffy assistant as they went around LA solving murders. I wondered if they were astute enough to unravel the mystery of Jane Rigg's death. Then again, they were just actors. Probably couldn't do anything without a script.

An hour passed. The show ended with the bad guys getting carted off by the police and the detective conquering another personal challenge. Outside, the bay was covered by darkness. The only sight was my own reflection in the windows as I wore a path on the wood floor.

"Patricia, come sit. What are you so anxious about?" Puppa patted the open spot next to him on the love seat.

I stopped and fiddled with my hands. "Oh, just worried about Brad. I'm more and more convinced that he'll never change course." My voice hitched. "It's hard, you know, accepting him giving up like this. I just don't understand it."

Puppa stood and came over to the windows, staring through his own image to the blackness beyond. "It is hard. But for Brad, it's an understandable choice. Health was important to him. He'll never have that again."

The tension in my chest exploded. "It's not understandable." I was a mass of ranting rage. "Of course health was important to him. It's important to everybody. But when something like that happens, you make the best of it. I know plenty of people who had bad things happen to them and they didn't give up on life. They kept on living. They walked again even though they didn't have legs. They worked again, even though they were stuck in a wheelchair. They loved again, even though their hearts had been cut out by greedy pimps." I flung around and stared him in the eyes. "Brad's choice is not understandable. And it's not acceptable. But if that's how he wants it, then Brad is safe from me. I can't bear to see him like that. It kills me. And if there's one thing I plan on doing, it's living."

Puppa stared at me, a dumbfounded look on his face.

I took a deep breath, gearing up for Act Two, when the phone rang. The digital tones jarred me out of my rampage.

Puppa answered and handed me the phone. "It's for you."

"Thanks." I snuck off to Grandma Olivia's old room and shut the doors.

"It's Koby," came the voice on the other end. "How are you holding up? You ditched us for the holidays, huh?"

I tried to smile. "I'm doing good. But I need to get this item taken care of so I can get back to Del Gloria. How are Celia and Portia doing?"

"Portia's home and healing," he said. "They told her to plan on six weeks before she could get back on the project. Celia's out of the woods, but will probably be off the team for the duration."

Guilt swelled up in that already overwhelmed area of my chest. How could I do my part for the team if I was chasing down Candice LeJeune? I made some calculations. It was December 23. That left two weeks before the new semester at Del Gloria. If I worked quickly, I could do what had to be done Candice-wise, and still get back to California to help the team finish on time.

"I'm glad the girls will be alright," I told Koby. "But I feel so terrible. If it weren't for me, Simon Scroll would never have firebombed that place."

"How could you have known? We're just glad you're okay."

I swallowed, humbled. "So. What did you find out?"

"It was pretty tough without a social security number," Koby said. "But I did what I could. Which do you want first, the good news or the bad news."

I closed my eyes. "Good news first."

"I found a trail. Leads to a place called Churchill Falls. Middle of nowhere. Like falling off the edge of the world. Travel was booked for—"

I heard the sound of paper crinkling.

"Here it is—late May."

"That's it." My heart raced. Only a matter of time. "What's the bad news?"

"She never arrived. Never used the tickets. Changed her plans. I don't know."

I looked around the bedroom and gave a discouraged sigh. "Back to square one, huh?"

"Not necessarily. Ask yourself, who does she know in Churchill Falls? What made her choose that place over any other?"

I shrugged. "Beats me. I never heard of it. She was probably just hoping to disappear."

"Maybe. But most people select a location for a reason. They don't just disappear without thinking it through. Weird thing is, Churchill Falls is a company town. Population seven hundred. Exists solely for the employees of the world's largest underground hydroelectric plant. Not exactly a tourist trap or a hot retirement spot. Makes it pretty hard to blend in. Maybe she's visited there before. Maybe she has friends, family, a job opportunity. Can you check around and see if it rings any bells with anyone?"

"Candice is a photographer. Why would she relocate to the end of the world?"

"To take pictures? I can guarantee she's not there taking soil samples. The place is practically in the Arctic Circle. Temps get pretty nippy."

"Can I ask . . . how did you find these travel plans?"

"If I tell you, I have to kill you."

I smiled and shook my head. "What if . . ." I squeezed

my eyes shut and thought for a moment, "what if Candice wanted people to think she'd gone to this place, but then didn't go. Maybe headed the opposite direction?"

"It's possible. But it's also possible that something prevented her from going there. I checked later lists, for both air and land travel, but never came up with that name. But she could have changed her name and arrived later."

"Hmmm. Or, maybe she just drove."

"Doubtful. There's one road in and out of that place. It's pretty desolate."

"So how do I get there?"

"You're crazy."

"I'm serious. I have to check out this lead. Just in case."

"It'll boggle your mind."

"Try me."

"You asked for it. Hypothetically, you could get on a plane leaving Marquette tomorrow and land three stops and one day later in a place called Goose Bay. From there you could take Provincial Air to Churchill Falls. But not until the twenty-sixth. No flights Christmas Day."

"Book it."

"What?"

"Please, Koby. I'm on a mission. I have to find this woman and get back to California before the semester starts. No dilly-dallying."

"You haven't heard the price tag."

"Price doesn't matter. I'll spend my last dime if it means finding Candice."

"Some Christmas present. Your grandfather must really love her."

I swallowed and gritted my teeth. "Oh yeah. Yeah. He sure does. Getting her back would be the best Christmas present ever."

"Alright, then. I'll book your travel and email your itinerary to you. Your flight leaves tomorrow at 2:30 from Marquette. When do you want to return?"

"Give me a week. That should be long enough."

"With travel time, that puts you back in Port Silvan on Jan third. I'll give you a couple days to recover, then you're taking a flight to Del Gloria. I'm booking it now. You WILL be on that plane."

I gave a quick laugh. "Thanks, Koby. You're the best. I'll transfer the funds tomorrow."

"And Tish—it sounds weird to call you that—God go with you. Do what you have to, then get back here where we need you most."

I nodded, though his words brought only a vision of Brad lying in River's Edge, longing for my return.

"Thanks, Koby. You're a true friend." I hung up the phone, hoping I'd find the energy, and the courage, to do what needed to be done.

31

First thing in the morning, I headed to the bank to take care of financial details. With a little finagling, I was able to access my accounts.

"Lucky for you your estate hasn't reached probate yet," the teller reported. "Thought for sure you were dead. The church ladies put on a good funeral luncheon. Heard the food was delicious."

"Nope. Just a big misunderstanding." I cleared my throat. "I hope you'll keep my visit confidential. To some people, I'm better off dead."

She nodded, her brown hair bobbing. "I understand. It's all hush-hush where I'm concerned." She counted out the cash I requested and put it in an envelope.

I smiled and thanked her, figuring it didn't matter if she blabbed about my return. I was flying out in a few hours anyway.

Back at Puppa's, I took a few moments to tie up loose ends. Scrounging up a piece of stationery from his office, I sat down to write.

Dear Professor Braddock,

Thank you for allowing me to stay in your beautiful home and helping me further my education. I am enclosing a check, an approximate payment in full for all the expenses you incurred during my stay, including tuition. I am no longer in need of your patronage and will make my own arrangements for lodging when I return to Del Gloria next semester.

Many blessings,
Patricia Amble

I stared at the note. Couldn't be more to the point than that. At least now he could start looking for a new heir. I didn't want anything from him. Not after the way he'd dealt with Brad.

My pen slipped out of my hand and I covered my face at the memory of the exchange between Brad and his estranged father. Here I'd been caught up in my own family's dysfunctions when all along Brad had a wacky family too. But with Brad, you never knew it. Before his injury, he didn't obsess over the fact that he was half orphan like me. He'd come to terms with his parentage.

Sadly, Brad's state of mind had changed in the past seven months. Even though I was angry with Denton, I still empathized with the professor when it came to Brad's lifetime of treating him as less than a father. What else could Denton do but use greed and jealousy to try to get Brad back on his feet? I'd stooped to low tactics myself. At this point, anything was worth a try.

Already weary, I sealed and stamped the letter. I would drop it at the post office on my way to the airport.

Upstairs, I repacked my meager belongings. When I was done, I sat on the edge of the bed, staring at the suitcase that belonged to Denton. I'd scrounged it from his attic before I took off on my jaunt from Sacramento to Manistique. The contents fell short of appropriate for winter gear for the Upper Peninsula I could only imagine how inadequate my clothing would be in a place like Churchill Falls, the day after Christmas.

Another cup of coffee, then out to the waiting truck. Puppa had agreed to drive me to the airport, but only after some major convincing.

"Who would think to look for me in a place like Churchill Falls? Come on, it's the perfect hideout."

He shook his head, doubtful. "Too small. Too remote. Too far away."

"Like I said, it's perfect." I didn't tell him I'd be returning in a little over a week. He might not be as open to driving me if he thought I'd deceived him.

On our way out, I waved to my horse. Poor Goldie. Would I ever get a chance to spend time with her? My life felt like one of those rides I used to love at the fair when I was young. Life spun so fast, I spent most of my time plastered to the wall. And when things slowed down, I was too motion sick to feel like doing much of anything. It seemed any attempt to slam on the brakes backfired, only adding to the chaos. Still, I couldn't help but feel there were just a few more loose ends flying in the breeze. Once those were tied up, I'd have that peaceful, serene life I wished for.

We drove through town, passing the bank, Sinclair's

Grocery, and the Silvan Bay Grille. I pointed to the post office.

"Can you stop a minute? I've got a letter to mail."

Puppa pulled up to the drop box and posted it for me. Then we were headed to Sawyer International, a fancy name for the airport south of Marquette. Past the sign for the cider mill, where I turned to get to Candice's house for tea every Thursday. Past the sign for Valentine's Bay Lodge, the house Sam and Cousin Joel stole from me. Past Silvan Corners and onto US-2, headed west, the same direction I'd taken that day I'd run away from everything . . . and everyone. A quick stop at the convenience store in Rapid River, then north on 41.

"You sure about this?" Puppa asked as we neared our destination.

"Very."

"You don't know anyone there. How are you going to get along? How will you get a job? Where will you live?" Puppa asked.

"Come on," I said, swatting his arm. "You're taking all the adventure out of it. It's not fun if you've got everything planned ahead." I stole a glance his way. "Have you even heard of Churchill Falls before now?"

To my surprise, he nodded. "Once. A long time ago."

I gave him a questioning look.

"Jake, your dad, was looking into it when he was young," Puppa said. "Thought he'd like working at a power plant. A lot like the paper mill, he figured. But, I never heard of it again."

My brain churned. "Do you think . . ."

"No," Puppa cut me off. "I already looked into it. No Jacob Russo in Churchill Falls."

The snap in his voice shut down the topic.

I stared at the snow-covered pines flying past and tried to swallow the lump in my throat. Why did I even get my hopes up when it came to my father? Couldn't I just accept the fact the guy had dropped off the face of the planet, or more likely was dead? But it seemed the fairy-tale princess inside me wanted to believe in magic. Wanted to believe she had a father out there somewhere who wasn't a penniless frog, but a king in disguise, ready to throw a banquet for his long-lost daughter the moment of their reunion.

My knuckle caught an escaping tear. I slouched in my seat, afraid to say anything more in case my voice came out a pathetic *croak*.

We followed the signs to the airport. Puppa parked the truck and came inside the clean, modern facility, visiting with me as I printed my boarding pass at the kiosk, then brought my suitcase to the small-town baggage checkpoint where my luggage was inspected on a table while I watched. The guard rubbed circular white pads on the inside surfaces, in case I was some terrorist with bomb-making residue on my clothing. Other passengers scrutinized the process as they waited in line, leaving me glad I packed my undies on the bottom. The security officer put the chemical pads under a sensor, then gave me the green light.

Puppa and I headed toward the waiting area, where he could sit with me until the boarding call. At that point, airline passengers would go through security screening to a separate waiting area that had everything but a restroom.

"There's no guarantee you'll be safe from Majestic and his goons even in Churchill Falls, you know," Puppa said.

"I know. But I figure if anyone gives me trouble, law enforcement can step in."

"I don't know if you're faithful or foolish, Patricia. Sometimes you ask God to perform a miracle to cover your back, when you're someplace you shouldn't be to begin with."

I gave a nervous chuckle, remembering my bargain with God on the cliff that day. God had certainly held up his end of the deal and got me out of my tight spot. But here I was, about to do something else stupid. Was God obligated to rescue me from this whopper of a mission, or had he already done his part and could now just sit back and laugh as I dangled from the next tricky spot?

With revenge my prime directive, I resolved it was too much to ask of God to go with me anyway. I'd have to leave God here at Sawyer International and hope he'd be waiting for me when I returned.

The call for my flight came over the loudspeaker.

Puppa stood. "Well, Patricia. I'm going to miss you. I wish you could have stayed put awhile. I sure enjoy your company."

"I'll be back. Don't worry. You'll see me again, maybe sooner than you think." Yeah, but would he ever speak to me again after what I had planned for his girlfriend? Maybe that "friend's" apartment in Havana was waiting for the possibility of Puppa reconciling with Candice.

If that were the case, Puppa might not appreciate my quest for justice.

We hugged.

"Take care, Patricia. I love you," Puppa said, walking me to the security line.

"I love you too. I'll be fine. Now go." I gave him a playful swat and watched him leave the building, wishing I could have my revenge and still keep my grandfather. But somehow, I knew I couldn't have both.

32

A night in an airport lounge chair and a night in a Goose Bay hotel room. I was convinced there was no difference between them when it came to quality of sleep. Maybe it was my nerves that had kept me awake, or maybe second thoughts. Either way, I felt caged sitting in the commuter plane on the last leg of my journey, a bundle of pent-up energy ready to explode or expire. I looked through the scratched-up Plexiglas window as the noisy Provincial liner circled the Churchill Falls field.

From my seat in the air, the town looked like a wheel with two sides lopped off. An extension of long, straight roads ran off in one direction, ruining any symmetry that might have pleased visitors from outer space. To the south, hills rose on the horizon. And to the north, there was nothing but a flat expanse of snow and water.

With a final turn, the plane landed and the sparse array of occupants disembarked. Inside the terminal, I claimed my oversized suitcase and hooked up with a local woman heading to town.

The middle-aged brunette gave me a running commentary on the company-owned settlement as we headed to the inn, where Koby, my thoughtful travel planner, had booked a room for me.

The car traveled east on Churchill Falls Road and hung a right toward the lopped-off wheel part of town. We turned on a street that began with an *O* but was impossible to pronounce. And by the time we reached our destination, I'd given up on trying to read the French-Canadian and native Inuit words.

According to my hostess, the Churchill Falls power plant and the community that served it had been built in the early seventies. My hotel room confirmed the story, the architecture and amenities testimony that no updates had been made since then.

But beds were beds, and within moments of bolting the door to my room, I climbed under the covers and fell asleep. I must have been dreaming, but I could have sworn I heard the doorknob jiggle, and the door creak open. A man entered the room. It was Brad. He'd found me and come to take me home. He snuck over to the bed and leaned over me. I could feel his hot breath on my cheek, the heat of his skin where his hand touched my neck, the brush of his lips to mine . . . Still dreaming, I jerked open my eyes. Brad dissolved like a vapor, gone. I sat up in bed, checking the room. Empty.

Disappointed, I flopped back to my pillow and tried to shut down my brain.

A few hours later, I woke to the squawk of hunger pangs. I sat up, throwing off the green and yellow floral bedspread, and yawned. When we'd pulled up to the inn, my driver had called the building the Town Center, mentioning that the complex also housed the school, theater, library, bank, post office, and most importantly, a restaurant.

I freshened up in the mirror, running a brush through the hair I'd managed to save from Maize's scissors. The California summer had bleached the ends to a straw color now topped by dark winter roots. With my daily wardrobe consisting of a sweatshirt, jeans, and a ponytail, it was easy to forget there was such a thing as style. I threw on a dab of makeup, hoping to perk up my still-sleepy eyes. A fresh coat of lipstick, a cardigan over a turtleneck, and I was headed down the hall toward food.

But when the restaurant appeared dark and closed, I walked to the front desk instead.

I cleared my throat hoping for the clerk's attention.

"Excuse me, where would I get something to eat?" I asked.

The woman laid the novel she'd been reading facedown on the desk and stood, walking to the counter.

"Sorry. Restaurant's closed. Chef quit last week."

My stomach gurgled. "What about the grocery store? Isn't there one in this building?"

"Grocery store, bank, post office, school, you name it, it's in here. But you can't shop until Thursday. It's closed for the holiday."

A squeak from my intestines. "But Christmas was yesterday."

"It's always closed Sunday and Monday, but since they fell on holidays, the employees get two extra days off. That's the way it is with The Company."

"Oh." *Squeeeeeek*. My stomach roiled with hunger.

The look on my face must have earned her pity.

"Here." She handed me a slip of paper. "It's a voucher for the mess hall. That's where the plant workers eat. Probably better than what you'd get here anyway."

I took the paper like it was manna. "Which way do I go?"

She pointed at the front door. "Out there, then take a right on Naskaupi. It's about a half kilometer down."

"Thanks." I walked back to my room to bundle against the frigid wind, glad for the attack of good sense that overcame me during my layover in Boston. I slipped into my new hip-length cream parka with fur trim, feeling chic enough to put Lara Croft to shame. A pair of snuggly wool-lined boots, hat, and mittens, and I was ready to take on the frozen tundra.

Not another soul braved the weather. I hiked alone down the street, grateful everything I'd need during my stay was contained in a one-mile radius. Snow had begun to fall and a steady breeze kicked up swirls that stung my cheeks. I pulled my hood tight around my face and stood under the glow of a streetlight looking at the building marked Staff Dormitory & Mess Hall. My stomach plunged, suddenly no longer hungry, as I wondered what I'd really do to Candice LeJeune if I actually found her. I resisted taking another step, the voice in my head screaming, "Go back! Go back!"

But the thought of Brad, wasting away at River's Edge, never again to be mine, kept me moving toward the door. I pulled it open. Light streamed onto the snow. I stepped inside and brushed off the flakes. A scattering of plant employees sat around several cafeteria-style tables. An array of steaming food was set up off to one side, the smell of turkey and stuffing curing my temporary nausea. After briefly making eye contact with a few curious onlookers, I bellied up to the buffet, handed over my voucher, and piled my plate high.

The recluse in me saw a solitary spot at a far-off table. But the bloodhound in me led me toward a table of four.

"Mind if I join you?" I gave a big, friendly smile to the three men and one woman.

"Go ahead." The woman gestured for me to take a seat.

I set my tray down and scooted into a chair.

"What brings you to town this time of year? Family?" she asked.

I mulled over my answer. Candice could be considered family. She'd always said I was like a granddaughter to her. "Yes. Family."

"What's the name? We probably know them." The man spoke with a French accent.

The group gave a laugh.

"I suppose you know everybody in town." I smiled along with them.

"If they've been here any length of time, we know them," said the French-speaking man.

"Ah," I said. "What about one who arrived recently?" I dug in my purse for the picture of Candice I'd packed for a moment just like this.

"Sometimes. If they've been over to the bar," he chortled.

"I'm looking for my grandmother. Her name's Candice LeJeune, but she may be here under another name."

"Ah, she is running from an ex-husband, no doubt."

I shrugged. "Something like that." I set the photo on the table. "Have you seen her?"

The dark-haired Frenchman picked up the photo. "She is very young and beautiful. It is easy to see why she is being hunted."

"The photo was taken more than twenty years ago. She's in her midsixties by now. But she looks about the same as she did back then."

"It would not be wise to hide in Churchill Falls if you are an older person. Here, they must leave town at retirement age. The Company only rents to active employees. All others must go."

I watched as the group passed the photo, looking at Candice's picture and shaking their heads. Disappointment swelled in my throat.

"Thanks. I'm staying at the inn, if you happen to see her. I'm Tasha Stewart, by the way." At the last moment, I decided that my pseudonym would be a safer route, though my travel arrangements had been made under the name Patricia Amble. I could imagine the innkeeper's confusion if someone did try to contact me.

I dug into my meal, savoring the juicy breast meat and gravy. In my mind, I thanked God for the Christmas feast, even though I didn't deserve it. I dabbed at my mouth with a napkin, catching the Frenchman looking at me. I blushed, uncomfortable under his gaze.

"I am sorry to stare at you. You remind me so much of a girl that is a friend to my daughter."

I nodded and waved a hand. "Oh, I get that all the time." Back in Rawlings, I turned out to be the virtual twin of a total stranger.

"Do you see it, Therese?" he asked the woman. "Doesn't she remind you of Monique?"

"Very much. Even her mannerisms." She turned to me. "Perhaps you are related?"

"I don't think that's possible."

"What makes you think your grandmother came to Churchill Falls? This isn't a place you come by accident," the Frenchman asked.

What could it hurt to just tell them the truth—or at least most of it?

"She made travel arrangements to this area last May. But the tickets were never used. I thought it was worth checking out. Just in case she arrived later, by car or something."

He nodded. "We have tourists along the Trans-Labrador Highway all summer. Perhaps she visited then."

"Maybe." Discouragement crept into my voice.

"How long are you staying with us? You must take a tour of the power plant while you are here."

"I'm here a week."

"Wonderful," Therese said. "Tomorrow you must come to dinner at my house. It is my daughter's birthday and we are having a party."

I almost declined, but the thought of spending a week alone in my hotel room made me nod in agreement. "Thank you. That's very kind. I'll enjoy that."

Therese gave me directions to her home. Then the group took their leave.

I nibbled at a glob of cranberry sauce and watched as workers entered and exited the mess hall. Finished with my meal, I cleared my tray and poured a cup of coffee, helping myself to a slice of chocolate layer cake for dessert. My fork played with the smooth frosting. I sipped my steaming beverage, hoping I wasn't dooming myself to a sleepless night.

Across the room, several workers walked in. One of them was a slim older woman. The group got in line and I watched as they laughed and loaded their dishes with food. I studied the woman's movements and facial features, thinking that beneath the long blond hairdo might be short gray hair and the face from the photo. As the five workers sat down, I nixed the idea that one could be Candice. Or maybe I just hoped it wasn't her. My bravery quotient had dropped from ten to zero since my arrival in Churchill Falls.

I headed back to my hotel room, glum. Would I be able to carry out my plans against Candice even if I had the opportunity? Just what would I do if I found her? *Be a good girl, Candice, and stay put while I get the police.* She'd laugh in my face. I had no leverage. As far as I could tell, there was no gun shop in Churchill Falls. And probably no tazers lying around either. That left the option of wrestling her into submission, which seemed unlikely given her remarkable strength for a woman of her age, or hitting her in the head with a heavy object, which would probably require some element of surprise. The way I was gallivanting around town, looking more like Tish Amble than Tasha Stewart, she'd see me coming 2.5 kilometers away.

The more I thought about it, the angrier I got. I gave a savage kick to a mound of snow in my path. Maybe I wouldn't wait for the cops. Maybe I'd be the one to give her what she deserved, then and there. As scenarios of vengeance scuttered through my mind, I played each of them out to their violent end.

Back at the inn, I stomped my boots on the entry rug and took the stairs to my room. Who was I kidding? Maybe I'd had it in me to sprinkle some pills in my suffering grandmother's arthritic hands, but when it came time, would I really have the gumption to deliberately kill someone? Especially where blood was involved?

I tamped down my anger, reverting to plan A. Turning her in to the cops, extraditing her to Michigan, testifying at her trial, seeing her go to prison . . . that would be my revenge. On the other hand, knowing Candice's history, she wouldn't let the cops take her anyway. She'd escape, or die trying.

My mind flashed to the day at the lodge, with Brad lying on the floor, his chest covered in red. I'd felt his blood on my hands, not comprehending at the time what it meant to my future. Not comprehending that it would lead to this day, this moment, this place.

Wasn't that enough reason to seek my revenge? Blood for blood. Her life for the life she took from me.

33

Inside my hotel room, I showered, hoping to wash away the images I'd concocted in my mind. I dropped into bed and watched an hour of lousy cable programming, then fell asleep, tossing and turning through the night.

By morning, my mind was back on food. This time I headed straight for the hotel desk for a breakfast voucher. With a clear sky above and only a light wind, I took the long way around to the mess hall, heading left out the front door instead of right.

I found myself on another street with a name too difficult to pronounce. I passed a group of apartment buildings and turned down Raven Street, the outside circle of the lopped-off wheel. Boxy prefab houses in various pastels lined both sides of the road. Labradorians, or perhaps just The Company, seemed to lack the notion of porches or trees, making the neighborhood feel antiseptic. Behind the homes, a ridge of snow-covered pines reached for the sky.

Now and then a car pulled past, the occupants giving

me a curious stare as they drove by. I angled up Eagle Street, the cold starting to penetrate boots that promised more than they delivered. Ahead was the mess hall. I pushed inside, joining the crowd for coffee and a hot meal.

I sat kitty-corner from a klatch of men and women gearing up for their day. I tried to blend in but noticed several stares, nods, and muted conversations around the cafeteria. Perhaps I was paranoid. Then again, the workers probably were speculating on my visit to town, perhaps having heard about my search for a missing person.

A gust of wind blew past my feet as another group came in from the cold. Finished with my oatmeal and eggs, I cleared my tray, pausing on my way out to zip my coat. I walked without looking as I fiddled with the pull—and collided with the chest of a plant worker.

My head shot up. "I'm sorry," I gushed, catching his startled look. "Just trying to bundle up before I hit the door."

I tried to brush off the incident, but the fifty-something man stood stock-still in front of me, staring. Eyes wide, mouth open, stepping backward as if he'd seen a ghost.

I squinted at him, confused by his reaction. "Are you okay?"

He nodded, mute, then twirled and dashed off toward the restrooms.

That was the first time I'd gotten that reaction. Never thought my face could make a man ill.

I slipped on my hat and mittens, pulled my hood tight around my face, and walked directly back to the hotel, wishing the library wasn't on the same holiday schedule as the grocery store. I'd left the book I'd borrowed from Denton's shelf of classics back at Puppa's for safekeeping.

To pass the day, I watched cooking shows and twiddled my thumbs, not having the faintest clue where to start looking for Candice beyond the mess hall. After a fascinating lesson on fluffy cheese soufflés, I stretched out on the floor, loosening up muscles tight from traveling. With my face so close to the ground, I could fully examine the lint and miscellaneous other particles that had landed on the carpet. I got up and dusted off, then got ready for Therese's party, thrilled to have been invited to dinner by a complete stranger my first night in town.

I double-checked for Candice's picture in my purse, ready to show it at the gathering should the opportunity arise. With parka and boots on, off I went to the party. I stopped at the hotel desk for an envelope and put in a generous gift for the girl whose friend looked a lot like me.

A few blocks away, I found the gray-sided house. Several cars were parked in the drive and a couple more along the curb. As I knocked on the door, I wondered how all those people would fit in the tiny space.

Therese opened the door wide. "Tasha. Welcome."

I stepped in, surprised that the interior felt roomy and open. A group of partygoers filled the living room. I smiled at the blur of faces, nervous to be surrounded by strangers.

Therese led me through to the kitchen. "This is my daughter Renee. Renee, this is Tasha Stewart, visiting from the States."

I shook the hand of the dark-haired beauty, who glowed like a candle atop a sixteenth-birthday cake. "It's nice to meet you," I said, amazed at the radiance of youth.

She returned the compliment, then joined a group of young people at the table.

Therese led me around the house, introducing me to her clique. I lost track of names, and before we were done, the faces began to look the same. We'd made a circle through the living room and were headed back into the kitchen.

"Oh," Therese exclaimed, "you haven't met Monique yet. Wait until you see her. You will be amazed."

Heads turned when we reached the table of teens, as if I'd already been a topic of conversation. I spotted my look-alike right away. Long, reddish-brown hair, and a nose and mouth the same as mine. I'd always thought the bottom half of my face was run-of-the-mill, but Monique was beautiful. Her eyes were brown, not green like mine, and had a rounder shape, but somehow our eyebrows had the same arch to them.

Therese introduced us. "She belongs to Suzette and Roger Jamison."

We shook hands. Neither of us spoke, probably stunned speechless. There seemed no credible explanation, except that we both had Noah as a common ancestor. After a moment of silence, those around the table began to fidget, no doubt as uncomfortable as I felt.

"Please help yourself to some food, Tasha," Therese said, helping me out of an awkward spot.

I gladly dove into the array of breads, meats, cheeses, and side salads. Filling my plate, I wandered into the living room, looking for an opening in a conversation. The group on the sofa discussed the state of the Labrador/Newfoundland economy. I steered away when I heard grumblings over some sort of lopsided agreement the power company had with Quebec. Two couples standing near the hallway had extreme weather on their minds, with battery chargers and the high cost of fuel their main concerns. I drifted toward the front door where a man and a woman ate their sandwiches in silence. His back was turned to me, but she seemed to watch my every move.

I smiled at the eye contact. Then, feeling foolish and alone in the center of the room, I beelined in her direction. She seemed to panic as I drew near, her forty-something forehead scrunching as she made some sort of eye signals to the man across from her. I almost let the behavior chase me away, but I figured I might as well take a risk. What were the chances I'd ever see any of these people again?

I stuck out a hand as I drew near. "Hi. I'm Tasha."

She fumbled with her plate, nearly dropping it. "Suzette. Nice to meet you." Her hand felt sweaty in mine.

"Oh, you're Monique's mom."

I turned to the man, expectant. "And you must be Roger. Therese couldn't wait to introduce me to your daughter. From the looks of it, Monique and I could be sisters." I was the only one laughing.

Keeping his head down, Roger stuck out his hand. "Nice to meet you," he said.

I grabbed his fingers in mine. A shock of static zapped us on contact.

"Woo. Sorry about that," I said. At my words, he looked up and I got a peek at his face. "Hey. You're the guy I ran into at the mess hall. We're just doomed to have one painful encounter after another." I'd hoped he'd loosen up at my joke, but he seemed to have the same sickened reaction as our last meeting.

"Excuse me," he said, heading off down the hall.

Suzette covered for him. "He's not feeling his best today."

I nodded, surreptitiously wiping my hand on my pants to get rid of any virus before I touched my food again.

She jumped in to fill the silence. "So you're from the States?"

"Yes, I am."

"What brings you to town this time of year? Skiing?"

"Good heavens no. It'd be like a giraffe on ice skates." I got the smile I'd hoped for. "I'm actually here looking for a lost relative."

Her face seized up. I was touched by her concern.

"What have you found?" she practically whispered.

"Nothing yet. But here—" I dug in my purse for Candice's photo. "This is what she looks like."

Suzette took the picture from me. Her body visibly relaxed. "She's very lovely."

"Have you seen her?"

"No. Never," she said, handing it back to me.

I took the photo. "I suppose it would be too simple if she were here."

Suzette pulled at the collar of her blouse. "What makes you think she's in Churchill Falls?"

"Travel plans made but never used. I thought maybe she arrived here later, by some other means." I shrugged. "Might be a wild goose chase."

"Best of luck to you," she said.

Therese called from the kitchen. "Time to sing. Gather round, everybody."

I made my way to a corner near the refrigerator and fought tears as we sang to the beaming birthday girl. I tried not to compare my special day with hers. Why go there? But I couldn't stop the tug of memories. Gram's kitchen back in Walled Lake. The guests were her church friends, gabby women who somehow thought a sixteen-year-old would prefer a round of bridge over capture-the-flag with people her own age. I took my slice of cake into the living room, curled up on the couch, and read *Jane Eyre* for the third time. It was late when the gaggle left. Gram said good night, and I cleaned up the mess.

Therese gave her daughter a big hug. "My baby is sixteen!" She held her by the shoulders and smiled. "Just look at you. So beautiful! I love you, Renee."

"Love you too, Mom." The girl returned the hug, tears in her own eyes.

I looked out the window and stared at the pattern of lines made by blue siding on the house next door. Aluminum made a very practical covering for homes this far north. Very practical, I decided, as Renee screamed in glee from her dad's bear hug. I probably would have gone with tan. The baby blue gave me a headache.

"You are the best daughter a man could have." The affectionate voice cut through my musings.

I brought the lines back into focus. Yes, tan would have been a better choice. Much softer on the eyes.

The crowd in the kitchen started to break up, and I turned toward Therese, my head pounding. "Thank you for the invitation. I had a wonderful time."

She took my hands in hers. "It's been a pleasure. I hope we will see you again while you're here. Let us know if there is anything we can do to make your stay more comfortable. Anything at all."

"I will." I located my outerwear and hurried to put it on. "Goodbye," I said to the faces behind me and walked out the door.

The cold shocked me into action. I took off at high speed toward the inn, the rub of my parka against my ears and the thud of my feet hitting the ground the only sounds in the darkness.

The hotel clerk had her nose in her book again as I hurried through the lobby and up to my room. I shut the hotel room door behind me. The slam echoed in the emptiness, reminding me I was alone. I leaned against it, focusing on the rasp beneath my breath, hoping to drown out the sounds of family and friends gathered for a special occasion.

After a minute, I blew out a puff of air and hung my coat. Boots off, I went to the bathroom and splashed water on my face. The towel felt rough on my skin, increasing circulation to my capillaries as I rubbed. My headache lightened up with the massage. I stared in the mirror, face red and raw. How come I was the one inside this body? Why couldn't my soul have been born in that girl Monique instead? Same mouth, same nose, same face, but a thousand miles and two parents difference.

I leaned on the counter and gave a disgusted sigh. Why did I always do that to myself? Why did I think everybody else had it so much better than Patricia Amble? I met my eyes in the mirror. The green seemed extra bright through tears. Mother dead when I was eight, father out of my life since birth, raised by a drunken grandfather and a bitter grandmother, a prison sentence, betrayed by a friend, a boyfriend dying by his own free will, house pilfered by an almost sister-in-law, and now stuck in the middle of an arctic wasteland looking for the only thing that could possibly make me feel better. Revenge.

I was pathetic.

I took two aspirin and curled up under the covers. I could feel myself sliding down that dangerous but somehow soothing path toward despair. It was no state of mind to be in before ending the killing rampage of the woman who virtually ended Brad's life. I had to stay sharp, pull myself out of this slump if I was going to get the job done. Of course, I had to find her first.

But, too emotionally exhausted to do anything about it tonight, I stretched to reach my suitcase on the floor by the bed and pulled out the envelope of photos I'd brought along for the trip. I set the pile on the bed next to me and picked up the top one. My mother. A line of tape ran down the center of the photo where I'd patched it together. Cousin Joel had torn it in two in a fit of rebellion when he first learned I was moving into the old lodge, a home he once considered his inheritance. My fingers tightened their hold on the shiny paper. And now the traitor and his wife had snatched it from me.

I looked at my mom's playful eyes. I'd almost forgotten what her face looked like, but now I could remember her smile.

"Bedtime, Tish," she'd say.

"In a minute, Mom." I never obeyed the first time.

"Uh oh. Here comes the tickle monster."

"Eeeek!" I'd scream and run and she'd chase me and grab me in her arms and haul my little body to the bedroom. Then we snuggled and read bedtime stories. I yawned after the first one, but whined until I got a second story. Then it was kisses and a tuck in.

My eyes went back to the tape stuck across her beautiful face. My mom. Taken from me the day Frank Majestic's clowns forced her Ford into the quarry. Maybe I should be going after Majestic instead of Candice. He was the true source of my pain.

I tried to block out images from the birthday party, but the thought of Therese hugging her daughter invaded my mind. The more I tried to push it away, the more I could feel my mother's arms around me, tickling, holding, loving.

My hands flopped to the bed, the picture landing facedown. Oh, how I loved to torture myself. I left the photo where it was and grabbed for the next one. Why stop now? I was on a roll, reaching for my next dose of pain like an addict.

Mom and I at the beach, compliments of Candice LeJeune Photography. I really needed that reminder of Candice's ploy to infiltrate my life, only to destroy it. I slapped the picture onto the comforter.

The two of us on the woods path. Me on a swing. Each

photo only made me angrier. I flipped to the next one—and froze. Brad and I. Sharing a Coney at Sam's Diner back in Rawlings. I'd never seen the picture before. Brad looked so handsome in his polo shirt and khakis, so full of life. And I had a huge smile on my face. I squeezed my eyes closed, remembering how it felt to be happy. I opened them and tried to remember when the photo had been taken. Must have been a Sunday after church. We'd always gone with a crowd to eat and visit. I flipped it over.

Brad, thought you'd want this! Love, Pastor John.

How had it gotten among my things? It belonged to Brad. I bit my lip. He must have gotten rid of anything to do with me. I looked at the shot, tears pouring down my cheeks. I could understand why Brad hadn't kept it around. Who wanted to be reminded about what might have been?

From deep in my chest, a wail gushed up. I threw the photos to the bed. They scattered across the comforter. I flung back the covers and got up, pacing the room, wondering how I could get rid of this pent-up rage. What had Candice told me one day over tea? That it was best I'd been raised without my father's influence. It gave me a chance to escape the Russo family curse. Well, it hadn't mattered. Father or not, the curse had found me. Everything had gone wrong with my life. Maybe I shouldn't waste my energy taking things out on Candice. Maybe I should just end my agony here.

The thought splashed like a bucket of water across my brain. What was I thinking? Where was I headed? Time to step back and take a breather.

I turned on the shower, hoping I'd get a fresh perspective after a good dousing. I gave the water a chance to warm up, heading back to the bedroom to clean up my mess. I gathered the photos, careful not to let any of them register in my mind and fan the flames of my fury. But despite my efforts, one image leaped out at me. I took the picture in my hands. It was my mom and dad, sitting together at the Watering Hole the night my mom died.

As I squinted at the photo, studying my father's features, I realized I'd just seen an older version of that face. It belonged to Roger Jamison.

Hands shaking, I drew in a breath and blinked away the insane thought. But there was no denying it.

I'd found my father.

34

I'd come here to find Candice LeJeune. Instead I found Jacob Russo. I collapsed on the edge of the bed.

His hand. I'd touched his hand and I hadn't even known he was my father.

Somewhere above my twisting stomach was a lump that pushed against my heart. The pressure threatened to crush the delicate organ.

The man who had been a cloudy, faceless blur in my memory was right here. Right here in Churchill Falls.

I didn't even know what to do with that information. He wasn't some homeless bum on crack. He was a responsible member of society, an employee at a power plant, a husband to Suzette . . . a father to—I raced to the bathroom and wretched into the toilet, the convulsions stopping only when the sixteenth birthday party was flushed away. Wracked with chills, I crawled under the shower and scrunched up like an infant in the tub, letting the heat warm my bones. Steam filled my lungs and I struggled to take slow, even breaths.

It's okay. It's okay. It's okay.

I let the chant block any thoughts from my mind. Water pelted my face and body. The constant drone against the painted metal blotted out all other sounds. But the sensory barrier was only temporary.

Despite my efforts, Monique's face exploded into my head.

All those years.

All those years that I had been without a father, she'd had one. She'd had *mine*.

I couldn't stop the little whining sounds from coming out of my throat, like a sad little puppy left out in the cold.

Monique looked about the same age as her friend Renee. My fingers wiggled as I did the math. When I was seventeen and graduating from high school, Grandma Amble the only family member in the audience, my father was having a baby with another woman. I did some calculations. That would have made him thirty-sevenish. Just a little older than I was right now.

My fist smacked the water puddled in the tub. How dare he?

He was supposed to be with *me*.

"Me." I said the word out loud.

Didn't he know Mom died that night and I was all alone? Didn't he care that I cried myself to sleep a whole year? Didn't he hear me calling for him in the night?

"Daddy. Daddy, please, come get me, Dad. Don't leave me here. Dad, I want to be with you."

One night, somewhere around eleven years old, I told myself that he must be dead too and that's why he wasn't coming and I was completely alone in the world. And as long as he'd been dead or destitute, I'd been okay. But now—how could this happen? How could he be fine and doing well and living life? All without me?

It was wrong.

Spiraling into shock after an overdose of reality, I sat up in the tub, as if stuck on automatic, and wiped the streams of water from my face. I washed up and dried off. With a towel around my hair, I stepped to the bedroom and slipped into comfortable pajamas.

The remote sat on the bedside table. I clicked it and stared at the blur of images across the TV screen, not caring what was on. The hours slipped by. At some point I escaped into sleep.

—ɯ—

My eyes flicked open, alert after a sound penetrated my slumber. I lay still, listening. The heating system hummed, doing its job. A few minutes passed and I decided the noise had been imaginary. Only in my dream.

The digital clock read 6 a.m. Way too soon to be moving. But my mind was already awake and processing its latest information. I felt better this morning, ready to put the kibosh on the whine-and-cheese party and take some action instead.

I dressed for the day, contemplating my next move. I had to confront Roger Jamison, alias Jacob Russo. The man was not getting off the hook a day longer. Thinking back over his first reaction when he saw me, I realized he had known who I was. He'd known I was his daughter. And what did he do? Run to the bathroom.

And his wife Suzette. She'd known who I was too. I was sure of it. Only Monique and I suffered in ignorance.

Monique. I even liked her name better. What kind of name was Patricia anyway? Everybody was named Patricia. If it hadn't been for the saving grace of my nickname Tish, the name my mother had always called me, I would have made myself a Sabrina or a Victoria or a Genevieve. Something a little more romantic than Patricia.

Still, that was the name Puppa called me. *Patricia.* He made the word formal, proper . . . important. Special even. I kind of liked the name when it came from Puppa's lips.

Puppa. In the bathroom mirror, the brush paused, inches from my hair. Monique was his granddaughter too, but she had never known him. She'd never been to the lake house, ridden horses, eaten supper, or harassed sick people with him.

My cheek quirked a smile at the memory of Puppa congratulating me on kissing my sleeping prince.

The brush continued through my hair. Monique had no idea what she'd been missing. We lived opposite halves of the same life. She got—I swallowed hard at the thought—she got our father. But I got our family. Puppa, Joel, Gerard, Grandma Olivia. Maybe I should be feeling sorry for Monique instead of myself.

With the new perspective, I realized there were plenty of things Monique missed out on. Summers at the lodge on Valentine's Bay, the Fourth of July celebration in Port Silvan, playing ambush with cousins on pine-needle covered trails . . . Maybe when she found out about Dad's family back in Michigan, she'd feel as gypped as I did when I thought of growing up without a dad.

That in mind, I decided to go easy on Monique when I told her the truth about why we looked like we could be sisters.

We *were* sisters.

I inhaled a sharp breath at the thought, somehow realizing for the first time that I had a sister. A little sister. We shared only half blood, but blood nonetheless.

While I plotted my strategy for chastising my deadbeat dad, I also planned how Monique and I could become friends. More than friends. *Sisters.*

Finished with my morning routine, I scoured the bedside table for the local directory. It only took a second to find the number for Roger Jamison on Osprey Avenue. I picked up the phone to dial. But at the sound of the tone, I put down the receiver. What was I going to say?

"Hi, this is your firstborn, Patricia Amble. Can I come by for a cup of coffee?" I'm sure Suzette would be thrilled to welcome into her home the daughter of her husband's ex-fling. Dear Old Dad would probably spend the whole time in the bathroom with the dry heaves, anyway.

No. I'd go with the more intrusive, in-your-face approach. I'd just show up at their door and throw a tantrum on their snow-covered lawn until they asked me inside.

Yeah. That was mature.

I put my boots on. What did I care what they thought of my emotional maturity? My short time in Del Gloria couldn't undo thirty-three years of conditioning overnight.

I tugged on my parka. They'd just have to deal with it. Love it or lump it. With my primary mission focused on dousing Candice's lights, did it really matter which they chose? Anyway, Candice wasn't anywhere near Churchill Falls or I'd have found her by now.

I walked to the dresser for my purse.

A rhythmic knock sounded at the door. I paused, not sure if I'd heard right. The quiet tapping came again.

It was all of 8 a.m. Who could be knocking on my door?

It had to be my dad. I stared at the door. It seemed to warp away from me, like a view through the wrong end of binoculars. I breathed into my hands, telling myself to stay calm, he was family. A final deep breath, a pasted-on smile, and I pulled back the slide bolt and opened the door.

An elderly woman stood there, bundled in a long coat and carrying an oversized tapestry tote. I recognized her loopy-curled wig. My cohort from River's Edge.

I shook my head in utter, confused surprise. "Mrs. Callahan? What are you doing here?"

She pushed past me into the room. I shut the door, still speechless.

The old woman stood at the end of the bed. "Tish. Thank God. I see I got to you before he did."

She pulled her wig off and I cringed. Short silver hair spiked up underneath. She peeled off some sort of rubbery stuff from her cheeks.

I gave a cry of astonishment. "Candice! It's you."

35

With her disguise gone, Candice lost twenty years. An almost wrinkle-free face disputed her true sixty-something age.

I wanted to be angry. Had she been spying on Brad at River's Edge? What was that about—to make sure he died if he didn't kill himself?

I wanted to scream in rage. How dare she show up in Churchill Falls? And just as I was going to visit my long-lost father.

I wanted to strangle her. How could she walk into my hotel room like an old friend after what she did to Brad?

I kept it all business. "What brings you to Churchill Falls?"

"The same thing that brought you here." She tossed the tapestry bag on the bed and pulled it open.

I flashed a fake grin. "And what would that be? I came here looking for you."

"Oh, I think you're here looking for more than that."

Candice unbuttoned her frumpy pink old-lady blouse, revealing snug black sleeves beneath.

"You're right. I am looking for more." I was looking for revenge.

Crossing my arms, I observed as she slid out of fuchsia polyester slacks, uncovering tight black leggings.

"We don't have time for games, Tish. I took the plane from Goose Bay. I think he has an ATV and is coming in on the Trans-Labrador, which gives us only a few extra hours."

"Who? What are you talking about?"

"Just book your tickets in your real name, why don't you? It's like a neon sign flashing 'Follow Me!'"

"Using a false name isn't exactly easy anymore. Besides, you booked travel using your real name. Why do you think I'm here?"

"I did it because I knew they would look the opposite direction from Churchill Falls as soon as they saw I hadn't used my tickets. They'd know it was a bluff. Hence, everyone would remain safe."

I rubbed fingers to my temples. "I'm not following. Who are 'they' and 'everyone' in this story?"

"'They' are Frank Majestic and friends. 'Everyone' is Jacob Russo—your father—and his family." Black jeans came out of the tote. She stepped into them, pulling them over her leggings, as she brought me up to speed. "And 'he' is a hired gun, the assassin paid by Majestic to finish the job. He's hot on your trail. We have to get you out of here, and somehow make it seem like you didn't find what you were looking for. Once we get you safe on your way, I'll double back and warn Jacob."

She took a sweater out of the bag, dragging something with it. A pistol landed on the bedspread. She picked it up and casually tossed it back in the tote. Then she put on the sweater, smoothing the soft gray angora into place. Looking in the dresser mirror, she tousled her hair. "There. Now I feel more like myself."

And with the gun in the bag, I could tell she was ready to act more like herself too. Which man would die this time around?

I tried to look natural, even as I plotted a way to get at the gun. "I was just headed over to my dad's house now. I'll warn him when I get there."

Candice swung toward me. "Single him out, Tish, and he's dead. Right now he's just another plant employee. It'll take awhile for the killer to narrow it down." She pointed a finger at me. "But you walk up his front steps, and it's like giving him the kiss of death."

"You're full of malarkey." I walked to the bed and dropped onto it, one leg tucked under me. "You shot Brad. Why? To spare me from the possibility that things wouldn't work out twenty years down the road? That is so lame. And I'm supposed to believe you came all this way to rescue my father? He abandoned me as a child. That's a far bigger crime than anything Brad could ever do to me. For all I know, you're just using me to find my dad so you can kill him yourself."

She sat next to me on the bed. "No. I love your dad. He's . . . ," she looked away, "he's Bernard's son. How could I not love him as much as I love everything else that belongs to Bernard?" Her eyes pleaded for understanding.

"Touching. Really. But I've seen how you express your love. Did you ever think about consulting me before you killed the one I love most?"

She stood and walked toward the window. "I suppose you're still mad about that. I meant to take a clean shot at his heart." She clasped her hands together, head bowed. "But at the last moment I had second thoughts and went for a lung instead. I feel bad I nicked his spine." She clasped her fingers over her mouth, looking out the window.

I leaned forward, hand in the bag, feeling around for the pistol. "You shot him, Candice. He almost died. He wishes he was dead." I aimed the weapon at her.

She turned back to me, her eyes registering the gun, but not even acknowledging it. "Brad surprised me. A big macho man like him, heartsick over his girlfriend's death. He'd rather have died than live without you. It was very romantic." She walked toward me.

"Stay where you are." I couldn't let her get to me. Her voice was hypnotic, soothing. It was just a means to distract me.

She smiled. "Tish. Come on. There's no time for games. Get your things packed so we can get you out of here."

I jerked the weapon. She stopped a few feet from the bed.

"I'm not going anywhere until I talk to my dad."

She leaned on one foot, and casually crossed her arms. "What really convinced me I was wrong about Brad," she said, "was the way he reacted that day I helped you get into his room."

I sighed in disgust at the memory. "He threw me out. I think he's done with me."

"Austin had a crew of doctors and a physical therapist there for him the next day." She lifted her eyebrows. "I think you changed his mind about cashing in his chips."

I sucked in a breath. Brad wanted to live? The pistol in my hand wavered and lowered a notch.

Candice took a step toward me.

I yanked the gun to the level of her eyes. "Hold still."

She put her hands up in mock surrender.

I jabbed the weapon in her direction. "I want you to see something. It's in my suitcase over there."

She nodded. I could tell her mind was churning, trying to keep one step ahead of me. She slowly walked around the end of the bed.

"In that envelope." I pointed with the gun, swinging it back toward her.

"Okay." She slowly bent to pick up the envelope.

As her head lowered, I took a step closer and cracked the butt of the handgun across the back of her skull. The blow made a sickening *thunk.* She didn't go down right away, just hovered a moment before collapsing face-first into my suitcase.

I gasped and fought the roiling of my stomach.

Tucking the pistol into my purse, I raced out of the hotel room to the lobby. I blew past the innkeeper and out the front door, cutting across the parking lot toward the residential area behind the town center. If I remembered right, Osprey Avenue was a block past Gull on the way to the mess hall. I tore between houses, feeling foolish as I caught the startled look on a face in one window. Snow piled into my boots. Back on the street once more,

I angled up Osprey, searching for the address numbers from the phone book. A group of children playing in a front yard stopped to stare at the woman sprinting through their quiet town.

I found the single-story home with its WELCOME TO THE JAMISON HOUSE sign on the door. I hammered with my fist, the sign thumping along with me.

I stopped to listen. Footsteps came to the door. I waited, sensing hesitation on the other side. A smile on my face, I tried to catch my breath. The knob turned and the door opened. I adjusted my eyes down to the height of a girl around ten years old. Dark hair, brown eyes, and the mouth, nose and eyebrows of Monique. Another sister.

"Hi," she said, hiding half behind the door.

"Hi." I stared at her. If she was ten, I would have been twenty-three when she was born. I'd been sitting in a jail cell on the day of her birth. "Think I could come in?"

"You're that person, aren't you?" Her eyes were huge as she studied every inch of me. "The one Dad said might come around some day?"

They knew about me? I looked both ways up the street, getting that horrible feeling that someone besides kids in snowsuits could be watching. "Is your dad here?"

She shook her head.

"Is your mom?"

She shook it again, no closer to granting me entry.

"Hey." A girl's voice came from behind her. "Let her in."

The ten-year-old stepped back, swinging the door with her. Monique stood in the center of the living room as I made my way inside.

"Thank you."

The door closed behind me.

"Let me take your things," Monique said, eyes somehow hopeful.

I shook my head. "No, I can't stay."

"Then please sit down. Can I get you something from the kitchen?" Her voice was gracious. Her manners impeccable.

I stepped out of my boots and walked to the sofa, considering whether or not I could eat with my stomach twisted in a knot. "No, thank you, I don't care for anything right now." I sat. My fingers fidgeted with the bottom zipper on my parka as I thought about what to say next.

The two girls sank onto the love seat opposite me, fingers busy as well.

"So," I said, breaking the ice, "you guys seem to know something about me." I figured since I was the eldest sister, I'd better be the one in charge.

The two girls looked at each other.

The older Monique spoke first. "Dad said he had a child with a woman a long time ago. He said you might find him someday."

I nodded, too choked up to speak.

Meagan perked up. "He said if you found him, that was a bad thing, because that meant other people might find him too."

I put a hand over my mouth. A bad thing. He'd told them I was a bad thing. Tears welled up. Why was I doing this to myself?

At any rate, Candice had been right. I was the mouse

that led the assassin to the cheese. By coming here, I'd not only endangered my father but his new family as well. Why couldn't I have just minded my own business? Settled down with Brad and had a family of my own? Let my dad have his life, wherever he was, and be content with living mine?

I sighed and cradled my head in my hands. That would have been impossible for me. It simply went against my nature to live an uncomplicated existence. I seemed to thrive on theatrics and chaos.

I looked at my sisters, who seemed a little freaked out. "Okay," I said. "Here I am. I found you. And Dad was right. That's a bad thing."

"Wh . . . why is it so bad?" Meagan wanted to know.

No sense sparing any details. "When Dad was younger, he got mixed up with a big drug dealer, but Dad did the right thing and turned him in. Problem was, the guy wanted to get back at Dad for tattling and has been looking for him for the past, I don't know," I threw my hands up at a loss, "twenty-something years."

Monique jumped in. "So they watched you, waiting for the day you'd lead them to Dad."

"Bingo," I said.

"Didn't you know any better?" sweet little Meagan asked. "Didn't you know you should stay away from him?"

I tried to control the black cloud that edged into my mind. "All I knew is, I had a dad out there somewhere who pretty much left me alone since I was born. I figured he was dead. But sometimes I thought he was still in trouble, doing drugs somewhere, wasting his life. Then," my teeth gritted, "I end up in Churchill Falls for an entirely unrelated reason, and I keep running into this guy who gets sick every time he sees me." I nodded my head at Monique. "And I meet a teenager who could be my sister. The pieces fall into place and I realize I found my father." I gave Meagan a pair of don't-mess-with-me eyeballs. "Yes, I'm going to come see him. I want to know why he left me alone and then went on to have some whole new family."

The room was quiet as I finished my tirade.

"Are you mad at us?" Meagan asked.

Monique poked her on the thigh.

I sat back on the couch, looking at the two of them. "Yeah. I was pretty mad at first. But how could I stay angry when I realized that Dad's new daughters are also my sisters? I always wanted a sister. And now I have two."

"Three, really," Monique said. "Mallory's away at college."

I tapped at my lips with a finger to keep a bellow from escaping. After a moment I asked, "And how old is Mallory?"

Meagan answered. "She's twenty-two. She graduates this year."

I pursed my lips and nodded. Dad's big do-over raising daughters seemed to be going pretty well. His firstborn didn't make it past her sophomore year at Michigan State University, but the eldest in his next batch was getting her degree this spring. Couldn't ask for better than that.

I did more math. This Mallory was twenty-two. I'd

been eleven years old when she was born, still hollow from the grief of losing my mother.

I clamped a vice on my pipeline of thought, cutting it off. There was no sense taking my ire out on the girls. They were victims like me. I'd save my resentment for the head muck-a-muck himself, our father.

"Where can I find Dad, anyway?" I'd better warn him, give him a piece of my mind, then get out of here before all our lives were ruined.

"Mom and Dad are both working shifts today," Monique said. "Dad said if you came over, I should invite you to dinner and he'd talk about things then."

"I'd just love to catch up on old times with Dear Old Dad over supper, but I really need to get a hold of him right away."

The girls just sat and stared at me.

"Seriously," I said. "Right now if you want him to live."

Monique stood. "Come on. I'll take you over there."

36

Monique looked at her younger sister. "You stay here."

I shook my head. "No, she can't stay by herself. Just in case."

Monique sighed. "Fine."

We scrunched three across the bench seat of a small-model pickup.

Monique put the truck in gear. "It's just a few minutes to the plant."

We curved through the streets and onto Churchill Falls Road. A few minutes later, a forest of metal towers connected by wires appeared on the horizon.

Meagan pointed. "That's the switchyard. The power goes all over from there. Even to the States."

"Cool," I said, not really interested in anything other than getting to my father before his assailant.

Monique turned at a sign. CHURCHILL FALLS GENERATING STATION, it said. A digital board told passers-by the current megawatt output. I assumed the numbers were meant to impress.

A few minutes later, we parked near a building that

looked like a couple shoe boxes topped with an oatmeal canister. Scattered across the snowy grounds, sharp posts poked skyward.

"Come on," Monique said, taking charge.

I grabbed my purse and slid out of the truck.

"You don't have a gun in there or anything, do you? We have to clear security," Monique said.

"Ummmm, I think I'll leave my purse in the car." I tucked my passport in my jeans pocket, then flipped my handbag to the floor of the truck and joined the sisters on a walk toward the building.

A group had gathered in a central area, apparently waiting for a tour of the facility.

"Come on," Monique said. "Mom's working control."

We stopped for an ID check.

"Who's your friend, Monique?" the employee asked.

"Believe it or not, she's my sister. Details later, okay?"

We left the woman sputtering.

"That's Aunt Veronica. Won't she be surprised to hear about you," Monique remarked as the three of us took off down meandering hallways.

Red carpet paved the floor of a room that resembled the bridge of the Starship Enterprise.

"Mom," Monique said as we entered.

At her voice, Suzette Jamison and a fellow employee glanced up from the bank of buttons and dials.

Suzette stiffened when she saw me. "Hello, Tasha."

I gave a nod. "I'm sure you've figured out by now that it's Patricia."

"Yes. So it is." She walked toward us. "Roger is working down in the powerhouse today. He thought we could get together over supper to discuss . . . ," her hand searched the air, ". . . whatever it is you wanted to discuss."

I couldn't blame her for wanting to wall me out of her life. "Thank you for the invitation, but I can't wait until supper. I really need to talk to him right away."

"His shift ends at—"

Monique cut her off. "Mom. It's seriously important. Take us down there. Please."

Hands on her hips, Suzette gave a sigh. She looked toward her partner at the controls. "Can you man the helm while I take care of a family emergency?"

The worker nodded. "Take your time. Everything's normal on the board."

"Thanks, Pete." She followed the carpet out the door. "This isn't exactly protocol," she murmured as we hastened to keep up with her. She swung a finger in Monique's direction. "You and I are going to have a little talk later."

"Sorry, Mom. I just know how I'd want to be treated if I were in her position."

A shelf filled with hardhats lined the wall. We sized them up and put one on. Suzette remained quiet as we waited for the elevator.

I couldn't take the smothering silence. "This is all my fault."

Suzette raised her eyebrows as if to say a sarcastic "really?"

I grimaced. "I should never have involved your daughters, but it's urgent that I speak to . . . Roger. Monique offered to drive me here, and Meagan couldn't stay at the house by herself, just in case."

Suzette's arms twisted like giant pretzels. "Just in case what?"

Meagan rushed to fill her in. "Just in case the bad man is after us. He's coming, Mom. Patricia said he might already be in town."

I flapped my hands in denial. "No, no. I don't know. Maybe someone might be following me, who can say?"

"Just as Roger feared," Suzette said in a weary voice.

"Please," I said while the elevator continued its descent. "This is completely unintentional. I had no idea my dad was in Churchill Falls when I arrived."

"Just one big coincidence," came Suzette's cynical reply. "I have a hard time believing that."

"No one is more surprised than me." My stomach began floating into my rib cage. "How far down does this thing go, anyway?"

Monique answered. "Close to three hundred meters." She must have seen the lack of comprehension on my face. "Almost a thousand feet to you Americans."

A fifth of a mile. That was almost half the distance from the highway to the lodge on Valentine's Bay. One-third the distance from the bus stop in Del Gloria to the row of houses on Rios Buena Suerta. A tiny fraction of the distance that now stretched between Brad's heart and mine.

The elevator slowed and dropped to a halt. We followed a clammy tunnel toward the sound of churning machinery. The passage opened into a cavernous room that looked as long as a football field. Chunky boxes colored red, yellow, blue, and green made a line down the center, like a Rubik's Cube tournament for giants. Next to each square was a railed-in flight of stairs, heading below ground. The walls were home to more buttons and dials along with color-coordinated doors, each with a number lit up above.

"This is the powerhouse," Monique explained in a voice loud enough to conquer the roar. "The electricity made here every year from harnessing the Churchill River takes a conventional power company 158 thousand barrels of oil a day to produce."

"Kudos to the tree huggers," I said, watching two men in hardhats walk along the far wall, wondering if one of them was my father.

"Let's hustle, girls," Suzette said, taking off at a brisk pace toward the other end.

Cubes passed by in a whiz of color.

Suzette slowed and hailed the men, arm held high. "Roger. We need you a minute."

My father turned his head at his wife's voice. His eyes met hers, skimmed over his daughters, then shot to me. For a minute he looked like he might be sick again. Somehow he fought it off. He turned to his partner, gave some kind of explanation, and walked our way.

My hands shook as he came closer. What would I say to him anyway? Hey, Dad, nice meeting you, I'd love to talk, but there's this evil dude coming after you and we really ought to leave town for a while?

He stood in front of me, Suzette talking in one ear, his daughters in the other. I just stared. Captivated. Jacob Russo in the flesh. My father. All the heartache he'd caused my mother—driving drunk and letting her take the rap, doing drugs and not being there for her, leaving her pregnant and alone, making Mom raise me by herself—somehow I couldn't see any of those flaws when I looked at the man under the hardhat. His eyes were as blue as Puppa's. Same high cheekbones and rounded chin, faintly wrinkled. His eyes searched mine as if seeking acceptance. Acceptance from *me*. As if I might somehow hold against him all the years we'd been apart.

I supposed I could make him pay for the sins of his youth, turn my back on him, refuse to call him father . . . the way Brad had made Denton pay. I would certainly have my revenge, if crushing a man's spirit was a substitute for justice. But maybe I'd seek something better . . . maybe I'd decide to look more closely on the things my dad and I could share from here on out rather than the things we missed out on and could never have back.

The other women had quieted and were simply watching us.

I stretched out a hand toward him. "So. You're my dad."

37

My father nodded. "There's a really good explanation for why things happened the way they did—"

I touched my finger to his lips. "No explanations necessary. I'm guessing you did the best you could at the time. Besides," I gestured toward Monique and Meagan, "if things had happened any other way, I would have missed out on them." Tears started gathering in my eyes and it felt like a cork was trapped in my throat. "I'm so happy to have sisters."

At the other end of the plant, a tour came out of the tunnel onto the main floor. The voice of the guide echoed through the vast space.

By now I was holding my dad's hands.

He squeezed my fingers. "Sometimes I look back and wish things could have been different. But then I see Suzette," he looked at his wife with adoration, "and my girls," his eyes swelled with tears, "and I know God worked it all out. And I knew He was watching over you. I trusted Him to keep you safe."

Some snotty part of me wanted to demand why he

thought he could be off the hook just because he turned me over to God's care. But I shut that old voice out, wanting to hear more of the voice that said, yes, God had taken care of me my whole life. He'd taken good care of me. Exceptional care. And when I was ready, He'd led me to this place a thousand feet below ground to meet a man I'd only dreamed about. Jacob Russo had turned out to be far better a man than I had expected. Wouldn't Puppa be proud to know his rabble-rousing son had found a steady job and had a loving family that included three more granddaughters to disrupt the stillness of the lake house?

Because of course they would come visit the lost branch of their family tree in Michigan. The blight brought on by Frank Majestic could be overcome. We'd simply stop giving Frank power over us. Light would conquer darkness. Right would prevail over wrong.

The voice of the tour guide faded as she led her flock the opposite direction.

Fingers clasped around my father's, I swung his arms with mine in a fast, happy rhythm. "Now that we're together, I don't even know what to do." I glanced around the powerhouse. A gash of rocks showed where the ceiling stopped and the walls began. "Can I hug you?"

He nodded, a smile spreading across his face.

I slung my arms around his neck. He bent to accommodate our bare difference in height.

He held me tight and for a moment I could see myself as a baby, wrapped in a striped blanket, fresh from my mother's womb, being rocked in the arms of my adoring father. It didn't matter that it wasn't true, that it had never really happened. It only mattered that it felt true at the moment. Jacob Russo loved me. He adored me. My heart could feed forever on the joyful vibes of the moment.

His embrace loosened and I let go my hold around his neck and gave him some breathing room.

Without letting go of his elbows, I met his eyes, forcing myself back to reality. "You know that it's not a good thing I'm here."

He nodded, in sync with my meaning.

I swallowed, reluctant to let reality settle in. "Frank Majestic's goons followed me. I guess my whole life they've kept tabs on me, looking for you. And I've led them right to you. I don't know what you plan to do, but you're not safe here anymore." I nodded at Suzette and the girls. "Neither are they. It's only a matter of hours now before he catches up."

He shook his head. "I don't have a plan. I always knew today would arrive. I've feared it. I've lost sleep over it. But running is a thing of the past. Our lives are here in Churchill Falls. We'll just have to take this as it comes."

I held his hands like a child. "Maybe we could start by notifying the authorities. At least they can be on the lookout for anyone suspicious."

He looked to the ground. "I lied about my name, I made up my past. If someone's coming for me, it'll have to be Roger Jamison they're after. That's who I am."

"Go ahead and be Roger Jamison. I won't contradict your story. Listen—" I glanced at my sisters and Suzette. The three watched us with curious faces. "I have to get going. I just wanted to warn you about what's coming your way . . . and wish you and your family the best."

"Thank you." He choked up. "I'm really glad to have met you, Patricia. You're beautiful, just like your mother."

I nodded, tears too thick in my eyes to see anything clearly. "I love you, Dad."

A guttural cry came from his throat. He grabbed me in his arms again. "Let me kiss my baby once before she goes."

Eyes closed, I savored the feel of my father's lips against my temple. Tears streaked down my cheeks. I opened my eyes to the view past my dad's shoulder, catching a glimpse of a stray tourist looking our way. The guy's hands were tucked in the pockets of a bomber jacket worn over blue jeans. Dark hair curled from beneath his white hardhat. His face seemed intent as he stared, and somewhat familiar.

I stiffened in my dad's hold. The last time I'd seen that man's face, it had a purple birthmark over half of it. But even without the garish marking, there was no mistaking my classmate Simon Scroll.

Understanding rushed over me. The birthmark had been a simple disguise that let him blend in at the college. From the menacing glare of his eyes, Simon Scroll was here to kill my dad. I realized now why I'd never trusted the guy.

I tore loose from Dad's grip, as if that could somehow undo the kiss that revealed his identity.

"He's here," I whispered breathlessly. "You might want to change your policy."

My dad turned just as Simon started toward us.

"Run!" I screamed and grabbed my half sisters by the arms.

Suzette ran with us.

"George!" she yelled to the man at the far wall. "Get security down here now!"

Dad followed a few steps behind us.

In the corner of my eye, I saw a shape leap toward my father, bringing him to the ground.

I skidded to a halt. "Keep going," I yelled to my sisters and Suzette.

The girls ran toward a far doorway. I did a 180 back in my dad's direction.

With Jacob Russo facedown on the ground, Simon stepped on his back and cuffed him across the head.

"Dad!"

I plowed into Simon at full speed, knocking him to the metal floor. He grabbed me and threw me aside like a crash dummy. My skull landed against the sharp corner of a green cube. White dots arced across my vision.

By the time I got back on my feet, my father was draped against the safety railing of a down staircase, tossed there by Simon, who was revving up for his next blow.

I crawled toward them, reaching for Simon's ankles, hoping for a swift takedown. But a blur of movement from across the plant reached Simon before I did. The figure collided into our attacker, pummeling him over the rail and onto the staircase below.

"Candice!" I stared as my once-friend raced down the steps after Simon.

My father crumpled to the floor, holding his head in his hands.

"Dad, are you okay?" I made it to his side.

At his nod, I poked my head through the wide rails to see the fight below. Simon had turned the tables, with Candice now the one flailing on the stairs.

"Hang on! I'm coming!" I yanked on the rail and got back to my feet, racing to the steps.

A couple hardhats headed across the plant floor toward the commotion. I took the stairs two at a time, descending to the level of deafening turbines. Supersized gears and gadgetry whirred as the machines generated enough power to light up North America's eastern seaboard. The steep run ended in an eagle's nest suspended above the panorama.

With help from the steel toe of Simon's work boot, Candice tottered over the platform rail, grabbing the ledge at the last moment, only to dangle above a distant floor. One less contender to worry about, Simon turned in my direction and came up the steps. I froze in panic. A single prod from his shoulder would be enough to send me flying. I gripped the rail with both hands and lashed out at his face with my foot as he came into range. But one deft hold-and-turn of my leg as he blew past left me clinging to the metal treads in pain.

"The professor was stupid to trust you." I lashed out with words since my body was no longer cooperating.

"He was stupid to trust that Rigg woman." Above me, Simon peered across the plant floor, leaving me to wonder about his words as I crept toward the dangling Candice.

Simon must not have liked what he saw coming his way. In a few short seconds, he was back in my face, one arm wrapped around my neck in a chokehold.

"Hostage time," he said, his voice slithery in my ear.

My heart raced. I blinked and closed my eyes even as he forced me up the staircase, a sharp object jabbing my ribs. I kept my mind on breathing, attempting to slow my metabolism down and drop my pulse to a reasonable level. Calm sea breezes and sandy beaches filled my inner vision, warding off the hostile hormones that would rob me of reason. Panic would not eclipse my memory this time. Whatever happened today, I would be a conscious witness. I would have perfect recall of every move, every decision. I would be in command of my mind and body. No paralyzing fear would overcome me today.

Serene beaches, beautiful sunsets, soft breezes, a loving God. . . I forced the images into my mind as we reached the plant floor. Three men with the CF logo on navy windbreakers huddled around my father, now looking up as Simon called to him.

"Get up, Russo. Majestic wants to kill you himself. Come quietly and I won't kill your daughter."

The men helped him to his feet. He groaned and hobbled our way.

"Stay back," Simon said to the duo in hardhats as they surged after my father. A shot of pain in my ribs and I let out a holler. The men backed off.

I fought panic.

Lapping waves, pretty seashells, the cry of gulls . . .

Our backs were against the wall.

"Open it," Simon said to my dad.

Dad pulled open a metal door.

We backed through and Dad closed it behind us. A few more steps and we were in some kind of tunnel. Rock walls looked patched in places, explaining why hardhats were in fashion at the plant.

"Dad!" Monique's voice came from farther down the tunnel. They must have entered from another door.

"Stay back, honey," my dad called.

"Are you okay?" It was Suzette's voice this time.

Dad gave a loud exhale, his body tense as he kept up to the swiftly moving Simon. I tripped along, awkward in the stranglehold as we drew closer to the voices.

"We'll be alright, Suz. Get to safety, hon. This guy's a nut."

"Watch your mouth, Russo." Simon ground the sharp point of his weapon into my back.

"Ahhh!" I screamed in pain.

The tunnel angled up, making the going even more difficult as Simon dragged me by the neck.

We came to an intersection. Simon hesitated.

"Which way out of here?" he asked.

My dad looked at the two possible routes, eyebrows scrunched. A sign with the words EXIT lay on the ground, pointing in the direction we had just come from. I smirked at the thought of the girls staying one step ahead of us, knocking the exit sign off its fasteners, just to make Simon's life more miserable—and hopefully shorter.

"The left tunnel," my dad said after some thought.

A flash of headlights and the sound of a vehicle came from the gloom of the left tunnel.

"Then we'll take a right." By now Simon had my head tucked under his arm like a football, making it easier for both of us to move quickly.

"You can't get out this way," my dad said, huffing to keep up.

"Sure you can."

Simon tightened his hold and I grabbed his forearm, trying to pry it away from my esophagus.

"I . . . can't . . . breathe . . ."

Simon laughed. "Get used to it. It'll be a permanent condition as soon as I see daylight." Simon slowed as the incline grew steeper. He let out a chuckle at some private thought. "You have no idea how pathetic you looked sitting up on that roof all night."

"You were the one who took the ladder?"

"You were way too comfortable in Del Gloria. You needed a little fear factor, a little prodding to get you moving. I couldn't wait forever for you to go looking for your father. The ladder, the writing on the wall . . . you're pretty slow."

"I can see you messing with me, but Celia and Portia? They could have died in that fire."

"Don't blame that fire on me. I had nothing to do with it. I wasn't trying to kill you, just get you moving."

"If you didn't start that fire . . . then who?"

"Like I said, the professor shouldn't have trusted Alexa Rigg. I did warn him."

"Ms. Rigg? What did she have to do with it?"

He gave a low laugh. "She was once known as the Debutante of Dublin. A dazzler by day but part of Dublin's retribution bomb squad by night. She retired to the

U.S. to raise her daughter in safety. She was one mistake I'm sure old Ambassador Braddock paid for the rest of his life."

My knee banged the tunnel wall as he dragged me around a corner.

"I'm only glad the Debutante of Dublin blamed you for Jane's death instead of taking out her revenge on me," he added.

38

My legs scrambled to keep up to Simon's fast pace. "You killed Jane?"

"The professor was paying me to protect you. Majestic was paying me to track you. And Jane got in the way. She knew too much and was using the information to get more of the Braddock fortune. I could have cared less until she tried to get a piece of my action. You elbow in on a hit, you end up at the bottom of a cliff."

I dug my fingernails into the skin of his hand. "That's disgusting. It was Thanksgiving Day."

He cried out in surprise and slugged my temple. "You're right. I should have waited until it wasn't a national holiday."

I blinked back tears, determined to remain in control of my emotions during crisis. I craned my neck around, but all I could see was Simon's chin. "Can we take a break? I can't keep going this speed with your arm cutting off my air."

He waved his weapon in front of my face. A thick, straight piece of wood, like the handle of a wooden spoon, sharpened to a deadly point. Simple, nonmetallic, and effective in gaining my cooperation.

We passed a couple signs on the wall. SURGE CHAMBER, said one. REFUGE, said the other. Both arrows pointed ahead.

"Which way, Pops?" Simon twisted my neck as he asked the question, earning a good yell.

My dad was bent over, catching his breath. "You can't get out this way. I already told you."

"Come on, old man. There must be an escape tunnel somewhere."

Dad shook his head. "The refuge is where you go if the escape tunnels collapse. There's food and water in there."

"I feel a breeze," Simon said, holding out a hand to catch the air. "Where's it coming from?"

"The vent shaft for the surge chamber," Dad answered. "It's a straight shot up. Unless you're Spiderman, you can't get out that way."

Simon squeezed my neck. I started to gag.

"Unless I see daylight pretty quick, you're going to watch your daughter die."

"I don't know what to tell you." Dad gestured helplessly with his arms. "They're coming for you. I suggest you give up without a fight."

Simon dragged me through a metal arch toward the sound of rushing water. Dad followed behind. Another vast cavern, this one with a railing and a straight drop to swirling foam below.

"It's a dead end," my dad said.

"Dead end for you, maybe. Where's this thing go?" Simon gestured to the water below.

Dad shook his head. "You wouldn't have a chance. If

you made it out of the lower chamber alive, it's still almost two kilometers through the tailrace to open water."

"Then you better hope we can backtrack through the escape tunnel. I only get paid when Majestic gets his man."

A sound like a footstep, or a rock falling, came from the route behind us. Simon turned, yanking my head around with him. The sharp pointy stick prodded my jugular.

Candice stood in the archway.

"You're okay." My voice came out squeaky under pressure.

From the shadows came Suzette, Monique, then Meagan.

"Suzette, get the girls out of here," my dad said, panic in his voice.

"Mr. Scroll is outnumbered, Jacob," Candice purred. "I think he'll put his kabob stick down and give up quietly." She stood with her arms crossed, looking sleek in her black clothing. The other women followed suit, standing in menacing formation.

Simon laughed, each shake of his body driving the point farther into my skin. "Afraid of a bunch of girls? You look like more hostages to me."

I grabbed his forearm, nudging the solid mass of muscle away from my air pipe. "Don't mess with Candice. Trust me. Put the weapon down and run for your life."

"It's good advice, Mr. Scroll," she said. "I'll give you ten seconds to comply."

Simon laughed.

Candice dug into her pocket and took out a slim squirt bottle, as small as a breath mint dispenser.

"What's that? Anthrax-on-the-go?"

"Something a little more fast-acting," Candice seethed. With a quick thrust of her finger, a shot of liquid arced across the space between them. I felt a drop land on the back of my hair, even as Simon hollered and bent down, rubbing his eyes with both hands.

My head was still locked in his grip, but while he writhed, I made a sharp twist and jerked myself free—not without a jab to the neck.

"It's amazing how effective good old-fashioned pepper spray can be. My own recipe too." Candice grabbed my arm and pulled me out of reach of my captor.

I held a hand to my neck. Wet, oozing blood stuck to the fur of my new parka. "Jerk," I said, grateful Simon had missed a major artery.

Simon slashed out with his pointy stick, slicing at my father's shirt. Dad jumped back, perhaps considering whether it was worth trying to subdue the raving man.

Eyes red and watery and still completely closed, Simon screamed as he gashed the air with his weapon. "You're going to die, Russo. You and your daughter both. I'm not done with you. Don't try to leave."

My dad walked away from the screaming lunatic and swept his wife and younger daughters into his arms and urged them back into the tunnel. "Come on, Patricia," he called to me.

Simon made a blind lunge toward the sound of his voice, and caught hold of Candice's jacket.

"Let go." Her voice was low and threatening.

But Simon had the opposite intention. He pulled Candice to him and drove the point of his stick through the leather into her side.

"Ahhh!" Her scream echoed through the surge chamber.

Simon flung her body around blindly, stabbing wherever his weapon found a weakness.

"Candice!" I screamed and ran toward them.

Blood ran from her face, her legs, her arms. She looked ripped to shreds. Candice screamed and flailed, but the angry man kept lashing out, showing no mercy.

I kicked at the back of his leg, popping it out from under him. He hollered and whirled, letting go of Candice and coming toward me, eyes barely slits across his face.

A slew of insults rolled across his lips. I dodged him, no plan in mind as I raced along the rail, heading through the gloom toward a blank rock wall.

"Really smart, Tish," I chided myself as I ran along.

In seconds I'd reached the end of the line. Panting, I turned to face Simon, too late to dodge the brute force that plowed me into the cavern wall. The air rushed out of me the same time my head made a deafening crunch against the stones. I opened my eyes in time to see his fist coming toward my face, weapon in hand.

I ducked to one side, feeling the point rip across my cheek and harpoon an earlobe exposed beneath my hardhat. No breath to scream, I rolled under Simon's arm, feeling a tug and burning pain at the side of my head as the weapon pulled free of my skin. I scrambled away, my only thought survival, as Candice limped past me to confront our attacker.

"Just run," I gasped.

She ignored me, fixed on her target. I turned to watch in horror as the older woman wrangled with Simon, the tip of the weapon only inches from her heart.

With a cry, she landed against the rail, leaning backward over the flowing water as she tried to avoid getting stabbed again.

Footsteps sounded behind me. I glanced over my shoulder to see my father. He reached me, putting his arm around me just as Candice screamed and slipped over the rail. At the last moment her arms reached up and clung to Simon's neck, bending him forward in a precarious dip over the railing. He tried pushing her away, but she swung her dangling body, knocking him off balance and tumbling him forward until only his back end was still on our side of the barrier. With a final grunt, Candice yanked him clear of the metal rods.

"Candice!" I screamed and raced to the rail to see two bodies plummet to the swirls below. The double splash was barely audible over the sound of rushing water.

"Dad! Do something!" My fingers clung to the cold railing.

His arms held me, his silence answer enough.

I stared into the black water, reaching as if I could somehow pluck Candice from the maelstrom.

"I'm sorry, sweetheart. Was she special to you?" My dad's voice broke through my vain attempt to raise Candice from the depths with prayer and wishful thinking.

I broke into a loud moan, only able to nod my reply. How foolish was it to be sad that the woman I came here to put out of commission was now dead? Shouldn't I be rejoicing? I hadn't even dirtied my own hands.

But this wasn't the ending I'd really wanted. Yes, I'd wanted to hurt Candice in revenge for shooting Brad. But I could never have killed her. Forgiveness would have somehow welled up at the last moment and stopped any deadly blow. After all, hadn't she come to Churchill Falls to save my father? That favor deserved better than death. Besides, Candice hadn't actually killed Brad. If he was dying now, it was by his own choice.

Tears dripped onto my knuckles, still clenched around the iron rail. "Is there any hope at all?" I whispered.

My dad's hand rubbed over my back. "We've been running at low capacity for repairs, so the flow is down and divers can retrieve the bodies if necessary. But no, honey. I don't think it's possible to make it out alive."

I nodded and crumpled, forehead to my hands against the banister. There was no chance now of Happy Ever After for Puppa. His love story had come to an end here in the cold dampness of a man-made cavern, the bare glow of overhead lamps illuminating the freezing waters of an underground river.

Lifting my head, I gazed across the expanse. Yet because of Candice and my hunger for revenge, I found my father—and my sisters. Perhaps without realizing it, Candice had given far more than she'd taken.

Humble and sad, with a glimmer of understanding for the whole warped thing, I turned to my father. "I imagine we've got some questions to answer. But when we're done here," I took a deep breath for courage, "am I still invited to supper tonight?"

He laughed through his tears, holding me in a fierce grip. "Always, Patricia. Always."

39

Divers found Simon's body the next day, tangled up in the tailrace portal. The only sign of Candice was her leather jacket, frozen stiff on the riverbank. They figured they'd find the rest of her downstream come spring.

During questioning, I'd gladly given police the weapon Candice had brought to my hotel room, along with all the details I could think of regarding Simon Scroll's deadly connections, and Candice's attempt at saving our lives. Of course, I listed "visit family" as my reason for being in Churchill Falls, rather than "punish Candice." The chief gave our five-member family unit a stiff warning as to the dangers of getting involved with people who engage in illegal activities and the seriousness of causing a near international incident at a major power company. Before dismissing us, he contacted authorities in Del Gloria for me, informing them of Alexa Rigg's act of vengeance.

We thanked him on our way out the door.

—∾—

"What's going to happen with your job?" I asked Dad during my last supper at the Jamison home before catching the puddle jumper for Goose Bay.

Dad speared a chunk of roast beef. "I laid it all on the table—running from Majestic, changing my name—and thank God the police chief is a reasonable man. We're pretty close-knit here in Churchill Falls and I think they'll want to keep Suzette and the girls around." His eyes sparkled as he looked around the table at his family. "I'm guessing they'll cut me some slack."

Suzette used the edge of her fork to chop up her baked potato. "I think they'll miss more than just Suzette and the girls, honey. You're a very valuable employee." She turned her gaze to me. "Your dad performs every function at the plant well, from repairing the communications network, to troubleshooting the turbines. He's not one to sit at the bar or be late for a shift or snooze on the job. I'm sure the results of the investigation will be in Roger's favor."

"What about you guys?" I asked Meagan and Monique. "Have I totally humiliated you by showing up here?"

"No way!" Meagan got a big smile across her ten-year-old face. "I can't wait to tell my friends about my cool new sister. You rocked. That guy was going to kill you and you were so brave."

Monique piped in. "Yeah. I don't know how you stayed so calm. I would have been freaking out."

I smiled and waved a hand in dismissal. "Well, when you get to be my age and you live through a few things, little stuff like that doesn't even get to you anymore."

Meagan's eyes got big. "Cool."

A burst of pride rose in my chest as I looked around the table at my newfound family. I had a dad. And a stepmom. Two—no, *three*—sisters. And they loved me. They accepted me. I couldn't wait to tell Brad.

My fork halted midair, steam rising from buttery, golden corn. I couldn't tell Brad. There was no Happy Ever After for Tish and Brad in this new reality.

The fork clinked as I dropped it to the plate, my appetite as gone as my love life.

"Everything okay, Patricia?" Dad asked, face scrunched in concern.

Elbows on the table, I leaned my head in my hands. "No. Candice shot my boyfriend and he gave up on life and never wants to see me again." My blubbering sounded stupid, even to me.

The table was silent and I could just imagine everyone looking at each other like I'd finally lost it. Roger, just get her to the airport, Suzette must be thinking.

"Hey," sixteen-year-old Monique touched my shoulder.

I crossed my arms and looked at her.

"The same thing happened to Renee when her boyfriend got hurt in wrestling last winter," Monique said. "He was feeling really bad about himself while his leg was messed up and tried to break up with her for her own good. She basically told him it wasn't going to happen. He could break up with her when his leg was healed, but not before. She stuck it out, even though he was really hard to be around for a while. Today, they're still together and really happy." She gave a hopeful shrug. "Maybe you could try doing that?"

Out of the mouths of babes. I stared at Monique. Maybe her idea would work. It was worth a shot.

Suzette cleared her throat. "I think it's probably a little more complex than that, Mo."

Monique tilted her lips. "Doubt it."

I took a bite of corn, hungry with new hope, savoring my last moments in Churchill Falls before embarking on my journey home.

We cleaned up our supper, laughing and smiling on top, but unable to ignore the bittersweet beneath.

"Do you think you'll be safe here now?" I asked Dad as he handed me a wet plate to dry.

"I think so. After I told him the whole story, the chief made it sound like the Canadian government could do some arm-twisting to get Frank Majestic put away once and for all. What happened here was a matter of international concern. They're not going to let some pot dealer mess around with the employees at a plant that supplies power to a good chunk of North America. Frank will get shut down and no one will hear from him again. I guess in a way, it's good this happened. I feel free at last. And," he looked at me, perhaps with that same adoration in his eyes as with his other daughters, "I finally got to meet my Patricia."

I put the plate in the cupboard and turned to him. "I can't imagine having gone a second longer without knowing where you were and who you were and how you lived your life. In a way, I'm glad everything happened just the way it did." But at the thought of Candice falling into the murky waters of the underground river, a cry gurgled up in my throat.

Dad put his arms around me. "I know, sweetheart. At what price?"

I waited until my voice was under control. "She had a really bad life. I wish something good could have happened to her. Just once. But then this."

"Maybe to her, this was the something good. She saved you, didn't she? Maybe it was that final act of redemption that will give her peace."

I sniffled and wiped my eyes. "Maybe. I guess I'll have to think of it like that."

"Time to go, everyone. The plane won't wait." Suzette shooed us all to the car for the drive to the airport. We said our goodbyes on the way, the setting sun orange on the horizon.

"I want to come visit you," Monique said. "Where will you be? Michigan?"

The question caught me off guard. "I'm supposed to be finishing up my degree in California. I'm just one semester away. After that, I don't know where I'll be."

I thought of Brad. Even if he wanted to be with me, could we make things work? He was a guy from downstate Rawlings who got stuck in Michigan's Upper Peninsula while he recovered from a gunshot wound—or expired from it, whichever he decided. And I was a nomad now.

"Well," Monique said, "wherever you are, I'm going to visit."

"You just want to go to the States," Meagan said, a tease in her voice.

"Duh," Monique replied. "And I want to see my big sis again."

"I'd love to have you, Monique. All of you. Any of you. You're all welcome wherever I end up."

Dad made the turn to the terminal building. "We'll take you up on that, honey. I only wish you didn't have to leave so soon. We've got thirty-three years of catching up to do and we've covered, what? Two of them so far?"

He parked.

I held his hand and we walked into the building together. The others followed, bringing my suitcase.

Tearful goodbyes, and soon the plane was in the air, circling the lights below one last time before turning east to Goose Bay.

The travel home was grueling with far too much time to think. Busy enjoying my last moments with family, I'd barely noticed the lump on my head, the sore muscles, the cuts and bruises. But now they consumed my thoughts, along with guilt and remorse over Candice's death, frustration at Brad, anger due to the fire in Del Gloria and the injuries to my friends, annoyance at Samantha and Joel for taking my house, and sorrow that I didn't know when I'd get to see my dad, stepmom, and sisters again.

I popped acetaminophen like breath mints until I was safely back in Michigan airspace. My final connection touched down late afternoon, two days after I left Churchill Falls. I rented a car for the trip back to Port Silvan, glad to have the freedom of my own wheels the next few days before flying back to Del Gloria. I could visit Brad and take care of loose ends without inconveniencing Puppa, who'd already bent over backward to accommodate my resurrection. Besides, I'd left my grandfather with the impression I'd taken up permanent residence in Churchill Falls. I had enough explaining to do.

The familiar backdrop of snow-covered pines whizzed past on the highway. Most of all, I dreaded telling Puppa of Candice. His words rang in my head: "not infected with cancer . . . infected with love." How would I tell him his love was dead?

And what of my love?

Rapid River, then Silvan Corners. The drive flew by, my mind no closer to a strategy for dealing with Brad, college, or the lodge. Cupid's Creek, the sign for the cider mill. Then the blink-and-you-miss-it drive through Port Silvan.

I pressed on the gas at the curve out of town. A mile up, I slowed at Puppa's white fences, turning down the driveway to the lake house.

He was at the door, a surprised look on his face, as I walked across the porch.

"What happened? Are you okay?" He hugged me, then ushered me to the living room.

"Long story," I said. "Do you have any tea?"

"I'll make a pot. Sit." He left the room.

I stared out the bank of windows at the snow-globe scene on the other side of the bay, with its row of cottages on the shore and church steeple in the distance.

In a moment Puppa joined me.

"Tell me everything," he said.

"Not sure you want to hear everything." I blinked back tears. "It's not all good."

But somehow I made it through the detailed version

of Candice showing up at the hotel room, my dash to warn Dad of trouble, meeting the sisters I never knew I had, the near-death experience at the plant, and Candice's final act of love toward Puppa's family.

Somewhere between Simon Scroll showing up and Candice falling into the river, the teapot whistled. Puppa set us up with two cups and urged me to continue.

He hadn't said a word during my entire monologue. And now, as I wrapped up the details of the missing Jacob Russo's life, Puppa just sat there, tears streaming down his cheeks while he listened.

When I was done, Puppa shook his head. "My boy turned into a fine man. I'm glad you got to meet him, Patricia."

I sniffled and wiped at my eyes. "Me too. And I know you will again someday."

From his seat in Grandma Olivia's rocker, Puppa stared into the distance. "That's not so important anymore. All God's promises came to be. He took care of Jacob when I couldn't. He took care of you when Jacob couldn't. And—" he stopped to gain control over his voice—"He even took care of Candice, giving her another chance to make things right before she died." He wiped his hand across his brow, then covered his face.

I watched him fight his grief, then finally succumb. I gave him a moment alone, then walked over and joined him, crying on his shoulder as I hugged him from above.

He patted my hand. "At least we have each other, Patricia. I don't know what I'd do if you weren't in my life."

Memories of Grandma Amble's guilt-grip over me

flooded my mind. I took a deep breath. "I know how hard this must be for you. You thought you lost me, then you lost your mother, and now Candice." I stepped back. "It's going to hurt for a long time. Maybe the rest of your life. But I've got to move on with mine." My future plans suddenly became crystal clear. "I'm going back to Del Gloria in a few days to finish up my degree. It's not going to slip through my fingers this time."

He looked at me, confusion, or maybe abandonment written on his face. "That's not what I expected. I thought now that it's safe enough to stay, you would . . . ," he paused as if searching for a delicate way to put it, "you would at least stick around for Brad's sake."

I sat on the chair across from him, excited at the clarity cropping up in my plans. "On the way home, I asked myself what I could do that would change Brad's mind about dying. What could I do that would make him want to live? And I decided that it's out of my control. It's really his decision." I leaned forward, my hands emphasizing my words. "All I can do is show by my example how to choose life. That means I can't give up on my dreams because someone I love is suffering. That means I move forward with my own plans, cheering him on should he decide to join the living again. It means taking the risk that I could lose him by not catering to his depression. And being even more grateful in the end if we pull through it together."

Puppa stared at me. "What are they teaching you in California?"

I sat in momentary horror that he disapproved of my reasoning.

A smile broke out on his face. "You're doing it, aren't you? You're figuring life out. I think you may have already passed up this old man in the maturity department. I'm really proud of you, Patricia." Puppa crouched beside me, taking my chin in his hand. "I think that's the spirit Brad fell in love with. And it's exactly what he needs to see now, if he's going to survive."

I leaned my forehead against his. "It's going to be really hard. Every instinct is screaming, 'Stay and take care of him.' But," I shook my head, "that's not the right thing for either one of us. We'd just feed off each other's weaknesses until we destroyed every bit of love between us, like what happened between me and Grandma Amble." Another deep breath. "This way, we stay strong for each other, building each other up as we conquer the obstacles in our own lives. We'll fight a common enemy instead of making each other the enemy."

Puppa looked baffled. "Who taught you that?"

I shrugged.

"You're going to make it, Patricia. You're going to do just fine."

"Thanks, Puppa. I probably would have made it anyway. But now I can make it in style." I scratched my head, grasping for a term that escaped me. "What's the word used in the Bible?"

"Abundance," Puppa said. "Now you can live an abundant life."

"That's the word I was looking for. I think for me it means a life without fear. I'm sick of deciding stuff based on fear. One thing I've figured out—God is with me even if I make a big mistake. And while I want to make the best decisions possible, I don't have to be afraid of every possible outcome. It's still His world in the end. And His will."

He squeezed my shoulder. "If I was only half as trusting as you." A smile hovered on his face.

"Oh, come on," I said with a playful smack on his shoulder. "Who do you think taught trust by example? You did. And I'm so grateful. Now," my gaze flicked to a cobweb in the corner, "I have to see what Brad's position is on all this."

"Let's get supper going and you can visit him first thing tomorrow morning."

My stomach growled at the mention of food. "Good idea." I forced my heart to stay calm at the thought of seeing Brad again, pushing back the fear. I was going to be direct with him. Firm. Take charge, just like Monique's girlfriend had done. And Brad would be thrilled to see me and happy to hear everything I had to say.

But even as Puppa and I walked to the kitchen, I knew that nothing about tomorrow was going to be fun—or easy.

40

Puppa and I ate breakfast together, a silent meal peppered with private emotion.

"Thanks for the eggs," I said, bringing my dish to the kitchen and rinsing off traces of yolk.

"I'll do the cleanup, Patricia. You get on with your day." He squirted dish soap into the sink as it filled with water.

"I don't mind helping." I wet a dishcloth and wiped down the dining room table, knowing that any delay in going to see Brad could only be a good thing. I scratched at a piece of food stuck to the wood. What if he still refused to see me? Candice had said that after I left his apartment last time, he had a crew of doctors in with him the next day. But what if his plans for recovery didn't include me? Could I handle it?

I gave a final swipe with my cloth. Of course I could. I had plans of my own. That was the whole point. Lives that were separate, but together. Just like things had always been for us.

In the kitchen, I tossed the cloth into the sink. How

dumb did that sound? If Brad and I were going to be a couple, we should be together, not apart. But I didn't want to give up on college. Not this time. Not again. Not for Brad, or for anyone. Finishing up at Del Gloria was something I had to do for myself. I could be part of a couple and still have my own goals, couldn't I?

By the time the swirling thoughts subsided for a moment, I had both hands planted on the kitchen counter and was on the verge of hyperventilating.

Puppa dried his hands. "Hey. Don't make this bigger than it is. Brad loves you. It's going to be okay."

I nodded and evened out my breathing. "You're right. I know you're right. It'll be okay."

"Get moving, before you talk yourself out of it." He flicked water at me with his fingers.

I gave a little scream and laughed. "Okay. I'm going."

Upstairs, I checked my hair and makeup one last time, smoothing on a fresh dab of lipstick.

My eyes, with their downward turn in the corners, sparkled in the mirror. My cheeks were rosy, my hair glossy. I looked like a kid on Christmas morning ready to rip open every gift under the tree. I blinked hard, hoping I wasn't setting myself up for more disappointment.

I made the drive to Manistique. As the snowy landscape passed by, I realized I hadn't experienced this area in the summertime since I was a kid. I still hadn't swum in the lake, or watched the fireworks on the Fourth of July, I hadn't hiked down the jetty to the lighthouse in Manistique Harbor, or explored the boardwalk along the shore. I'd wanted to save all that for Brad. Now it looked like I'd have to do it on my own after all.

The turn for River's Edge appeared in front of me, as if I'd driven on automatic all the way. I pulled in, hands shaking, stomach cramping, brain seizing.

Inside the assisted living home, I forced my feet to move in the direction of Brad's apartment. A brass number shone on the door in front of me. I stared at the digits as if they offered some magical escape route. Then I knocked.

Austin answered, wearing his trademark blue scrubs. "Oh. It's you. Thought you moved to Canada or something."

"Hate to disappoint you. Can I come in, please?" I tried to keep my voice casual and steady.

"Wait here. I'll see."

Austin shut the door, leaving me in the hallway. He reappeared a moment later, an amused look on his face. "Yes. You may come in."

I blew out the breath I hadn't realized I'd been holding. "Thanks." I stepped inside and glanced around the tiny living room/kitchenette combination. I pointed to the bedroom door. "May I?"

"Absolutely." He stepped aside, one hand ushering me closer to the dreaded moment.

I looked with wonder at Austin, amazed how his attitude had gone from "no way" to "okay" in just over a week. "All right, then. Thank you." I turned the knob, easing the door open. My eyes shot to the bed. Empty.

"You came back." Brad's voice came from a chair by the window. All I could see was the top of his head over the tall, leather back. Pillows in white cases spilled over the sides.

I stepped toward him, coming into his line of vision.

"Hi." I leaned against the window ledge, studying his face in the cool light. He'd gotten thinner since I'd first seen him across the fence that separated our backyards in Rawlings. His cheeks seemed a touch on the hollow side, the laugh lines around his eyes looking more like deep wrinkles these days. His body was wedged into the chair and supported by puffs of pillows.

"It's good to see you out of bed," I ventured, convinced that anything I said would probably be the wrong thing.

"Thank you." He seemed to struggle for words. "I'm surprised to see you here."

My fingers twisted together and I simply stared at him. We were like two strangers who'd never spent time looking into each other's eyes. Who'd never touched and felt the electricity flow between them. Who'd never put their hearts on the line and told each other their secret hopes and dreams. I could accept that and leave things the way they were, or I could take charge and fight back.

"Of course I'm here. A little bellowing won't scare me off. You'll have to do worse than that if you never want to see me again."

His eyes flickered, as if afraid to hope. "I heard you went to Canada. I didn't think you'd be back."

"Long story short, I went there to find Candice and bring her to justice. Instead, I found my father. He's married and has three daughters." My face broke out in a smile that couldn't be suppressed. "I have sisters now." But dark events blotted out my happiness. "In the end, Candice gave her life to save mine. She paid for what she did to you." My eyes watered. "I wish I could say I felt better about the whole thing."

His finger twitched against a pillow, as if asking for comfort. I reached out, slowly, and touched the skin of his hand. I closed my eyes and remembered the soft feel of it against my cheek. Then suddenly I was on my knees in front of him, crushing the warmth of his hand to my face. The blankets on his lap caught my tears as I rubbed his palm to my temple, my cheek, my neck, then my lips. I held his hand there, weeping over it, glad for the warmth and life it contained, but saddened by Brad's inability to respond to my love.

At the sound of a sniffle, I looked up. Tears ran in rivulets down Brad's face.

"You still love me?" he asked.

"How do you stop loving someone who is a part of you? My past, present, and future are wrapped up with yours. I'm not giving up my dreams because of a little bullet. You still have your life. Your mind. You're still the man I fell in love with."

A cry ripped from his throat. "I want to hold you and I can't. I want to take care of you and I can't. Nothing works anymore."

"Shhh." I scooted up and put my ear to his chest, basking in the simple sound of his heartbeat. I looked into his eyes. "Your heart works okay. You can still love me."

His head tilted back against the leather and he looked at some point on the ceiling. "You make it sound so easy. But how's this going to work in the real world?"

"It'll work if we say it works." I gave a shrug of my shoulders and a timid smile. "Neither one of us has lived cookie-cutter lives. Do we really care about what's considered normal in a relationship?"

He swallowed hard and conquered his voice. "Before all this, you were going to be my wife. We were going to move to Rawlings, have kids, keep the lodge as a summer home, and eventually try living up here. None of that is even a possibility anymore. Would you really give up the hope of a normal life just to be with me?"

I thought hard before I answered. "No. I won't give up the hope of a normal life to be with you."

His face clouded over.

I squeezed his hand. "I gave up the hope of a normal life awhile ago when I realized normal and Tish Amble don't belong in the same sentence. Life's always going to be a struggle. But I'm making progress. And maybe out of all the chaos I've survived, I even have something to offer you—the hope of a happy life without being normal." I intertwined his fingers with mine. "We can just be ourselves, the people God made us, broken bodies, broken spirits, and all. And maybe we can even help others struggling with the same junk figure out how to be happy too."

"So," he choked on his words, "you'll still marry me?"

I watched his Adam's apple bob as he swallowed. I couldn't lie to him. Not when he'd already come so far.

"No. I won't marry you." The words came out a whisper.

He turned his head, withdrawing from me. "Why not?" Only a whisper.

"Because it's what I wanted to do when I was trying to be normal. You know, get married, buy a house, have kids, the whole American formula for happiness." I leaned my head into his shoulder, breathing in the smell of zesty guy soap. "But I want more. I want to marry you because it's my heart's desire, not because it's the thing to do." I pulled back and looked at his strong profile. "And I just think that where we're at, with the separation we've been through, with the obstacles we both have to overcome, that now isn't the time to be talking marriage."

He looked at me, his old quirky smile on his face. "Then come back tomorrow. We'll talk marriage then."

I broke into a grin. "You're an incurable romantic." On a whim, I climbed onto his lap, snuggling his body to mine. "Am I hurting you?"

He closed his eyes. "Can't feel a thing."

I pressed my lips to his ear, swooning in the jolt of electricity from that simple act.

"Listen," I whispered. "I'm going back to Del Gloria. I'm finishing my degree. I won't be home until summer."

There was no answer for some time. I let my lips trail along Brad's neck as I waited.

Finally he spoke. "You were in here when Denton visited. You must have heard everything."

I nodded against his cheek. "I did."

"I'm not proud how I handled it. I love him so much, but I still hold so much against him."

"I want you to know I stand by you, whatever you decide with him. I sent the professor a letter thanking him for his support, but I won't be staying with him when I go back out there. It wouldn't be loyal to you if I did.

He said some really hurtful things to you. And as close as I felt to him for several months, his money and his esteem mean nothing to me compared to you."

Brad turned his face to mine. "Thank you."

Our lips were impossibly close. There was no resisting the magnetic attraction. Our mouths touched, timidly at first, but becoming braver with each heated moment. He tasted as delicious as I remembered. I showered his face and neck with kisses.

I took a deep breath. "I love you, Brad." I wanted him to know it before I left.

"Then come back tomorrow. We'll plan our marriage."

I leaned my forehead against his. "I'm not coming back until summer." I rubbed my fingers through his hair. "But don't worry. I'll be back."

He caught my eyes with his. "You're always leaving me. Do you realize you've left me three times in just over a year?"

I giggled and shrugged. "Just a personality quirk, I guess." I became serious. "Really, Brad. I don't want to leave you. But I have to do this or live with more regrets."

"I know, Tish. I have plenty to keep me busy while you're gone. I'd like to walk my wife down the aisle after our wedding, if it's okay with you."

A rush of love washed through me. "I'm going to hold you to that. No more talk of marriage until you're back on your feet."

"Then you'll marry me?"

I swatted him. "You're incorrigible."

"Yes," he said, his voice tickling my ear. "When it comes to you, I just won't give up."

"I'm flattered. Now if we can just get you to say that about yourself."

He nuzzled me with his mouth. "I won't give up on myself. How's that?"

His lips tickled and I laughed. "That'll do."

I stayed all day and late into the night, hating to leave him, wanting to take back my promise to Koby that I'd be on the plane to Del Gloria, and instead stay and get married and wake up in Brad's bed come morning.

41

But instead of staying, I left him. Again. I drove my rental car to Sawyer International and got on the flight back to California. And by late afternoon, I was there, taking the bus to Portia's apartment complex, the place I'd call home for the rest of my college career.

She hugged me when I walked in the door, a clingy embrace that said everything without words. By the time I stepped back, we both had tears running down our faces.

"Look at you. You're all bandaged up." I held her arm-distance away. White pads were taped to the side of her face and head.

"Just had surgery a few days ago," she said. "But the prognosis is good. Professor Braddock paid for the best plastic surgeon Hollywood has to offer. There won't be any scarring."

"You're so beautiful," I said. "I'm glad you'll be okay."

She gave a shy smile, a charming look for the once-hardened woman. "The doc was pretty torn up when he found out his housekeeper was the guilty party. Can

you imagine finding out you've been harboring a former terrorist?"

I turned a shoulder to her, staring at white linoleum. "What about Celia?"

"She's in the burn unit in Sacramento," Portia said. "At first, they only gave her a few days to live. But that girl is invincible. They expect she'll be fully recovered by summer."

"Thank the Lord," I whispered. "Now, let's get that Covenant Award. Celia deserves it."

—∞—

With winter break over, classes began. I filled my days with homework and houses as the team forged ahead, working long hours to meet project deadlines.

As we repaired, prepped, and painted, I shared the details of my trip to Churchill Falls.

"I knew Simon Scroll was a scum bucket," Dagger said, his gang clothing covered with paint. "You could tell by looking at him he was up to no good."

I arched an eyebrow his way. "Careful. Turns out you're right about Simon, but I've been wrong about people over and over when I try to sum them up in one glance."

Dagger hiked up his dropped waist. "Even without him we can finish in time. Some of my people said they'd help out."

"If they're anything like you, your people are the best." I smiled his way.

Koby edged the woodwork with white paint. "So this guy Brad. He's pretty messed up now, huh?"

I looked at Koby, with his two artificial legs. At Portia, with only one hand. At Maize, with her nervous energy. Dagger, with his persecution complex. Timid Gwen, with her obsessive perfection disorder. And of course, me with my hang-ups and letdowns.

A shake of my head. "Nope. He's not messed up. He's got a few challenges ahead," I shrugged, "but he's pretty much just like the rest of us."

Koby seemed disappointed at my answer. "So you plan on getting back together with him?"

"We never broke up."

He went back to painting. "If there's ever anything I can do for you, Tish, just say the word."

"Thanks, Koby. You're a good friend."

As we completed individual homes, families began to move in. I helped coordinate the process, lining up strong backs from the college and the community to haul furniture and boxes for the new inhabitants of Rios Buena Suerta. In return, many of the grown-ups pitched in with the finishing touches on the project. The possibility of meeting our May deadline was becoming a reality.

A month had passed since my return before I got up the nerve to visit Professor Braddock. We'd seen each other in the halls and in various classrooms, but averted our eyes, both suffering too much to discuss our losses.

I knocked on the door of his office at Walters Hall.

"Come in." His voice sounded weary.

A turn of the knob, a push of the door, and I faced the birth father of the man I loved.

"Hi." I barely knew what to say.

He gestured toward a chair. "Sit. Please."

I made myself comfortable, refusing to back down or chicken out. "I'm sorry about your housekeeper."

He smiled sheepishly. "And I'm sorry about your bodyguard."

Our mutual misfortune brought a chuckle from us both. The tension broken, I leaned toward him, pushing an embossed book across his desk. "Thank you for lending me this."

He picked up the volume and rubbed the leather cover. "*The Count of Monte Cristo*."

"I took it home to finish."

His voice was husky. "Did you enjoy the story of a man who exacts vengeance from those who ruined his life?"

"I didn't care for the ending."

Denton flipped the pages at random. "Ah. The ending. You wanted him to reunite with the fair Mercedes."

I nodded.

"An impossibility. You must have realized it in advance."

"The romantic in me never gave up hope."

"Life is so different than we expect, isn't it?" His eyes misted over. "We spend so much time chasing after what we think we want, only to have it turn to ashes in our hands."

I leaned forward. "But the Count ends up getting better than what he wanted. Just not in the way he thought."

He sighed and looked out the window. "And so the story becomes just another fairy tale."

I studied his pained profile, my heart reaching out to him. "Don't give up on Brad. He loves you. He wants you in his life. There can be a happy ending."

His face crumbled. I went to him, gripping his hands in mine. "I know what Brad's feeling. I felt it with my father too. Of course Brad is angry with the way things happened between you. Call him. Talk to him. You can work things out. I know you can."

The professor sat a moment in silence. "So," he said, "the student becomes the teacher."

"Just think about it. Anyway," I gave his hands a final squeeze, "thank you again for lending your book."

He nodded, looking bereft.

I left him to his thoughts, my feet echoing in the empty hallway as I walked to the elevator.

—∞—

The semester was almost over, the deadline upon us. We pulled some all-nighters in order to finish before graduation ceremonies. As we put the final touches on the last home, I couldn't believe I'd survived. There would actually be a college degree with my name on it. All the years of disappointment over not having a diploma were over. Now I could cheer for the MSU Spartans again.

And in the past two years, I'd done everything I needed to do. I'd put to rest my guilt over Grandma Amble's death, found out my mother had been an amazing photographer, met my father and sisters, and finished college. And it turned out, as weird and messed up as I thought my life was, it was actually pretty cool. I had great relatives, good friends, and a boyfriend who loved me through it all.

I rubbed at a window with a cloth. It was a shame Brad couldn't be here for the big day. He congratulated me over the phone when we'd talked the other night. But somehow it wouldn't be the same without him. His health had been steadily improving over the past months, but his doctors wouldn't give him permission to travel.

A final look around by our gang of overworked, exhausted, thirty-something college students. Everything sparkled.

"Perfect," said Gwen.

"If she says it, then it must be true," Dagger commented.

"Let's get the clutter out of here." Portia kept on us as we gathered up the cleaning supplies.

"Take care, everybody," Portia said. "Tomorrow's the big day. I guess we'll find out if all the effort pays off."

"See you guys tomorrow," Maize called, skipping out the door.

Portia and I walked to the Dogpatch station, swinging buckets of cleanser and Windex on our arms.

"Have you heard back on that camp position in Michigan?" I asked.

She looked at me, eyebrows raised. "Yes. They want me to interview for associate director."

"That's great. What town was that again?"

She laughed. "Just north of Big Rapids. It didn't look

too close to Port Silvan on the map, but if I get the job, maybe we can get together once or twice a year."

I threw an arm around her neck. "Definitely. That's so awesome."

"What about you?" Portia said. "Have you decided what you're going to do yet?"

"I have." A smile crossed my lips. "I'm going back to Port Silvan. I'll live with my grandfather for a while and work at the Coney up the road—"

"Coney?" Portia interrupted. "You mean the restaurant in your old house? I thought you were trying to get them out of there."

I shook my head. "Nope. I decided it was a perfect fit for Sam and Joel. That's why I bought it in the first place—fix it up and sell it to the right customer. I'm really glad this time it turned out to be family." I kept going with my story. "Anyway, Samantha had her baby in March and she's looking forward to having me help out while she does the mom thing."

"I'm surprised you'd do that to yourself."

"Nah. I'll get to see my baby cousin every day, make a few bucks, and be close to Brad. Once he's over the rough stuff, he can come stay at Puppa's." I gazed at the spring blossoms on some exotic bush near the station. "We'll enjoy the view at the lake house. It's right on Silvan Bay, which is gorgeous this time of year. And you can hear the church bells."

Portia gave a knowing smile. "Speaking of bells, do I hear wedding bells in your future?"

The bus pulled up on schedule.

"Ladies," the driver said with a nod.

"Hey, Mr. Kim," Portia greeted the grinning man. "Tomorrow's graduation. Are you coming?"

"Young lady," he said, "I haven't missed a graduation ceremony at Del Gloria College in twenty years."

"Great. We'll see you there."

He slid the door closed and we were on our way, bouncing toward Cliff Edge Apartments.

—‿—

The next morning, I stayed in bed a few extra minutes, thinking about the day and what it signified in my life. Looking back, I was glad everything happened the way it did. I would have changed a few things if I could, like the trail of dead bodies that seemed to follow me from place to place. The years I'd spent in prison. The loss of my mother. Brad's life-altering injury. But who's to say everything didn't happen just the way it was supposed to, according to God's higher, grander purpose. It felt good to look back with acceptance rather than regret.

I got up and hit the shower, then dressed in my navy blue duds from my admissions interview almost a year ago.

"You look professional," Portia said, playing with the pleated collar of her summer fashion as we jockeyed back and forth for the lead position in the tiny bathroom mirror.

"Maybe we should trade outfits. You're the drill sergeant around here." I laughed.

"Graduated drill sergeant. I can't wait to be around undisciplined little kids instead of undisciplined adults."

"Come on. We weren't that bad."

She smiled. "You were all hard workers, you just needed direction."

"And as long as you were working alongside us and not shouting from the sidelines, we didn't mind taking orders from you."

Portia shook her head. "Bunch of rebels."

Laughing, we slipped into high heels and headed for the Dogpatch bench out front.

—w—

The graduation ceremonies were traditionally held on the expansive lawn in front of Walters Hall, with the steps and portico serving as stage. The gentle sunshine of late May and a cloudless sky made the location perfect again this year.

Students with hopeful faces sat in folding chairs arranged in rows, forming a patchwork of black and white graduation gowns—black for the men, white for the women. I squeezed Portia's hand on one side of me, Koby's on the other, as Dean Lester addressed the graduates along with the crowd of spectators behind us. After an uplifting speech, she introduced Professor Braddock to present the diplomas.

He took his place behind the podium, clearing his throat into the microphone. "Thank you for coming today. We generally like to start out every year by announcing the winner of the Covenant Award, a prize given to a team of students who show extraordinary growth, courage, and accomplishment in their final year at Del Gloria College." He paused as the spectators applauded. "This year, we have a special visitor who will present the award. This individual himself exemplifies the qualities embodied by the Covenant Award. A year ago, this man nearly died from a bullet wound."

I gasped, then calmed myself. He couldn't be talking about Brad.

"The bullet damaged his spine, leaving him virtually paralyzed." Denton glanced behind him at the doors to the building, then back at the audience.

My shoes squeaked a happy rhythm. My fingers twirled the tassel of my cap.

The professor paused, as if reining in his emotions. "Only through great courage and faith was this individual able to conquer the odds and be here today."

I told myself not to get my hopes up as the doors opened and a group of people came through, one man pushing a wheelchair. I squinted. That looked like Joel. The woman next to him, with long black hair sweeping over her shoulders, resembled Samantha Walters-Russo. And the man in the wheelchair . . . I caught my breath. It was Brad.

Tears burst forth like water through a dam. I bent forward in my seat, sobbing.

"What's wrong?" Portia's voice held urgent concern.

I just shook my head, too emotional to answer. He was here. Brad had come to my graduation. There was nothing but my white gown to catch the happiness falling from my eyes.

"Ladies and gentlemen, my son, Mr. Braddock Walters."

I looked up as Denton handed the microphone to Brad. He took it as if he'd never lost mobility in his arms.

Brad toyed with the mike a moment before speaking. "As a child, I was blessed by having two fathers. One, my birth father, is this man next to me, Professor Denton Braddock, who established this college and changed for the better the lives of so many hurting people. The other was my stepfather, Samuel Walters, for whom Professor Braddock dedicated this building as a memorial. Both men loved me deeply, and by example showed me how to live a rich life."

Tears ran in a steady trickle down my face as I listened.

"Not too long ago," Brad said, "I reached a low point. My only goal was to die. I wanted out of the disappointment and pain that circumstances had brought my way. But God," Brad held the mike away as he fought for composure, "God had different plans. Because of Him, I can be here today to present the Covenant Award to a very special group of people."

He fumbled in his inner suit pocket for a slip of paper, the microphone magnifying the rustling sound as he opened it. "Could I please have the graduating members of the Revamp Program come to the stage?"

A cheer erupted through the crowd, blotting out Brad's voice as he read off the list of names, including Celia's.

Portia grabbed me in an exhilarated hug. Koby joined in and soon we were standing and jumping in place, thrilled over our victory. The six remaining team members wove our way through handshakes, pats on the back, and calls of "You go, girl! You rock, man!" Our joy was dampened only by Celia's absence.

We climbed the steps and shook hands with an array of college staff and administration. Then we stood in a line behind Brad. I could barely breathe in such close vicinity to him when all I wanted to do was wrap my arms around his neck and kiss him.

Denton stepped up to the podium. "This group began as two teams in competition with one another. They embraced a larger cause, banding together to complete a project that quite frankly had an impossible deadline. Yet, they braved personal differences, conquered their fears, survived acts of violence, and worked long hours to meet the class requirements. As a result, eight local families now enjoy affordable, quality housing."

Another round of applause. I could barely see my classmates through the beads of water clogging my eyes. And every time I looked Brad's way, my vision only got worse.

Denton held up a hand to quiet the crowd. "I want to take a moment to introduce to you the member voted Most Valuable by the staff at Del Gloria. This woman challenges the status quo, questioning beliefs many of us leave unquestioned, until her faith and trust in God ring with an authenticity few can claim."

I clapped my hands together, in anticipation of congratulating Portia for her achievement.

"Ladies and gentlemen, please show your appreciation to Miss Patricia Louise Amble."

I inhaled. Did Denton have it right? I was voted Most Valuable? I looked around at my cheering, smiling team members. Humbled, I covered my mouth with my hands, blubbering like a Miss America pageant winner. Not caring that hundreds of people were witnesses, I walked to Brad's wheelchair, stared at him with love in my eyes, bent and kissed him. A round of hoots and cheers snapped me out of my daze and I stood up, embarrassed.

Brad picked up his microphone, "I have only one question for Miss Patricia Louise Amble." The crowd hushed, listening.

Joel came over from the side of the stage and took the mike from Brad. My ex-cop boyfriend gripped the arms of the wheelchair and strained to lift himself to a standing position. I could only stare in utter horror, worried he'd tumble and hurt himself on the hard stone beneath. He steadied himself, then he took a haltering step toward me. I tried to move forward to meet him, but Portia's sturdy grip held me in place. Another step. And another. Not strong, not confident, just miraculous.

Brad stood before me. His hand reached into his trouser pocket. Out came a tiny box covered in black velvet. He pulled open the lid. The sparkle of a single diamond set in white gold blinded me along with a renewed torrent of tears.

Joel handed Brad the microphone. Brad's voice echoed across the silent lawn. "Patricia Louise Amble, will you marry me?"

Not even the song of a bird broke the silence as I stared at him in amazement. All this . . . for me?

"Yes, I'll marry you." The words bounced off stone and glass, repeating themselves until scattered by the breeze.

A rush of wind as the crowd inhaled in unison, then let out a wild whoop. I laughed and cried, held close in Brad's arms until the noise dimmed into the background of our beating hearts.

He put the ring on my finger. "I love you," he whispered for my ears alone. Then we kissed as if we were on a deserted island. A round of hoots from the audience and we were transported back to Del Gloria. Joel situated the wheelchair and Brad collapsed into the sling seat.

The rest of the ceremony was a blur, my beloved diploma a mere afterthought on a day that had come to mean so much more.

Later, the crew from Port Silvan gathered around the hall steps. Samantha held her sleeping baby girl.

"My little cousin will officially be my niece soon too," I said, gazing with adoration at plump cheeks and wispy eyelashes. "Puppa must be so proud." I looked at the faces of my best supporters. "I wish he could have been here."

Joel spoke. "He wanted to be. But something came up and he left the country."

"What? Where did he go?"

Joel shrugged. "Havana."

"Cuba? What on earth?"

"He gave some story about the woman who went over Niagara Falls in a barrel. Everyone said it was impossible, but she survived anyway."

I bit my lip. Candice was alive. They were finally together.

"Puppa deeded the lake house to you. Said it was a wedding gift."

I nodded, all cried out. Maybe I'd never see my grandfather again. But I couldn't be sad over it. He and Candice finally got their happy ending.

Denton passed me an envelope.

"What's this?" As I pulled back the tab, I wondered if I could take one more emotional moment. Inside was a travel brochure showing a beach of white sand and water so clear it looked green. On the shore was a bamboo-and-thatch cabana. Kadavu, the letters above it read.

"Kadavu," I whispered and looked at Brad. "Our island in Fiji." We'd found it on the Web back in Rawlings, the day Brad decided to teach me something about computers.

Brad's eye crinkles were in full action, as if he'd had some part in the plan.

"You get a beach house all to yourselves. It's my wedding gift to you," Denton said.

I smiled. "Thank you. It's perfect. Everything's perfect."

"And when you get back, make sure you stop by Cliffhouse," he added. "I think you'll like what I've got planned for the exterior."

I shook my head, overcome. Denton and Brad were father and son again. The restoration of Cliffhouse would finally be complete.

The people in front of me blurred through more tears. My family. My friends. Things just didn't get better than this. I wanted to preserve the moment, bottle the aura of love and happiness. Because one thing I'd learned, life didn't stay this way very long. The lull was only temporary. And at any moment, my next adventure could begin.

Acknowledgments

Thanks to Joel B., the power plant repairman I met on an airline flight, for suggesting Churchill Falls as a location for a suspense novel and graciously assisting with my research.

Thanks to Jordan Lester and Austin R. for lending me the use of their names.

A huge hug and thank you to my editors Vicki and Barb for their support and labor on the Patricia Amble Mystery Series.

Thanks to the dedicated fans of Tish Amble for their notes of enthusiasm and encouragement throughout the years.

And special thanks to my dear friends and family for their love and endurance as I reach for my dreams.

Nicole Young resides in Garden, Michigan, with her children, cat, and tiny Yorkie. Home renovation is a way of life for the author whose first project was converting a Victorian into a thriving bed & breakfast. Nicole launched her writing career in 2004 with an American Christian Fiction Writer's Noble Theme Contest win for best of show, which featured an excerpt from the Patricia Amble Mystery Series. Along with writing and parenting, the author enjoys horseback riding and performing vocals and fiddle with a gospel bluegrass band. Find more about Nicole at the author's website, www.NicoleYoung.net.